Praise for the Gethsemane Brown Mystery Series

"The captivating southwestern Irish countryside adds a delightful element to this paranormal series launch. Gethsemane is an appealing protagonist who is doing the best she can against overwhelming odds."

– *Library Journal* (starred review)

"Gordon strikes a harmonious chord in this enchanting spellbinder of a mystery."

– Susan M. Boyer,
USA Today Bestselling Author of *Lowcountry Book Club*

"Charming debut."

– *Kirkus Reviews*

"A fantastic story with a great ghost, with bad timing. There are parts that are extremely comical, and Gethsemane is a fantastic character that you root for as the pressure continually builds for her to succeed...in more ways than one."

– *Suspense Magazine*

"Just when you think you've seen everything, here comes Gethsemane Brown, baton in one hand, bourbon in the other....There's charm to spare in this highly original debut."

– Catriona McPherson,
Agatha Award-Winning Author of *The Reek of Red Herrings*

"Gethsemane Brown is a fast-thinking, fast-talking dynamic sleuth (with a great wardrobe) who is more than a match for the unraveling murders and cove̶ ̶i̶d̶e̶d̶ ̶b̶y̶ ̶h̶e̶r̶ ̶various– handsome–allies and her irascibl

Auth

n,

es

D0813294

"Gordon's charming sequel to *Murder in G Major* finds sassy Virginia-born musician Gethsemane Brown still living in a postcard-perfect 200-year-old Carraigfaire Cottage... near Dunmullach, a village in southwestern Ireland...Gethsemane races between often-failed attempts to raise a ghost and her need to clear her brother-in-law's name, find a murderer, and thwart an international art scam. This is light entertainment at its best."

– *Publishers Weekly*

"Gethsemane Brown is everything an amateur sleuth should be: smart, sassy, talented, and witty even when her back is against the wall."

– Cate Holahan,
Silver Falchion Award-Nominated Author of *The Widower's Wife*

"Erstwhile ghost conjurer and gifted concert violinist Gethsemane Brown returns in this thoroughly enjoyable follow-up to last year's *Murder in G Major*....With the help of a spectral sea captain she accidentally summoned, Gethsemane tries to unravel the mystery as the murderer places her squarely in the crosshairs."

– Daniel J. Hale,
Agatha Award-Winning Author

"A delightful read. But then, how can one go wrong with music, murder, art, and a ghost."

– *Mystery File*

"In the latest adventures with Gethsemane, murder is once again thrust upon her and with determination and a goal, she does what needs to be done...The author does a great job in keeping this multi-plot tale intriguing...I like that the narrative put me in the middle of all the action capturing the essence that is Ireland. The character of Eamon adds a touch that makes this engagingly appealing series more endearing."

– *Dru's Book Musings*

KILLING
IN C
SHARP

The Gethsemane Brown Mystery Series
by Alexia Gordon

MURDER IN G MAJOR (#1)
DEATH IN D MINOR (#2)
KILLING IN C SHARP (#3)

A Gethsemane Brown Mystery

KILLING
in C
SHARP

ALEXIA GORDON

HENERY PRESS

Copyright

KILLING IN C SHARP
A Gethsemane Brown Mystery
Part of the Henery Press Mystery Collection

First Edition | March 2018

Henery Press, LLC
www.henerypress.com

Trade Paperback ISBN-13: 978-1-63511-304-4
Digital epub ISBN-13: 978-1-63511-305-1
Kindle ISBN-13: 978-1-63511-306-8
Hardcover ISBN-13: 978-1-63511-307-5

Printed in the United States of America

To my parents, as always

ACKNOWLEDGMENTS

Thank you to:

Rachel Jackson for bringing order to the chaos of my manuscript drafts;

Kendel Lynn and Art Molinares for believing in Gethsemane;

Paula Munier for being my swell agent;

My blog mates, The Missdemeanors and Femmes Fatales, for the good advice and comradery;

My parents and Aunt Wilhelmina for being my biggest fans;

Lifeworking Coworking for the marketing and promotional support;

Leslie Lipps for the cool graphics on short notice;

The Deerpath Inn for letting me hang out in the Hearth Room, liking my Instagrams, and having the best whiskey menu in Lake Forest;

My friends, readers, book reviewers, and fellow crime writers for the encouragement and support.

One

Gethsemane Brown frowned at her landlord across her kitchen table. "No. Absolutely not. Worst. Idea. Ever. No way."

Billy McCarthy, the source of her irritation, returned the frown. "'Twasn't a request, really. More of an ultimatum." His mellifluous brogue didn't disguise the seriousness of his statement. "Dredge up some of that legendary Southern hospitality you brought with you from Virginia."

"Or?"

"Or pack your bags and be gone."

Damn. Gethsemane glared at the handsome, dark-haired businessman who looked so much like his late uncle, composer Eamon McCarthy. Billy could have evicted her at Epiphany, as he'd threatened, but begging, pleading, and a word from Father Tim Keating, the parish priest, about Christian charity won her a stay. No negotiating room remained. But what he asked her to do—

"Paranormal investigators," she said. "Seriously? You're going to let paranormal investigators invade Carraigfaire to try to find proof your uncle's ghost exists?" She didn't mention the ghost in question stood scowling in a corner. His aura glowed an infuriated cobalt.

"Paranormal investigators who paid me serious money for access to this cottage and the lighthouse." His frown deepened. "And your cooperation."

"You own the property. You don't own me."

"But you owe me. After that stunt you and Uncle Eamon pulled, you're lucky I don't have the gardaí send you packing straight to the airport and an exorcist send my uncle packing straight to hell. Besides, I thought you watched *Ghost Hunting Adventures*."

"I watch it. Doesn't mean I want to star in it. Nor does Eamon." Gethsemane looked past Billy. Sparks crackled around his head and an orb hovered near his ear. Gethsemane shook her head slightly and willed him to hold still. Blasting his nephew with a high-speed energy ball wouldn't help. She turned her attention back to Billy.

"I don't have to see him to know he's back there." Billy, like most, couldn't see or hear Eamon. Which was good, because if he had seen his uncle's expression, an exorcism would have become a reality instead of a threat. "You tell him—"

"He can hear you," Gethsemane said.

"Then I'll tell you both. I stood to earn a fortune selling this place to Hank Wayne, but the two of you ruined that plan. The money from this deal with the TV show doesn't come close to what I'd have gotten from Mr. Wayne, but it will help pay to keep the lights on and the roof from leaking. If you don't ruin this, I might forgive you." Billy paused. "Maybe."

Eamon's aura darkened and his orb grew larger. Gethsemane spoke before he could launch it. "Eamon and I saved you from making a terrible, irreversible mistake." Hank, a slick property developer, had wanted to turn Carraigfaire into a tourist trap. Unlike Billy, he could see ghosts and he feared them. Eamon put on a paranormal horror show and sent Hank running for his life out of Dunmullach and Ireland, hopefully forever. Billy hadn't appreciated the effort. "You'd have regretted seeing your heritage destroyed and replaced with a tacky motel and a parking lot, regretted it every day for the rest of your life."

"Well, that cow's gone to the butcher, so we'll speak no more about it. But if this cottage wants to be kept, it'll have to start earning its keep. And if that means selling tours to ghostbusters, then anyone staying in this cottage—" Billy looked back and forth between Gethsemane and Eamon's corner, "—be they alive or dead, will just have to go with it. Understood?"

Eamon said something she was glad Billy couldn't hear. "Okay, okay, I'll accommodate the *Ghost Hunting Adventures* boys. But what about the other thing?"

Billy crossed his arms.

"Venus James? After the smear job she did on your uncle in that stupid book of hers?" Gethsemane had read enough of Venus's book about the McCarthy murders before she arrived in Dunmullach to deem it near-libelous trash. Like almost everyone else, the true crime author believed Eamon had murdered his wife and then killed himself. She hadn't released any official comment after Gethsemane exonerated the composer, but showed up on Carraigfaire's doorstep three months ago, at the same time as the paranormal crew. But while the ghost hunters had moved on to other haunted houses while their producer hammered out a deal with Billy, Venus had stayed in Dunmullach and sniffed around. And weaseled her way into the community. Helped, no doubt, by her trademark red lipstick and stiletto heels. Gethsemane couldn't stand her. "All those terrible things she said about him? The insinuations, the outright lies?"

"Stupid book? You mean the international bestseller that's being re-issued in an updated edition incorporating facts you uncovered when you exonerated Uncle Eamon?" Billy leaned forward and clapped Gethsemane on the shoulder. "Think of it as an opportunity to make sure Ms. James gets her facts straight this time."

He rose from the table, and Gethsemane followed him to the hall. "If you and Uncle will excuse me, I promised to meet Ms. James at the Rabbit. She's keen to interview me about my relationship with Eamon and Orla." He donned his mackintosh and cap. "The ghost fellas will be here in a couple of hours to look around the place and figure out what kind of equipment they'll be needin'. Be nice. Maybe tell them some stories about Uncle

Eamon."

Gethsemane scuffed her foot against the hall bench. She kept her focus on the floor so Billy wouldn't see the daggers she shot at him. "I can't use that type of language on a basic cable program."

Billy laughed and opened the door.

Gethsemane called after him. "What about school? I've got a job, remember? This month's busy. Aed Devlin's coming to write his new opera. He's agreed to give a series of lectures and hold master classes at St. Brennan's. I'm music director. I have responsibilities."

"In the eight or nine months you've been in Dunmullach, you've turned a disaster of an orchestra into championship musicians, convinced a millionaire to donate a new music room to the school and pay for opera house renovations, exonerated two innocent men of unjust accusations, and exposed two murderers. And," a grin played on Billy's lips, "saved a historic cottage and lighthouse from a greedy developer despite the owner's plan to sell them. Juggling a few celebrity ghost hunters, a crime writer, and a has-been composer should be a piece of piss for a woman as driven as you." He tipped his cap and closed the door behind him.

Gethsemane kicked the door. "Ow." She hobbled over to the bench and massaged her throbbing toes.

"Careful, darlin'." Eamon, his aura still an angry blue, materialized next to her. "I'm the one who can pass through doors."

"I wish I could disappear right about now. What a mess." She grinned at Eamon. "You handled yourself well. I'm impressed. I thought for certain you'd fire an orb or two, right at Billy's head."

"I behaved for your sake, not his. You'd have had a helluva time explaining what happened to the guards. To say nothing of the mess." He winked.

She elbowed him in the ribs. A buzz shot up her arm as her elbow passed through his ribcage. They both jumped.

"That tickled," Eamon said.

"Sorry, I keep forgetting you're not—"

"Real?"

"Solid. You're about as real as they come." She chose her next words with care. "So, maybe you should—go."

Eamon's aura turned a mixture of sienna and yellow. He dematerialized until she could see the woodgrain of the hall bench through his legs. "You want me to leave? Now I've gotten rid of Hank Wayne and Carraigfaire is safe?"

"You know me better than that." She poked a finger through his knee. "I don't want you to leave. I'm not trying to get rid of you. I just got you back. But—"

"You're afraid I'll make trouble."

"No. I'm afraid the *Ghost Hunting Adventures* boys aren't all show. What if some of those high-tech gadgets really can capture evidence of ghosts? What if they capture proof you exist?"

"So what if they do?"

"Imagine every paranormal investigator, psychical research society, psychic medium, religious zealot, curiosity seeker, and plain ol' quack lined up from here to Dublin wanting to see for themselves."

Eamon swore.

"Maybe you could go back where you came from. For a little while. Just until they give up and leave."

"Go back to limbo? I'd sooner cut off my hands. Limbo's worse than hell. At least in hell, you've someone to talk to."

"How about heaven? Or won't they—"

"Don't say it. Anyway, I can't go. I don't know how." He glowed a thoughtful ochre. "Unless Father Tim can find a spell in one of his brother's grimoires."

Father Tim inherited a collection of occult books from his late brother, an exorcist with the Catholic church. Several grimoires numbered among the collection. The priest had loaned Gethsemane the spell book she used to bring Eamon—and, unexpectedly, an eighteenth-century sea captain—back from the other side with the strict admonishment that she'd never ask for another conjuring spell. "I don't think he'd be open to the suggestion," she said.

"What about the girl, then? Saoirse Nolan."

"I'd rather not involve her." Saoirse, the younger sister of one of Gethsemane's students, was homeschooled. Both brilliant and prescient, she managed to sneak a few of Father Tim's spell books among the Latin and Greek texts he gave her to translate. "She's only twelve."

"Twelve going on thirty-five," Eamon said. "Good head on her shoulders."

Gethsemane waved away the suggestion. "I'm probably worrying about nothing. I've watched *Ghost Hunting Adventures* since its first season. Five seasons later and the boys have yet to turn up any hardcore paranormal proof. They usually just capture a bunch of bleeps and blips and unintelligible white noise. Siobhan turned up more convincing stuff." After a pause she added, "May she rest in peace." Siobhan Moloney, Dunmullach's resident fake psychic and blackmailer, had met an untimely end not long after Gethsemane's arrival. "Why should this investigation be any different?"

"Because this time there's a genuine ghost?"

Gethsemane rolled her eyes and stood. "You're supposed to reassure me, not validate my fears. We'll see what we're up against when they get here. Right now, I have to head over to St. B's."

"No school today."

"Aed Devlin wants to meet with Headmaster Riordan and me to plan the schedule. He's going to give three master classes as well as a couple of lectures."

"What's he going to talk about? How to make a right bags of your career?"

"Stop it. Anyone would think you were jealous."

"Of Aed Devlin?" Eamon laughed.

"Devlin is a gifted composer on a brilliant career trajectory." She corrected herself. "Who was on a brilliant trajectory." He'd been tapped to become music director at the Metropolitan Opera.

"Until he crashed and burned. Billy's right, he's a has-been."

"One negative article—"

"One scathing indictment in one of the most influential

classical music publications in the world did to him what one bad eruption from Vesuvius did to Pompeii."

"Granted, the article damaged his career." The vicious piece had scuttled Devlin's rise to the top.

"Destroyed, demolished, devastated."

"Hurt. But one negative write-up, even such an unusually vituperative one, doesn't equate to a lack of talent. This new opera's giving him the chance to rebuild—"

"Resurrect."

She ignored him. "—his career. A fresh start. Everyone deserves a second chance."

Two

Gethsemane twirled a pen back and forth between her fingers and tried not to watch the clock in Headmaster Riordan's office. She needed to get back to Carraigfaire before the ghost hunting crew arrived. The gray-haired, youthful-faced man seated near her in front of the headmaster's desk, Aed Devlin, perused his planner. Headmaster Riordan stood near the display case, home to the trophy Gethsemane and the honors orchestra won in the recent All-County competition, on the opposite side of the room. Riordan and Devlin, both St. Brennan's "Oul Boys," had attended school together. Gethsemane knew this loyalty had prompted Riordan to pull strings and call in favors to let Devlin premiere his new opera at the Athaneum, the village opera house. It had also prompted his suggestion that she include Devlin in her lesson plans. Not that he'd twisted her arm. Having a talented opera composer, even a disgraced one, available provided a rare opportunity for the boys.

A minute ticked by. Riordan coughed. Devlin looked up from his planner. "Sorry, Rick, Dr. Brown. I'm going ninety getting this opera ready. My schedule's pure murder. How about Thursday, first period after lunch? Does that work for you, Dr. Brown?"

"Yes," she said. "Perfect. A master class will keep the boys engaged, help them refocus after indulging in their tasty, nutritious midday meal."

Devlin addressed Riordan. "School lunch must have improved a helluva lot since we were here. I remember noon meal smelling like a bog and tasting half as good as peat."

"Dr. Brown's being facetious, Aed. Sorry to say lunch hasn't improved over the years. But the quality of the musicians has." Riordan pressed a hand against the display case's glass.

"Yes, congratulations, Dr. Brown. Your win is legendary." He nodded at the center shelf, crowded with Gethsemane's golden piano-shaped trophy. "About time St. Brennan's rare pearl had some company in there." His gaze dropped to the lower shelf, home to the only other trophy St. Brennan's ever won in the All County, seventy-five years prior.

"How many boys will you have time for in the master class, Mr. Devlin?" she asked.

"Five, if they limit their pieces to short ones." He consulted his planner again. "I could give two more master classes the following week as well as a lecture Friday and one the Monday after, if that's all right. I know I'm disrupting your schedule. And call me Aed."

"No disruption at all, Aed." She meant it. Artists of Aed's caliber seldom held master classes at the secondary-school level. He was a brilliant instrumentalist and a compositional genius. Almost as good as Eamon. And not everyone thought the review that did him in was deserved. Many, herself included, thought it was a hatchet job.

"That's settled, then." Riordan crossed the room and sat at his desk. "I'll have my assistant formally add you to the calendar, Aed, and give you a copy of the schedule so you don't forget. I know how single-minded you can be when you're working on a new piece."

Sounded like a ghost she knew. When they were alive, Eamon so engrossed himself in each new work that his wife, Orla, had to remind him to eat.

"You know me too well, Rick." Aed clapped his hands and relaxed back into his chair.

Gethsemane glanced at the clock. She hesitated. Yes, the ghost hunters were on the way, but..."May we have a preview, Aed?" She couldn't resist this chance. "No one's in the music room now. We could head over there and—"

Aed interrupted the suggestion with a wave. "No need for a music room." He closed his eyes and whistled. A soft adagio, notes so low that Gethsemane strained to hear them, intensified into an eerie allegro, reminiscent of a danse macabre. Gooseflesh pimpled her arms. She shivered and tried to convince herself the faint strains of Tchaikovsky's "Pathétique" that played somewhere deep in her head weren't warning her of impending disaster as they competed with Aed's ominous melody.

Aed shifted back to the bone-chilling adagio, then stopped. "The overture."

"Good Lord, Aed." Riordan, pale, pulled a handkerchief from his breast pocket and wiped his forehead. "If the overture's that unnerving, the rest of the opera must be positively demonic." His voice cracked on the last word. He cleared his throat and readjusted his jacket.

"Thank you, Rick," Aed said. "I aim to discomfit, if not outright terrify. After all, I am writing about a savage murder. Now," he clapped his hands, "how about we discuss something almost as important as music?" He paused. Gethsemane and Riordan remained silent. "Food. I haven't eaten in donkey's years, and the swill I ate on the plane makes the St. Brennan's menu seem gourmet."

"You'll dine with us, of course, Aed," Riordan said. "Maeve's dying to see you." The headmaster turned to Gethsemane. "You'll join my wife, Aed, and me for dinner?"

"Thank you for the invitation, sir, but I'm afraid I can't." She glanced at the clock again.

"A previous engagement?" Riordan asked.

"Not exactly." Leftover shepherd's pie from the pub did not count as a dinner engagement. "Some, er, inspectors are coming to look at the cottage."

"Nothing serious, I hope," Riordan said. "Leaky roof, dodgy pipes."

"Nothing disastrous." She rose. "But you know old houses. The inspectors might find all sorts of things if they look hard enough."

Aed rose as well.

Gethsemane waved him back into his seat. "One thing before I go. I wonder if I might convince you to squeeze one or two extra lectures into your already-bursting schedule. I'd love to show some of the less musically inclined boys that opera is so much more than fat women singing in a language they can't understand."

Aed laughed. "Plenty of grown folks think as much of opera. Or should I say, think so little of opera?"

Gethsemane, caught up in her idea, sat again. "That's wrong. So wrong." She slapped the back of one hand into the palm of the other. "Opera is passion, intrigue, love, death, betrayal, despair. It's, it's," she searched for the word, "fundamental."

"You're preaching to the choir, professor," Aed said.

Riordan cleared his throat. "You make it sound rather intense for impressionable schoolboys."

"Bollocks, Rick," Aed said. "Hardly worse than the penny dreadfuls, potboilers, and pulp fiction lads have been reading under the covers late at night since St. Brennan's opened its doors."

"And not half as bad as what they stream from the internet these days," Gethsemane added.

"You've sold me, professor," Aed said. "You pick the class and I'll make the time."

"How about Introduction to Music History? That's Friday, right before Advanced Music Theory, which you're already scheduled for."

"Perfect." Aed clapped his hands. "I'll regale the young skeptics with the tale of murder and revenge I used as the basis of my new work. Dark Hungarian legends are always a hit with the tween set."

"Aed..." Riordan cautioned.

"Don't be an old woman, Rick. I'll keep it suitable for daytime viewing. You won't be deluged with angry letters from parents complaining of bills for therapy to treat the wee ones' nightmares."

"Perfect." Gethsemane stood again and shook Aed's hand. "I really do have to run. Maybe we can meet later at the pub and discuss specifics about lesson plans?"

"Or we could drink 'til we're fluthered and piss the night away singing randy pub songs." Aed winked at Headmaster Riordan's blushing discomfort. "Ladies' choice."

Riordan, red to his hairline, fiddled with papers on his desk. Gethsemane managed to hold back her laughter until she reached the hall. She leaned against a wall, doubled over with mirth, and ignored perplexed stares from the custodian at the opposite end of the corridor.

The custodian looked away from her and sniffed. "D'ya smell that?"

Ending the laughter required some effort. "Smell what?" She wiped the back of her hands across her eyes.

The custodian inhaled deeply. "Grease. Pepper." He frowned. "They fixing slop in the dining hall today?"

A loud creak from the ceiling and a blast of Tchaikovsky in her head preempted her reply. "Look out!" she shouted.

The custodian jumped back seconds before an overhead light fixture crashed to the floor where he'd been standing.

Aed and the headmaster came into the hall.

"What the bloody hell happened?" Aed asked, stepping around broken glass, tangled wire, and shattered light bulbs.

Riordan studied the section of ceiling where the fixture had hung. He spoke to the custodian. "Call the safety manager and the electrician right away. And clean up this mess."

"Are you all right?" Gethsemane asked the custodian.

"Aye." He rubbed his cheek where a piece of flying glass had caught him. "I'm fine. Thanks for the warning." He said to Riordan, "I'll get right on it, Headmaster." He pulled a phone from his pocket and walked towards the exit.

"What happened?" Riordan asked Gethsemane.

She shook her head. "The light fell without warning." Except the Tchaikovsky, which only she'd heard. "Bam." She slapped her hands together to mimic the light's descent. "All of a sudden."

"Lucky no one got hurt," Aed said.

"Yes." Riordan shifted his gaze between ceiling and wreckage. "This could have been a disaster if students had been here."

The custodian returned with yellow plastic "caution" signs and set them up on both ends of the destroyed light. "Safety's on the way. Couldn't reach the electrician. I'll try him again later."

Riordan straightened his tie. "I leave this in your hands, then. Notify my secretary as soon as the hall's clear." He gestured toward his office and nodded at Gethsemane. "Please excuse Aed and me, Dr. Brown. And hadn't you better hurry? You'll be late for those inspectors."

Gethsemane swore and looked at her watch. She'd have to rush to make it. She wished she had a car instead of the Pashley Parabike on indefinite loan from the parish priest. Or that she had Eamon's ability to vanish from one spot and reappear instantly in another. She said goodbye to the custodian, eased past the wreckage, and hurried for the door.

Kent Danger filled Carraigfaire's doorway as he smiled down at Gethsemane. He towered over her five-foot-three frame by a foot. His quarterback build, wavy blond hair, and blue eyes numbered him among the beautiful people. He flashed perfect white teeth and extended a hand. "Hi, I'm Kent." His voice sounded higher pitched in person than on TV, closer to tenor than baritone. "May I call you Gethsemane?"

"Sure, Kent."

Gethsemane ushered him inside and counted as his entourage filed in behind him. She'd reached twenty-two by the time she closed the door after the last one. Who were all these people? "I recognize a few of you." She nodded at the faces familiar from the television program.

Kent laughed. "We're window dressing. Everyone else you see actually makes the show happen." He introduced the collection of tech people, stylists, researchers, and other behind-the-scenes types who formed the show's crew.

"How does this work?" Gethsemane asked. "I've never been the subject of a ghost hunt before."

"First, relax. You don't need to do anything other than answer some questions. I hope you'll answer them. Our investigations aren't meant to stress you or trick you. We try to minimize the disruption to your life."

"I've watched your show once or twice." No need to let them know she watched regularly. "Some pretty stressful and frightening things happened." *Ghost Hunting Adventures* reigned notorious for both its physicality and the amount of profanity that had to be bleeped out. Eamon swore like a choirboy in comparison.

"A lot happens in the editing room after the investigation wraps. The actual onsite part involves hours of sitting and waiting. Nothing anyone wants to see in today's one-hundred-forty-character world. It ranks somewhere below reconciling your bank statements on the excitement scale. So we cut out all the mundane stuff, add in some creepy graphics and spooky music, and voila, a nonstop, amped up, in-your-face ghost hunt."

"You guys get pretty amped up when you find evidence of a paranormal entity." She shoved her hands in her pockets to conceal the air quotes she put around the word "evidence." A light flashing, or an alarm sounding on a meter, an indecipherable noise captured on a digital audio recorder, an orb, or a shadow captured on camera counted as proof of the paranormal and triggered apoplectic excitement and shouts of vindication against innumerable skeptics. Who knew what the ghost hunters would do if they actually encountered Eamon in all his full-bodied, blue-auraed glory. Speaking of which—she sniffed. No hint of leather and soap, Eamon's telltale scent. Good. He'd taken her advice to lay low. At least she hoped he had. "Amped as in out of control."

Kent flashed the perfect teeth again. "I confess to kind of losing it when we capture evidence we can't debunk. After all, that's why we do this—travel the world, spend time away from family, put ourselves in dangerous situations—to capture irrefutable evidence of life after death. So," he encompassed the room with a sweep of his arm, "why don't we get started? The sooner we set up, the sooner we can get some of these people out of your way."

For the next hour, Gethsemane hung back as Kent's team tramped through the cottage with meters and recorders and cameras. They measured temperatures and electromagnetic fields, photographed empty corners, and recorded silent rooms. Gethsemane sniffed the air from time to time. No trace of Eamon. She said a mental thank you. She also listened. Whenever danger threatened, Tchaikovsky's "Pathétique" played in her head. She seldom heeded the warning, but it always sounded. Now, only silence.

She relaxed on the couch in the study with a glass of Waddell and Dobb bourbon—twelve-year-old, double-oaked single barrel reserve, Eamon's favorite libation—and a book on Hungarian folklore. Since Aed based his new opera on a Hungarian legend, familiarity with the subject would help bring context to lesson plans she developed as tie-ins with the composition.

"Magyar Moon," a male voice said behind her.

She swore and dropped the book.

The speaker, a young man in a t-shirt and jeans, with long dark hair in need of washing, picked it up and handed it to her. "Sorry, didn't mean to startle you. Hardy Lewis." The faintest trace of brogue tinged his New York accent.

"You're one of the tech guys," she said.

"I'm also a researcher. I wanted to talk to you, ask you a few questions. Kent will do the on-air interview, of course, but I hoped to gather some background on the hauntings." Her expression must have suggested she wanted to provide background almost as much as she wanted to chew broken glass, because he followed up with, "I don't mean to pry. Actually, let's be honest. I do want to pry. But I'll limit my intrusive, unwelcome questions to your experiences living in a haunted house. Nothing about childhood traumas or secret loves."

She'd promised Billy she would cooperate. Her continued shelter depended on her cooperation. She set her book and glass on the coffee table and rearranged herself on the couch. "I'm not sure what I'll be able to tell you, but go ahead and intrude." She waved him to a seat.

"Let's start with the obvious. Do you believe in ghosts?"

She hesitated. Did "cooperate" mean "don't lie"? Would things be worse if she lied and Hardy believed her? *Ghost Hunting Adventures* delighted in turning skeptics into former skeptics. No point making herself a target. Better to confess. "Yes, I believe in ghosts." The barest whiff of leather and soap and a note of laughter rewarded her honesty.

Hardy's head jerked around. He glanced into the corners of the room.

Gethsemane forced her face to remain neutral. "Something wrong?" Please, please, please let the question sound innocent.

Hardy stared at her for a moment, then smiled. He reached for her book. "Magyar. That's Hungarian, isn't it? I thought an Irish ghost haunted this cottage."

"That's homework. Aed Devlin—you've probably never heard of him. He's a composer, opera primarily. He's based his newest work on a Hungarian—what's the matter, Hardy?"

Hardy, frozen and pale, stared straight ahead but looked like he was focusing on something beyond the room. He gripped the mythology book, his knuckles white with the effort. He shook slightly and gave no indication he'd heard her question. Or even realized she sat a couple of feet away from him.

Gethsemane risked a look around. Nothing in the room explained his reaction. No Eamon hanging out by the window or leaning against the bookcases. The smell of peat drifted in on the wind from the cliffs, untainted by the scents of leather or soap. The only laughter came from the crew in the hall. Had she said something? "Hardy?" she repeated.

He blinked and snapped back from wherever he'd been. "Sorry. Did you ask me a question?"

"Have you heard of Aed Devlin?" Stringy hair and a t-shirt didn't preclude knowledge of classical music. Had Devlin's name spooked him?

"I have heard of him, actually. My mother's a huge opera fan. Devlin's her particular favorite. She's obsessed with him, almost a groupie. You should have seen her reaction to the review that blew up his career. Lucky for the reviewer she couldn't get to him. She'd have ripped his heart out." Hardy dropped his gaze and picked at a fingernail. "I, um, don't suppose you could introduce me to Devlin. Mom would be over the moon if I got his autograph."

"Sure." Aed would probably love to meet the son of a devoted fan. Who wouldn't enjoy meeting someone who kept faith in you, despite prevailing opinion? "I'm meeting him at the Rabbit—that's the pub—later tonight to talk about some lectures he's giving to my classes. You're welcome to join us."

Hardy's smile made him look like a kid who'd just learned Santa was bringing him the bike he'd been asking for all year. "This new opera, it's not a secret, is it? Can you give me a hint what it's about? I promise not to post on social media. Can't promise I won't tell Mom."

"The premiere's in a few weeks, so I guess it's no secret. It's called 'Kastély.' Aed based it on the Hungarian legend of a princess entombed in a castle wall as a sacrifice so construction on the castle could be finished in time to save the city from invaders."

"Zoltánfi Castle!" a voice exclaimed from behind them. "I know that place."

Gethsemane and Hardy turned to see the new speaker, a woman about Hardy's age. She sported robin's egg blue hair and piercings in every pierceable part of her head. "I did an investigation there before I joined the boys' crew. Cree-pee. Some dude's really writing an opera about the place?"

"Wrote," Gethsemane said. "It's finished."

The blue-haired woman, who Hardy introduced as Poe, went on. "Dude must have a pair the size of the moon. I'm the first one to challenge a curse, but I'd sooner play in traffic than mess with Maja."

"I'm sorry," Gethsemane said. "I have no idea what you're

talking about."

Poe gawped. "You don't know about Maja's curse?"

Gethsemane shook her head. "Not up on my curses, I'm afraid." She had enough to keep up with with a garden-variety haunting.

Poe sat on the edge of the coffee table. She leaned close to Gethsemane and lowered her voice, as if delivering classified information. "Maja was a Hungarian noblewoman—not a princess, by the way—back in the thirteenth or fourteenth century. She was rumored to be the most beautiful woman in the country. The smartest and kindest, too. She married the youngest son of the Zoltán family."

So far, this sounded like every fairytale ever. "Let me guess," Gethsemane said. "Her mother-in-law, the evil queen, hated her—"

"Nah, the baroness—not queen—was cool with her. Everything would've been okay if the Mongols hadn't invaded." Poe broke off. "Hey, Hardy, got a cigarette?"

"I quit eight months ago, and you can't smoke in guests' homes, anyway."

"Forgot. I'm used to telling this story with a cig in one hand and a beer in the other."

Gethsemane gestured at the bar cart. "You can help yourself to whiskey if you tell me what happened with the Mongol hordes."

Poe accepted the offer. She spoke as she poured her drink. "The Mongols invaded and pretty much destroyed everything—pillaged, slaughtered, you get the idea." She paused and sipped. "Hey, what is this?" She raised the glass to the light and studied its amber contents. "Liquid paradise."

"It's bourbon," Gethsemane said. "Waddell and Dobb Double-Oaked Twelve-Year-Old Reserve Single Barrel. From Kentucky."

"Say, isn't that the bourbon Eamon McCarthy—" Hardy began.

Gethsemane cut him off. "It's a fresh bottle."

Poe ignored both of them, her story of invasion and destruction seemingly forgotten. She poured another glass of bourbon, sniffed it as if she knew what she was doing, took her time savoring several more mouthfuls.

Gethsemane cleared her throat. "The Mongols?"

Poe returned to her perch on the coffee table. "So, yeah, back to the Mongols." She sipped bourbon. "Where can you get this stuff? It's better than—"

"Poe," Hardy cut in. "Try and focus."

Poe sighed and drained her glass. "The Mongols. They wiped out everything and everyone they ran into. Wiped out practically the whole kingdom. But some people, the king included, survived. After the Mongols cleared out, the king granted pieces of his remaining land to surviving nobles on the condition they build a castle on the land to protect the kingdom, in case the Mongols decided to come back. The Zoltán family got some land and tried to build a castle, but every time the walls got yea high," Poe extended her arm and held her hand above her head, "some disaster happened and destroyed whatever they'd built. They had to start all over again. This went on and on for, like, five years or something. The castle walls would not stand. Finally, the king threatened to take the land back and give it to someone else." Poe stopped.

"And?" Gethsemane asked.

"One sec." Poe hopped up and went back to the bar cart. Replenished, she returned to the table and continued her story. "Baroness Zoltán consulted a fortune teller. The seer told her she had to encase one of her daughters-in-law in a castle wall. If she did this, the castle would be built within the next three months and the walls would stand forever."

"That's whacked," Hardy said.

"Yeah, the baroness thought so, too. She wasn't a psycho, and she wasn't crazy about the idea of sacrificing a daughter-in-law, but she had eight. Killing one, compared to losing them all, plus her sons and her grandkids, to torture and mass slaughter in the next invasion, seemed like the lesser evil."

"How'd she choose?" Gethsemane asked. "Lottery? Show of hands?"

"Some versions of the story say she was supposed to sacrifice her eldest daughter-in-law, but she liked the eldest best, or the eldest was pregnant or something, so the baroness offered Maja, the youngest, instead. Some versions say Maja was the choice from the jump. Long and short of it, the baroness tricked Maja into going to the construction site where seven of the sons, all of them except Maja's husband, entombed her in the castle's stone walls."

"That's a horrible, horrible story," Gethsemane said. "Opera-worthy horrible. Probably why Aed chose it as the basis for his new work. However, it's not a curse."

"The curse." Poe punctuated her words with a finger jabbed in Hardy's knee. "Maja uttered the curse with her dying words. She swore revenge on the entire Zoltán family, from generation unto generation. She said Castle Zoltánfi would, indeed, stand forever, but the family would fall. She promised her spirit would come back and murder the firstborn son of every branch of the family. A keeper of promises, she delivered: the baroness's firstborn, the heir to the title, died by impalement on the first anniversary of Maja's death. Then the firstborn sons of all the brothers died gruesome deaths: disembowelment, beheading, you name it, and always on the anniversary of Maja's murder. To this day, in every generation of the Zoltán family, the firstborn son dies of unnatural causes on the same anniversary." Poe drained her glass. "Which is next Thursday."

"What happened to Maja's husband?" Hardy asked. "The eighth brother? Why didn't he stop his siblings from killing his wife?"

"They waited until he was out of town to do the deed. When he came home and found his wife dead, he took their daughter to a convent to be raised by nuns, then threw himself off one of the castle's parapets."

"I don't think Aed Devlin has to worry," Gethsemane said. "He's Irish, not Hungarian. And he's the third of five brothers."

If asked to describe Poe's grin, Gethsemane would have called it "devilish." "The curse has a second part," the blue-haired woman said. "A fifteenth-century addendum. By then the Zoltán family were social outcasts. No one wanted to marry into it. People ridiculed and whispered about them. Playwrights and poets considered their story fodder. Authors and composers who catered to the lower classes wrote bawdy plays and drinking songs about them. The then-baroness, named Maja after the infamous legend—"

"How's that for tempting fate?" Hardy whispered to Gethsemane.

If Poe heard him, she ignored him. "—decided to put an end to the shame. She practiced folk magic, and she modified her vengeful ancestor's curse. She decreed that if anyone ever wrote about, sang about, preached about, or publicly spoke about the Zoltán family curse, they would die in the same way as that Zoltán generation's eldest sons. She also swore a wasting sickness would claim the lives of any firstborn male who listened to or watched a performance of the doomed piece."

"Did it work?" Hardy asked.

"Oh, did it," Poe said. "Vlad Nagy, the Duke of Toth's favorite court musician, composed a ballad based on the legend. Right in the middle of the premiere performance, a freak wind blew out of nowhere, circled the banquet hall, whipped the duke's entire sword collection off the wall, and sent all the swords flying at Vlad. Every. Single. Sword. They cut him to ribbons. Three days later, the news arrived that the heir to Castle Zoltánfi died when a gang of assassins jumped him in an alley and cut him to bits. And Vlad wasn't the only one to suffer Maja's wrath. Both the duke's eldest and Vlad's eldest contracted a mysterious illness within moments of Vlad's death. They stopped eating, they couldn't sleep. They transformed from the dukedom's finest specimens of young manhood to withered, bedridden shells in twenty-four hours and were both dead in a week. And—"

Hardy raised a hand. "Enough. We don't need to hear anymore. Isn't talking about curses supposed to be bad luck?"

Poe shrugged. "Don't think so. Anyway, I'm almost done. Since about the sixteenth century, no one's even been able to finish a play or book or composition about Maja. Bad things happen if they even try. Careers implode, marriages dissolve, they develop disfiguring and fatal illnesses, you name it. Maja's curse is even more unlucky than the Scottish play. And, same as with the Scottish play, some people won't even speak the curse's real name. They call it the Jinx."

"You spoke about it," Hardy said. "At length."

"But I," Poe said, "only chase ghosts. I don't write about them."

The Jinx. "The ridicu—" Gethsemane began, then bit it off. She used to define ridiculous as a belief in ghosts. Look at her now. Instead she said, "Maybe the curse is broken. Aed's already written the opera. He hasn't been dismembered, stabbed, set afire, or grown a second head." True, his career had imploded and his marriage had disintegrated, but he hadn't written the opera yet. "He has one or two last-minute tweaks—"

Poe's devilish grin returned. "Then he hasn't finished it yet. Has he?"

"Sheesh, Poe." Hardy frowned at his colleague. "Do you get off on the thought of some poor guy having his guts ripped out just because he wrote a play or a song about a woman who's been dead for eight hundred years?"

"I just don't like the idea of a man profiting from the suffering of a woman."

Hardy stood and gestured at Poe. "When feminism meets sociopathy. I'm going to go check with Kent and see where we're at. Hopefully we can knock off for the evening." He frowned at Poe while he spoke to Gethsemane. "That drink at the pub sounds like a great idea about now."

Poe perked up. "Pub? You're going to a pub? Can I come with?"

"No," Hardy said.

"Sure," Gethsemane said.

Hardy stared at Gethsemane. "You want to hear more blood and gore?"

Gethsemane shrugged. Solving murders had improved her

stomach for blood and gore. "The Mad Rabbit has a way of making people forget about death and loss and the bitter tears of disappointment." She nodded toward Poe. "Once she gets a pint in her and someone picks up a fiddle and gets a sing-along going, thoughts of vengeful ghosts will be as far from her mind as Earth is from Jupiter."

Hardy and Poe both snorted.

"You don't know Poe," Hardy said.

"I don't sing," Poe said.

"You've never been to the Rabbit," Gethsemane countered.

Kent appeared in the doorway. "Rabbit? You've seen an animal ghost?"

Gethsemane laughed. "The only animals people see after a night at the Rabbit are pink elephants. The Mad Rabbit is the local pub."

"A pub crawl?" Kent clapped his hands. "I'm game."

"Not much of a crawl," Gethsemane said. "Only the one pub."

"I thought we were going to track down the local clergy and get the religious perspective on the Carraigfaire hauntings," Hardy said.

Kent looked at his watch. "It's kind of late. Tomorrow's Sunday. We'll attend services and speak to the priest afterwards."

"A few hours at the pub, Kent," Poe said, "and you'll need to go to church for more than just research."

Kent scowled at her, then tapped at his smartphone. "Father Tim Keating, right? He's the parish priest?"

Gethsemane guessed he meant the questions for her. She nodded. "You might find him at the Rabbit. He's a pretty broad-minded priest." And a better paranormal expert than anyone in this room.

"We're done for the night?" Hardy asked.

A woman appeared in the doorway behind Kent. Her silver hair pegged her around the same age as Aed and Headmaster Riordan. Her close-fitting t-shirt and jeans showed she wore her age better than either of the men. Chronologically, she could have been Kent's mother, but the way her hand caressed his shoulder suggested her feelings for the blond ghostbuster were anything but maternal.

Kent smiled down at her. "I think we're done. We have a plan for interviews tomorrow. Ciara and Poe can get some interior and exterior shots of the cottage in the morning light. Hardy, after church, you take the tech crew up to the lighthouse and see where we can set up some cameras, maybe some EMF pods, and digital recorders. I understand the ghost sightings occur primarily at the cottage, so we'll do our actual stake out here, but we still might catch some EVP or EMF surges up there. Have I lost you, Gethsemane? EVPs are—"

"Electronic voice phenomena and EMF stands for electromagnetic force." She had told him she watched the show. She studied Ciara. She remembered seeing her in the flux of people who'd invaded Carraigfaire earlier but couldn't recall actually meeting her. She offered the silver-haired woman her hand. "We haven't been introduced. Properly, I mean."

Ciara kept one of her hands on Kent's shoulder and shook Gethsemane's hand with her other. "Ciara Tierney." Her brogue sounded less musical than the local dialect. Gethsemane couldn't place it. "Poe and I are the crew's still photographers. Pleased to meet you. Properly, I mean."

"Quitting time means pub time." Poe twisted her blue mane into a bun and secured it with a scrunchie produced from one of the innumerable pockets that dotted her cargo pants. "You guys ready?" She directed the question to Kent and Ciara.

Kent touched Ciara's elbow. "I think we'll skip tonight's party."

Poe protested. "But you said—"

"We'd love to go," Ciara interjected. "I bet the craic will be ninety. We don't want to miss out on the hooley, Kent."

Kent's hand moved to Ciara's waist. "It's late, Cee."

"We need some local color for the show," she said, "some flare. It's what makes us different from the other paranormal shows. What better place to pick up local color than the pub? Ma always used to say gossip flowed through pubs and churches like water through cheesecloth. Since I prefer to leave the church-going to Hardy, I vote for a night at the former."

Hardy flushed.

"Is the pub haunted?" Poe asked.

"As far as I know," Gethsemane said, "the only spirits in the pub come in bottles."

"As far as you know." Poe phrased it as a challenge. "Maybe there are ghosts no one's told you about. Maybe you haven't asked enough questions."

Gethsemane Brown hadn't asked enough questions? She'd been accused of much since she arrived in Dunmullach, but not asking enough questions didn't number among her sins. A couple of people had tried to kill her to stop her from asking questions. "You're welcome to try your luck," she said to Poe.

"Skill," Poe countered.

"Skill, luck. Either way, here's a tip: buy a couple of rounds first."

"All settled," Ciara said. Kent's hand moved from her waist to his pocket. "Down to the pub, first round's on the crew. We'll pry loose a few secrets before the night's through. You driving, Hardy?"

Three

"You've got mad parking talent, Hardy," Poe said as Hardy wedged the crew's rented SUV into a space designed for a Mini.

Gethsemane, Poe, Ciara, Kent, and Hardy climbed out of the vehicle. They had—Ciara had—invited the rest of the *Ghost Hunting Adventures* crew to join them, but everyone else begged off, citing the need to call family back home or get to bed early. The four paranormal investigators followed Gethsemane to the Mad Rabbit.

Muted noise from the pub crowd bled out to the street through the closed front door and hit them with a blast when Hardy opened it. Gethsemane led the way inside, through throngs of locals, over to the bar where she elbowed her way to the counter. She greeted the barman by name. "Hey, Murphy. Any chance of getting a table?"

The stout publican mopped his glistening forehead with a bar towel. "See for yourself. Place is bloody packed."

"Bet Father Tim hears lots of confessions tomorrow."

"Including his own. He's here." Murphy jerked his chin toward where Father Tim sat in a corner with the church secretary and sexton. He'd worked his way through a pint. Gethsemane caught his eye and waved.

"Who're those fellas?" Murphy asked. His gesture included Ciara and Poe.

"Don't laugh. They're part of the paranormal investigation

team Billy invited to Carraigfaire to capture proof Eamon's ghost haunts the cottage."

"Was Billy ossified when he made that deal? Or perhaps not the full shilling?"

"More like mad at me and—" She almost said "Eamon." She glanced over her shoulder to see if Kent and the others stood within earshot. "Mad at me and wanting to mitigate his losses. Hank Wayne's deal would have netted Billy a huge payout."

"And ruined the village." Murphy pursed his lips as if to spit. He looked around, apparently not finding a suitable place to expectorate, and swore. "I'm glad you stood up to him. I've known Billy his whole life, and I'd be first to have his back in a row, but I swear I'd've sorted him out if he'd gone through with the sale." He glanced at the ghost hunters. "I still might teach him a lesson for inviting that bunch of nutters to put on a holy show."

"Hey." Poe muscled her way to stand next to Gethsemane. "Look in the back corner. Is that really her?"

"Really who?" Gethsemane stood on tiptoe to see over the crowd. An attractive Asian woman sat at a table tucked into the far corner of the pub. Statuesque even while seated, she smiled down at the admirers crowded around her table, like a queen holding court. Her red lips matched those in the headshot on the back cover of the hated book, the hatchet job that twisted the details of the McCarthy murders and painted Eamon as a wife-killing monster. Venus James. The queen of true crime—or the queen of libel, depending on which side of her pen you fell on—and ghost hunters, all in the same night. "Shite," she muttered. There wasn't enough Bushmills in the world.

"Ms. James!" Poe shouted. Heads turned. Gethsemane would have kicked her if not for the press of people surrounding them. "Ms. James," Poe repeated as she pushed past the stares of patrons and curses of jostled barmaids on her way to Venus's table. Gethsemane followed her, ignoring the angry faces that blamed her for this disruptive whirlwind. "Excuse mes" and apologies from the other ghost hunters trailed behind them.

Gethsemane arrived next to Poe in time to see her grab Venus's hand between both of hers. Poe gushed, "I am so, like, your biggest fan. I've read all of your books, I've followed you since you were a street reporter at KXBH, I read all of the exposés you wrote for the *Tattler*." She paused for breath. "Well, I read the online archived versions, but I read them."

Venus spoke in the accent-less tone of an American news anchor. "May I know my biggest fan's name?"

"I'm Poe." She gestured past Gethsemane to her colleagues. "I'm with *Ghost Hunting Adventures*. We're staking out an old cottage to capture evidence proving Eamon McCarthy's ghost haunts the place."

The pub erupted in laughter. Gethsemane prayed for a hole to open in the floor and swallow her. No, so she could push Poe into it. The blue-haired girl exhibited the subtlety of a rutting buck.

Venus flashed Gethsemane a honeysuckle-sweet smile. "Seems as if everyone's investigating you, Dr. Brown."

A familiar male voice chimed in before she could respond. "Evening, Sissy." Frankie Grennan, St. Brennan's math teacher and Gethsemane's sometime co-conspirator in her unorthodox crime-solving escapades, grinned up at her. She'd been so focused on Venus, she hadn't noticed Frankie seated at the table across from her. He'd replaced his usual too-big tweed jacket with a slim-fit herringbone blazer. Crisp pleats replaced his khakis' customary wrinkles. A sandalwood aroma wafted from his still damp, swept-back copper waves. He'd been growing a beard since he'd helped her clear her brother-in-law of theft charges, but he'd clipped and shaved the once-scruffy fringe. Now a neat, close-trimmed beard, a shade darker than the hair on his head, framed his face. Its hairs skirted the dimple in his left cheek by an inch. His new wire-rimmed glasses added stereotyped academic flair. Was he putting on a show for Venus, or had the writer, a bona fide fashionista, worked some kind of fashion hoodoo on him?

"Don't call me Sissy." He'd heard her brother-in-law call her by the hated nickname, and he insisted on needling her with it.

Could this evening grow worse?

"Sissy's a fine nickname," another familiar male voice said. Gethsemane cringed. Yes, it could grow worse. Garda an Síochana Inspector Iollan Niall O'Reilly, Dunmullach's only cold case investigator, sat next to Frankie. The handsome inspector vacillated between friendly antagonist and ally. He intermixed warnings about her interference in police business—and about what would happen to her if she persisted in interfering—with valued assistance and, occasionally, appreciation for her efforts. He'd grown his salt-and-pepper hair out some since she last saw him. A gray-flecked dark curl played on his forehead. His trademark stingy-brimmed fedora, an inheritance from his father, rested on the table. He'd also inherited his father's penchant for designer shoes. This pair of Italian leather double monkstraps looked new. A tailored gray pinstripe that matched the smoky hue of his eyes replaced his usual nondescript cop suit. Venus had enchanted him, too.

"Nice shoes," she said. "You must've won your weekly poker game. And Sissy's a perfectly dreadful nickname." She heard laughter in her ear and caught an unmistakable whiff of leather and soap. Eamon picked now to show up? What happened to lying low? She should have known he'd never be able to resist putting in an appearance, even if only a private showing for her. This evening had officially grown worse than a punishment from the eighth circle of hell. "Someone please get me a drink."

Hardy signaled a barmaid. The barmaid ignored him. "I'll get it," he said and started toward the bar.

"Bushmills Twenty-one, neat," Gethsemane called after him as he disappeared into the crowd.

Venus offered Kent her hand. "I bet you're the head ghost hunting adventurer. Tell me your name."

Ciara stepped in front of Kent and intercepted the handshake. "He's Kent Danger, head hunter. I'm Ciara Tierney, lead photographer. You've met Poe. Hardy, research and tech, went for drinks."

Venus smiled at Ciara as if they were lifelong friends. "Please, join us."

"There doesn't seem to be any room," Gethsemane said. The table sat four comfortably. Eight chairs crowded around it, filled by half a dozen others in addition to Venus, Frankie, and Niall. In one chair, a young woman Gethsemane recognized from the bookstore sat on the lap of a man Gethsemane didn't recognize as her boyfriend.

Frankie nodded at the chair-sharing couple. "You can sit on the inspector's lap, Sissy." He winked. People laughed.

She never knew what mood she'd find Frankie in. Sometimes irascible, sometimes gloomy, sometimes impish. Tonight, she got flirty. Whether he flirted with her or Venus, she wasn't sure. "Francis William Rowan Grennan, Abaddon holds a special corner reserved for you, your full name carved in stone over the door."

"Shh." Frankie held a finger to his lips and jerked his head toward Father Tim. "The padre's sitting over there. He might hear you and get ideas."

Niall cuffed him on the shoulder. "Be a gent for once in your life, Frankie. Stand up and let the ladies sit." He offered Gethsemane his chair.

Frankie offered his to Ciara. "Two chairs, three ladies. We're one gent short."

Poe stood close to one of the other men. "I don't mind sitting on a lap."

The man blushed and gave Poe his chair. Kent and Ciara smothered laughs.

Hardy returned with a drink-laden tray. Niall rescued his hat as Hardy juggled the tray onto the center of the table.

"You get a job here, bro?" Kent asked.

"Nah, just trying to expedite." Hardy nodded at an exhausted-looking barmaid. "She didn't seem to mind." The barmaid smiled back wanly. "I got your usuals," he said as he handed drinks to Kent, Ciara, and Poe. "And your Bushmills." Gethsemane accepted the glass of amber liquid. Hardy stepped back from the table, empty-handed, and left the others to sort their own drinks out. "I told the barman same again for everyone else."

"Same again?" Poe asked. "What's that mean?"

"It's a colloquialism," Ciara explained. "It means you'll have another of whatever was in your glass."

Poe raised her pint to her lips and spoke over the rim of the glass. "Since when do you speak Irish colloquialism, Hardy?"

Hardy stammered, "It's, uh, something I picked up somewhere. Just a phrase I heard." He found a patch of wall in a corner and pressed himself against it.

"Not drinking, fella?" the man with the bookstore clerk asked.

"I'm designated driver." Hardy shrugged.

Poe wrinkled her nose and stared into her empty pint glass. "He's applying for a position as altar boy next week."

"Shut up, Poe," Kent said.

An embarrassed silence followed Kent's admonition. Venus jumped into the lull. "Dr. Brown, tell me: you solve murders, you teach music, now you've added 'hunts ghosts' to your resume. How do you manage it all?"

Niall, who'd either developed psychic abilities or had gotten to know her well over the past several months, shot a warning look in Gethsemane's direction.

Her smile wasn't as sweet as Venus'. The woman didn't know how lucky she was she sat within an arm's reach of a law-enforcement officer. "Mad multitasking skills."

"Are you working on a new book, Ms. James?" Ciara asked.

Gethsemane could have hugged her for changing the direction of the conversation. "Ms. James is revising a previous edition of her last book. It contained several factual errors."

"What was the book about?" Ciara inclined her head toward Venus. "Sorry, Ms. James, no offense, but I don't read true crime. Seems innocents are always being hurt and the criminals always getting away with it. Makes for drama, I suppose, but it upsets me."

"She wrote a book," Gethsemane said, "about the murders of Eamon and Orla McCarthy. Like so many others, she wrongly concluded Eamon murdered his wife then killed himself. Now that

Eamon's been cleared of both false accusations—"

"Thanks to your clever detective work." Venus leaned toward Niall. "How did the gardaí feel about an amateur detective taking an active role in a murder investigation?"

Niall, caught mid-sip, coughed. Frankie patted him on the back. "You all right, Niall? Be careful. The truth can be hard to swallow."

Niall elbowed him away. "Dr. Brown provided the guards with valuable assistance." He mumbled something else. Gethsemane caught the word "stubborn."

Gethsemane continued, unfazed by Niall and Frankie's banter. A boon of growing up with younger brothers. "Ms. James needs to correct a few details before releasing the second edition of her book."

"The first edition sold out in record time," Venus said. "The public clamors for an updated account of events."

"Are you going to write about the reported hauntings in the updated version?" Poe asked.

Venus dismissed the suggestion with a wave. "I'm strictly true crime. I'll leave the paranormal to your team."

"Maybe we could work together—"

Venus cut Poe off. "I work alone."

Poe pouted. "I just thought—"

"Safety reasons." Venus flashed a disarming smile. "I'd hate to be responsible for someone being injured while assisting me. I'm sure you know, being a fan, I often run into unsavory characters."

"You needn't fear running into that sort in Dunmullach, Ms. James," Niall said. "This is a safe village. Not many murderous fiends lurking about." Frankie choked on his Guinness. Niall patted him on the back hard enough to knock him forward a step. "Not anymore, anyway, thanks to Sissy."

That nickname again. Did cussing out a garda violate any local ordinances? Activity near the door spared her the risk of finding out. Aed Devlin stepped into the pub and scanned the room. Gethsemane waved him over. "Everyone, meet Aed Devlin. Aed, meet everyone."

A few moments of introductions and chair rearranging ensued. Aed ended up next to Venus, across from Gethsemane.

Hardy stood behind him and reached down over his shoulder to shake his hand. "Happy to finally meet you, sir."

Aed looked up at him, puzzled. "Finally?"

"Ma's a big fan. I grew up listening to your works. Meeting you's—well, Ma will be thrilled when she hears I met her idol."

Venus laid French-manicured fingers on Aed's arm. "You won't remember me, Mr. Devlin. We met a few years ago."

"Of course I remember you, Ms. James. You attended the premiere of one of my operas, 'Plinth,' wasn't it? The music reviewer from the *Times* escorted you."

"You have a remarkable memory, Mr. Devlin." Venus squeezed his arm. "Call me Venus."

"I could never forget such a remarkable face. And it's Aed. How's your friend, the music reviewer, these days?"

"I've no idea. I haven't seen him in ages. Last I heard he married a cellist half his age and moved to Monte Carlo." Venus leaned closer to the composer and lowered her voice. "And may I say how sorry I am about the—incident—with *Classical Music Today* magazine. Not that I'd ever shy away from controversy in pursuit of the truth—"

Gethsemane choked on her Bushmills. She sputtered and tried to say what she thought of Venus's concept of 'pursuit of truth,' when an electric buzz zipped from the nape of her neck to the base of her spine. Leather and soap tickled her nose. She shivered.

"Are you all right, Dr. Brown?" Venus asked.

"Fine," Gethsemane said. "I, um, stubbed my toe."

"Sittin' still?" Frankie asked.

Gethsemane frowned at him. Punching a math teacher would definitely violate local ordinances.

Venus continued. "Nor would I ever suppress a critical story to spare someone's feelings. But what Bernard Stoltz did to you crossed the line. Straight up character assassination. I'm amazed you didn't sue for libel."

Frankie nudged Gethsemane. "What's that about?"

She whispered, "Bernard Stoltz wrote an article accusing Aed of plagiarism. He claimed Aed stole significant portions of music he composed for a film score from one of his music students. The student committed suicide a few weeks before Aed landed the movie deal. Bernard got his hands on some unfinished pieces from the student's apartment. They looked a lot like what Aed had done for the movie."

"Could have been coincidence. Not uncommon for students and teachers to create similar works."

"Not coincidence. But not Aed's fault. Truth was, the student had used Aed's work, not the other way 'round. She tried to pass it off as her senior thesis. She killed herself after her ex-boyfriend threatened to turn her in to school officials and have her expelled unless she took him back. He also stalked and harassed her. The police eventually arrested him. The real story came out in the local papers after the arrest, but the damage to Aed's career was already done. Scandal and notoriety stuck to Aed. The movie's backers spooked and pulled out of the deal, and the whole project ended up on the shelf. Aed was fired and blackballed. No one wanted anything to do with him."

"Didn't this Stoltz fella print a retraction, an apology?"

"Nope." Gethsemane shook her head. "Opposite. He wrote a follow-up piece implying that Aed and the student had a romantic involvement and that Aed was the reason she'd broken up with the stalker boyfriend. He suggested the student might still be alive if Aed hadn't been a cradle-robber. Only suggested, though. Nothing concrete enough to hang a lawsuit on."

Niall leaned in. "What'd Stolz get out of it? Sounds more like a personal vendetta against Aed than," he glanced at Venus, "purely commercial sensationalism."

"No proof," Gethsemane said "but the rumor at the time went Bernard was running a cash-for-good-reviews scam. He wrote for *Classical Music Today*, an influential publication. In exchange for hefty payments, he'd write good reviews and squash any negative publicity. He allegedly tried to shake Aed down, but Aed refused to pay. Bernard made an example of him to keep other musicians in line."

"Was there nothing Aed could do?"

"Without proof?" She winked at the inspector. "Who's always reminding me of the necessity of proof?"

Niall blushed.

"But you said the true story came out in the local papers," Frankie said. "Aed could've used that as evidence."

"True. I guess he didn't have the heart for the fight. Someone else brought Bernard down later, anyway. He tried his scam on a musician with a hidden camera and an active social media account. They smeared him all over the internet—"

"And if it's on the internet, it must be true," Niall and Frankie said in unison.

"Bernard lost his position with *Classical Music Today* magazine and couldn't get hired writing classifieds for a church newsletter. But Aed never pursued his case."

Unaware of Gethsemane's sidebar with Niall and Frankie, Aed stared down at his hands. "'Twould have been no use. The damage was done. A drawn out legal battle would only have prolonged the pain for my wife." He closed his eyes and whispered, "Ex-wife." A headshake and jovial Aed returned. "What's a fella got to do to get a drink in this place?"

"Another drink run, Hardy?" Ciara asked.

Gethsemane couldn't decipher his expression. "Yeah, sure." He jostled a few people on his way to the bar. He didn't apologize.

"What's with him?" Gethsemane whispered to Poe.

Poe shrugged. "I should know? What am I, his mother?"

"What brings you to Dunmullach, Aed?" Kent asked. "You don't mind if I call you Aed, do you? Or is that a privilege reserved for beautiful women?"

Several people laughed. Not Ciara.

"You can call me Aed, too," the composer said to Kent. "I'm

here to premiere my new opera. I've, uh, been out of the music scene for a while. I wanted to stage my return someplace familiar, comforting. I know Dunmullach from my school days, so..."

"Aren't you afraid everybody's going to die?" Poe asked.

"Jesus, Poe," Kent said. "Where do you come up with this crap?"

"No doubt," Aed said, "the young lady refers to the curse of Maja Zoltán. I'm impressed, Miss—Poe, is it? Few people are familiar with fourteenth-century Hungarian legends. I don't believe in curses or magic or the paranormal. I find the deliberate choices of mortals cause most of the evil in the world. No supernatural agency needed. However, some of my cast and crew disdained my skepticism, so I took the precaution of having the production blessed by an obliging Cailleach. There'll be no trouble from any vengeful noblewomen."

"I confess to being one of the many unfamiliar with Hungarian legends," Venus said. "Who's this Maja Zoltán? Is she fascinating?"

Poe didn't need further prompting to retell the blood-soaked tale of death, shame, and revenge. She got as far as the Mongol massacre when Hardy returned with another tray of drinks.

"For Christ's sake, Poe," he said. "Keep it PG-13. You'll put everyone off their feed."

Poe frowned at him but toned down the blood and gore.

"You must agree," Aed said when she'd finished, "it's operatic."

"Speaking of opera," Gethsemane said, "may I bring the boys in the honors orchestra to the theater on Monday to watch rehearsals? Some of them expressed interest. They'd love the opportunity to talk to musicians about the differences between opera orchestras and symphony orchestras. And, perhaps, hear a sneak peek of your new work?"

"I'd be thrilled to have the lads attend rehearsal. It'll be good for them to get out of the classroom and hear music performed in its proper setting." Aed raised his glass to Gethsemane. "Not suggesting you're not a fine teacher, but I recall my days in the honors orchestra. Nothing but rote memorization and repetition.

No wonder we never brought home the All County trophy."

"Before you go," Venus asked, "how about a sneak peek for the grownups?"

"Unless you have a piano tucked under your dress, Ms. James..." Ciara paused as Venus ran a hand along the skirt of her gray bodycon dress, cut just tight enough to let everyone know what was underneath without crossing the line into tacky. Definitely no piano. "What's he going to play on? I don't see any instruments."

Gethsemane looked around. Usually, at least one person would have a fiddle or a bodhran, but tonight the only things present in the Rabbit were voices.

"He could hum a few bars." A whiff of leather and soap accompanied Eamon's voice in her ear.

"Why don't you whistle a bit, Aed?" she said. And regretted, as "Pathétique" immediately followed the suggestion.

"Why the hell not?" Aed stretched and draped his arm along the back of Venus's chair. "I'm among friends." He closed his eyes and whistled as he'd done in Riordan's office. All conversation ceased as the notes of the overture filled the room. Fear and foreboding replaced the good cheer in the atmosphere, turning the pub's packed interior from cozy to claustrophobic. Aed whistled the final adagio. Gethsemane held her breath. The roof didn't collapse.

"That's all for this evening," Aed told the still silent crowd. He rose. "If you want to hear the rest or," he gestured at Poe, "you missed the young lady's vivid account of the fate of Maja Zoltán and want to know what became of the poor bure, you'll have to buy a ticket. On sale now at the Athaneum."

"If you're still alive." Poe's muttered comment echoed loud in the quiet room.

Hardy poked her in the ribs hard enough to make her yelp. "Shut up, Poe."

Venus laid a hand on Aed's arm again. "Would you be kind enough to escort me back to Sweeney's Inn? I don't doubt the inspector's assurances about Dunmullach's safety, but all this talk of death and curses has me..." She waved her other hand. "Well, you can't blame a girl for being a bit jumpy."

Gethsemane heard Eamon's voice again. "The woman writes about serial killers and mass murders with glee, but ghost stories make her nervous?"

Hardy glanced in Gethsemane's direction, then turned his attention back to Aed and Venus. "I can walk you back to the inn, Ms. James."

"Don't trouble yourself, lad." Aed hooked Venus's hand in the crook of his elbow. "I'm headed that way myself. Stay here with your mates and enjoy the craic." He spoke to Venus. "I place myself at your service, sweet lady. I'll defend your life against ghoulies, ghosties, and long-leggedy beasties with my own. You'll not fall into evil hands with Aed Devlin as your protector."

"I knew I could count on you." Venus revealed the true magnificence of her stature as she unfolded herself from her chair. She stood a head taller than Aed. Gethsemane stole a glance at her feet. Six-inch stiletto heels, as trademarked as her red lips.

The group watched them go.

"Who's going to keep Venus from falling into Aed's hands?" Poe asked.

"I didn't get the impression she wanted to be kept out of them," Ciara said.

Gethsemane snapped her fingers. "Hardy, you forgot to get an autograph for your mom."

"He seemed—preoccupied," Hardy said, "I didn't get the sense he'd be in the mood to sign autographs. I'll catch up with him later."

"How about rehearsals on Monday?" Gethsemane asked.

Kent spoke up. "Sounds like a plan. While you're there, Hardy, poke around and see if there's anything to this Maja curse. Maybe we can turn it into a location shoot in Hungary. But now," he made a show of looking at his watch, "it's late, boys and girls. Time for bed. We've got work to do tomorrow."

Ciara slipped her arm through Kent's. "And tonight. Hardy, if you'll see Poe gets back safely, Kent and I will walk back to the inn."

"I can see myself back, thanks," Poe said. "I'm not afraid of the boogeyman."

"Fine by me," Hardy said. "May I give you a ride back to the cottage, Gethsemane?"

"No, thanks, I'm good. You've done enough running around for people. Go on back to Sweeney's. Maybe I'll see you at church tomorrow."

Ciara, Kent, Poe, and Hardy filed out of the pub. Niall reclaimed a chair. He leaned back and grinned at Gethsemane, dimple in full force.

"What?" Gethsemane said.

"I didn't say a word."

"No, but you're thinking several."

Frankie chimed in, his grin as dimpled as Niall's. "He's thinking that only you could land in the middle of both a ghost hunt and a true crime exposé."

"At least there're no dead bodies this time," Niall said. "Try to keep it that way."

"I don't look for murders, Inspector." Gethsemane crossed her arms and slumped in her chair. "They just find me."

"You don't go out of your way to avoid them, either. I think you enjoy solving the puzzles, sussing out who done it."

Did she? Was that why she involved herself in criminal investigations despite the exhortations of cooler heads and common sense? The challenge of answering a riddle? Or a desire—a need—to do the right thing, to be on the right side of the battle between order and chaos, good and evil?

"Solving puzzles is in Sissy's nature, Niall," Frankie said. "She's the daughter of a mathematician."

The urge to tell him to stop using that stupid nickname fought with the urge to thank him for taking her side. She silently recited Negro League baseball statistics until both urges passed.

"You encourage her, Frankie," Niall said. "Don't bother denying it. I know who aids and abets Sissy in her escapades. Breaking and entering, theft—"

"You make us sound like the bad guys." Frankie laughed. The inspector's allegations didn't appear to concern him.

"Not bad guys. More like mischievous schoolboys," Niall looked at Gethsemane, "and girls. Except dead bodies are as far away from childish pranks as Earth is from Neptune. Keep poking your noses into criminals' business and you might find yourselves listed in a police blotter."

"Mischievous schoolgirl?" Gethsemane came out of her seat. Niall had no right to reduce her rational, adult decisions—even when they were wrong—to instances of childish naughtiness, friend or no. Before she could unleash her feminist ire, a high-pitched scream outside the pub ripped through the air and silenced all conversation just as Aed's overture had. No one spoke or moved for several seconds.

Frankie spoke first. "What the bloody hell?"

Niall knocked over his chair as he raced to the door. "Stay here," he called without looking to see if anyone obeyed.

Gethsemane ran after him, followed by Frankie, the pub staff, and most of the pub patrons. They pushed through the door and stumbled out onto the street.

Deserted. Parked cars lined the curb on either side of the pub, lights snapped on in surrounding buildings, but no living creature, human or otherwise, except for people coming out to investigate the commotion, could be seen on the street.

Gethsemane stood on tiptoe and craned her neck to see over the heads of the growing crowd of spectators. "Where's Niall?"

A man's footsteps approached at a run, in answer to her question. Niall appeared around the corner, out of breath. "Did anyone pass by the other way?" he asked between pants.

"No one," Gethsemane said.

"Not a soul," Frankie said.

"'Twas a banshee," someone in the crowd suggested.

"A banshee?" Gethsemane asked. "As in—"

"Portent of impending death," Frankie finished.

Niall rejoined them, mobile phone in hand. "I'll call it in, have some uniforms out to help search."

"Probably someone's idea of a joke," an onlooker said.

Gethsemane held her breath and listened. No Tchaikovsky to warn her of danger. She exhaled. "Not a great success as jokes go."

"Did you hear the one about—" Frankie began.

Niall cut him off. "Shut it, Frankie, I'm not in the mood." He sniffed. "Do you smell that?"

"I don't smell anything." Gethsemane inhaled deeply. "Except the ever-present peat and sea air." Not even Eamon's cologne. Where'd he gotten to? Unlike him to skip the excitement.

"I smell it." Frankie wrinkled his nose. "Grease and peppers. What's Murphy cooking?"

"I didn't smell anything inside," Gethsemane said.

"Nor did I," Niall said. "But the smell's definitely out here." He sniffed the air again. "Maybe one of Murphy's neighbors."

An elderly man stood beside Frankie. Gethsemane recognized him from around town, one of a group of elderly men who gathered on benches in front of the grocers on Saturday mornings to compare notes about gossip they heard Friday night at the Rabbit.

"Grease and peppers," the man said. "Know what that means?"

Gethsemane shook her head.

"It's a sign a minor demon lurks in the vicinity. Mark my word."

"Some old wives' tale," Niall asked, "or more of your Saturday morning gossip?"

"Old wives often have a point, young fella," the man said. "You might do well to pay attention."

"I've listened," Gethsemane said. To her maternal grandparents, born and raised on Virginia and Carolina tobacco farms. They told her stories of omens and portents and manifestations from as early as she could remember until her upwardly mobile mother caught them at it and insisted they stop. "I've never heard any such thing."

The man narrowed an eye. "An expert on old wives' tales, are you?"

"Not an expert. But I know about haints, boohags, gray men, conjure men," she ticked names off on her fingers, "bones, stones, and chicken feet. Nothing about demons who smell like pepper and grease. Sulfur, yes. Pepper and grease, no."

"Maybe pepper and grease're a local variation." The man winked. "In areas where sulfur's hard to come by. I'll bid you good night and take care." He shoved his hands in his pockets and strolled up the street, singing in an off-key baritone:

She stood on the rocks of the lonesome shore,
Her tears vain pleas to Dia above.
Suaimhneas hers, nay, never no more.
Bound go síoraí to the taibhse of the manach she loved.

"'The Taibhsí of Skellig Michael,'" Frankie said. "I hate that song. My ex-wife loved it."

"My ex-girlfriend loved it, too," Niall said. "Reminds me of her."

"You like it, then?" Gethsemane asked.

Niall shook his head. "Hate it like taxes."

"Which ex-girlfriend?" Frankie asked.

"Shut it, Frankie," Niall said.

"Gethsemane, gentlemen," a voice said behind them. They turned to face a waving Father Tim. "An eventful evening. Celebrity authors, ghastly legends, operatic whistling, a scream fit to curdle milk. I may have to rethink Sunday's sermon." He looked at each of the three in turn. "I hope I'll see at least one or two of you in pews."

"Father," Niall said, "would you drive Sissy home? I know she's fearless and fights tigers with her bare hands in between conducting symphonies, teaching school, and catching murderers, but just in case that scream wasn't a joke—"

"Or a banshee," Frankie interjected.

Niall continued. "I'd feel better if she didn't walk all the way back to Carrick Point by herself."

"I've got my car," Frankie said. "I can take her."

"No, you can't," Niall said. "One: I know how much you've had to drink. Two: I know she can talk you into helping her search for the source of that scream instead of taking her home, and three: I need you to help me search until the uniforms arrive."

Gethsemane swore at the inspector and the math teacher. "No offense, Father Tim."

"None taken," he said.

"Your brogue's improved," Niall said.

"Who do you think you are that you can just order me to go home and stay there like a good little girl?" She felt her face flush.

"The garda."

She jerked her head at Frankie. "He's not. Why does he get to stay? Because he's a guy?"

"Yes," Niall said. "You can call me in the morning and remind me what a sexist pig I am." He clamped a hand on Frankie's shoulder. "You're with me. Good night, Father. Sissy." He led Frankie across the street. Gethsemane started after them, but Father Tim put an arm around her shoulder.

"Of all the—" she said.

"Don't take it personal," Tim said. "Men occasionally forget their female friends are brave, competent, and capable of taking care of themselves and become overprotective. It's the combination of night air, testosterone, and alcohol. Prevents synapses from firing. You have to make allowances."

"That's a lame excuse, Padre. Niall and Frankie both know I can slay my own dragons. I don't need a shining knight to come to my rescue. The odd ghost, maybe, but not a knight."

"I'm afraid that's the only excuse I've got." They stood for a moment, then Father Tim spoke again. "If you want to search for the source of that scream..."

"Funny thing, I don't really. With half the gardaí in Dunmullach searching, I'm not likely to find anything they won't." She inhaled. "I still don't smell anything. Do you?"

"Aside from the normal pub-in-a-coastal-village smells? No. Neither pepper nor grease."

"What about what that man said? About pepper and grease being associated with demonic activity?"

"It's not a claim I've heard anyone make, old wife or otherwise. Doesn't mean it's not true. Evil manifests in more ways than there are hairs on your head."

"There's a cheerful thought. Here's another; the custodian at St. Brennan's smelled pepper and grease just before a light fixture missed his head by an inch."

Tim grasped her by the shoulders and looked directly into her eyes. "Blame it on the testosterone and moonlight. My turn to be overprotective. What are you scheming?"

"I'm not scheming. I just wondered if your brother's books might say something about demonic smells." Tim's deceased older brother, a priest and an official Catholic Church exorcist, willed Tim his extensive collection of occult books.

"You want to look."

"I do."

"Tonight."

"Strike while the hellfire is hot. Isn't that how the saying goes?"

"Not at all."

"So can we go look?"

"Will you promise to be careful?"

"The light didn't fall on me."

"I know," Tim said. "But you have a talent for turning others' burdens into your own."

"Everybody needs a hobby."

"I'm serious, Gethsemane. Leave the demon-hunting to the experts. If a human murderer gets the upper hand, the worst that can happen is death. The consequences of tangling with a demon are so much worse."

"I promise, Tim, I will not conjure, summon, call upon, provoke, or otherwise mess with any demonic entities. I'm strictly paranormal-light. Eamon is about as much of the otherworld as I can handle. So can we go look? Just to see if there's anything to the man's claim about the smell."

"All right." Tim laughed. "Frankie's not the only one you can talk into things. Come to think of it, Niall's not as immune to your powers of persuasion as he likes to think he is. Off to Our Lady, then. We've got a few hours before I turn into a pumpkin. Let's see what we can find."

Gethsemane dropped a stack of books next to the several already on Father Tim's desk.

"Achoo!" She batted dust away.

"God bless," Tim said.

She pulled a chair up next to him and peered at the brown-edged pages of the thick leather book spread open in front of him. "I'm sorry I'm not more help. I should learn to read Latin."

"Your back and forth to the garden shed is invaluable help to these poor knees." Tim slapped a knee with a palm. "Not that you're missing anything. There's not much to read, at least not in terms of what we're looking for. Nothing in all these," he gestured at books, "about unholy smells, pepper, grease, sulfur, or otherwise."

Gethsemane thumbed through a battered volume. "Nothing at all?"

"The focus is on summoning and banishing paranormal entities, not on what they look, smell, or sound like once they arrive."

"About a hundred more remain in the shed. At this rate, we'll be searching until doomsday."

He seemed not to hear her. "These are fascinating, if not immediately useful. For instance, did you know a nineteenth-century Italian horologist, astronomer, and occultist invented a spirit-capturing device? He used an alchemical formula to combine copper, quartz, and silica in a device that was part clock and part compass. He used banishing and binding spells to trap spirits inside the device. They could communicate with him through use of the compass needle. He ran into difficulties getting the spirits out of the device after getting them in, but—"

"But that doesn't help us with the smell issue."

"No, it doesn't."

The office wall clock chimed. They both jumped.

"Midnight," Tim said. "I think we'd better call it a day."

Gethsemane closed the book they'd been looking at and rested her chin on her hands.

"Look at the bright side," Tim said. "We didn't find anything suggesting the smell of pepper and grease means demons."

"We didn't find anything that said it didn't, either."

"Tell you what. I'll take you home so I can make a truthful account to our Inspector. Then I'll call some friends in the States, occultists, who might be able to provide some answers. I'll brief you on my findings after Mass tomorrow." He looked at the clock. "After Mass today."

She covered a yawn. "I'm too sleepy to argue. After service, then. Great incentive not to sleep in."

Four

Father Tim caught up to Gethsemane the next morning during the break between Sunday services. "Take a walk with me." They strolled from the cloister, across the church yard and cemetery, to the poison garden.

Gethsemane shivered as she stepped into the wrought-iron enclosure that separated the toxic flora from the rest of the church gardens. Not so long ago she sipped poisoned tea while sitting amongst the deadly nightshade and hemlock.

"Are you all right?" Father Tim asked.

"I'm okay. Just had a flashback to a mad tea party."

Tim smacked his forehead. "Thoughtless of me. We can go somewhere else."

"Here's fine. What news from America?"

"My friends, two of whom still perform exorcisms, assured me peppers and grease have nothing to do with demonic possession or infestation. That's the good news."

"Meaning bad news follows."

"One friend, a fella who came up a couple of years behind me in seminary, knew of a case of a poltergeist in Kilkenny. Cooking smells always preceded the poltergeist attacks."

"Poltergeists? I thought those were associated with angsty teens. No shortage of those at St. Brennan's, but the pub's a teenager-free zone. Your friend's sure it was a poltergeist?"

"He wasn't personally involved in the case. He heard about it third-hand. Scarce details. The family wanted to avoid publicity so they went to great lengths to keep reports out of the press and keep records of the investigation private."

"Poltergeists." Gethsemane looked toward the cloister where Poe and Hardy mingled with parishioners. They carried small digital audio recorders and an SLR camera. Prior to the service, she had overheard them arguing with the church secretary about bringing in more gear. They lost the argument. The additional gear had remained in the vehicle. "Those two aren't teens, but they have issues. Could one or both be the trigger, or source, or whatever you call it?"

Up at the cloister, a stooped elderly woman spilled tea on Poe's boot when the photographer got between her and the tea tray. Gethsemane continued, "Or could one of the crew have staged things to guarantee some excitement for the show?"

"You said the school custodian noticed the smell?" Tim asked.

She nodded.

"Your ghost hunters had no access to the school."

She thought for a moment. "Hate to say this, but Aed had access to the school. And the pub. Kind of out of poltergeist age-range, but...Do you think he'd stir up trouble to boost ticket sales?"

"I don't like to think so. But folks have done worse for money and publicity."

A commotion in the cloister interrupted them. The words didn't travel across the distance, but they had no trouble deducing what went on from the gesticulations of the Ladies' Hospitality Guild president, Poe's stance behind Hardy, and Hardy's attempts to keep Poe from reaching around him. Poe had gotten in the way of one too many cups of tea.

"Should we break that up?" Gethsemane asked.

"Nah," Tim said. "They'll sort it out. Ten to one in favor of the Guild president."

Poe backed down after a rude gesture and a few shoves from Hardy. She and Hardy moved away from the refreshments.

"These TV fellas are rather aggressive," Tim said. "Ghost

hunters I dealt with in the past tended to be laid-back sorts. But this lot..." He jerked a thumb toward Poe and Hardy. "They ambushed me as soon as I stepped out of the sacristy, bombarded me with questions about Eamon and Orla. I had the devil of a time getting away from them, especially the blue-haired one."

"The others aren't as in your face as Poe. But 'pushy' is their trademark style. It sets them apart from the other dozen paranormal investigation shows."

"I confess, I'm surprised you're putting up with them. You're not one to suffer fools gladly. An admirable trait."

"Billy granted them access to Carraigfaire and made me promise to be nice to them," she said.

"In exchange for not tossing you out on your ear, no doubt. If Billy ever shows up for confession I'll have him saying 'Hail Marys' until his tongue falls off."

"Thanks for that, but you get used to them. Off duty, they're surprisingly normal."

"Even the one with blue hair?"

"Okay, surprisingly normal except for her. She's—different. But she's still one of God's children, right?"

"That's my line." The priest laughed. They watched another group of parishioners rebuff Poe and Hardy. Tim's expression sobered. "How are you going to stop them?"

"Stop them?"

"Yes, stop them. Before some of their high-tech doodads capture something best not captured."

"Eamon's promised to stay out of sight until they've gone."

"Not good enough. One mistake, one flare of that famous temper...No, you need to get them away from Carraigfaire and the lighthouse all together. Getting them out of the village would be best."

"Did you run all of the paranormal investigators you met in the past out of town?"

"No, I let them poke about a bit, told them a few strictly-for-the-tourists ghost stories, and they went away of their own accord."

"Why's this time different?" she asked.

"Because this time, you're involved. In the past, there was zero danger of the investigators capturing any concrete evidence of life after death because the real ghosts were far and few. But you bring ghosts out into the open. From twentieth-century composers to eighteenth-century sea captains, you're a manifestation magnet."

"Captain Lochlan was an accident. I didn't mean to call him up." Conjuring Captain Lochlan proved fortuitous. The charming ghost not only taught her the key to summoning spirits—combining a conjuring spell with musical tones that set up a sympathetic vibration—he saved her life. "I was trying to summon Eamon, remember?"

"You didn't mean to, but you did. Guess how many people recited that conjuring spell over the centuries, how many people sung 'Heuston's Lament' without impact. Then you recite a spell you can't understand, sing a sea chanty almost by accident, and you're up to your eyeballs in ghosts."

Gethsemane held up a finger. "One ghost. Captain Lochlan was one ghost."

"And Eamon makes two. If you so much as think about that spell with Mahler playing on the radio, you're liable to end up with a third, fourth, and fifth. Call it a curse or a gift, but, in case you hadn't noticed, you don't have to try very hard to summon ghosts."

She'd tried hard to summon Eamon. She'd played the piano until her fingers bruised. Then a chance encounter with a metal railing that gave way with a harmonious creak had brought Eamon back as easily as falling off a balcony. Maybe Father Tim had a point. "I still don't see the need to remove the *Ghost Hunting Adventures* boys from the cottage."

"Because you're at the cottage, you're their best chance of capturing real evidence, and the cottage is the most likely place for that to happen. Imagine the chaos if they managed to capture Eamon's image or his voice with one of their fancy doodads. Never mind the flocks of curiosity seekers and hordes of psychic investigators who'll descend on Dunmullach like frogs in a Biblical plague. Think of the implications for the Church. For all religions. For science. Conclusive proof of the persistence of consciousness after the body fails, proof of life after death, would create an irrevocable alteration of our fundamental understanding of God, and of what it means to be human. We can't let that happen. The world's not ready for it."

And she'd only been worried about people tramping on the lawn. "You don't believe their gear really records ghosts, do you? I've watched their show for seven or eight seasons. They never record anything more than flashing lights and weird noises. No full-bodied apparitions or coherent speech. It's nothing more than electronic smoke and mirrors, strictly for entertainment."

"Do you want to risk it? We're not talking about a gang of actors debunking a scary story told 'round the campfire. Aren't they always creating new and better gadgets? Dangerous ground to tread."

"Strange devices engineered by mad scientists."

"Mad or sane, they're still scientists. One of them might actually put together something that works."

"All right, now that you've framed the situation in terms of the continued existence of life as we know it, I'm worried. But what can I do? I'll have to trust Eamon to lay low while they're here, like he promised."

"Eamon McCarthy keeping the lid on? How's that working?"

Disembodied voices and the cologne scent in the pub. Hardy's odd glances at her, as if he sensed something he couldn't identify. Blue-hot anger lurking in Carraigfaire's corners, orb ready to launch. "Like a two-year-old who's missed naptime, that's how. But Eamon can't leave. He doesn't know how. And I'm afraid to try a spell, even if you hadn't sworn you'd never let me use one of your grimoires again." The priest had pointed out she could just as easily have summoned a psychopath as a sea captain.

"All the more reason to get those fellas away from Carrick Point."

"I can't kick them out. Billy pulled no punches about that."

"Since when has someone telling you 'no' ever stopped you from doing what needs to be done?" the priest asked. "You don't have to kick them out. Trick them out. Decoy them away."

A cheery "Good morning" from across the cemetery ended their discussion. Aed, the speaker, and Venus approached. Tim greeted the statuesque author by name.

"You two know each other?" Gethsemane asked.

"Ms. James interviewed me about Eamon and Orla a couple of weeks ago."

"You're a loyal supporter of the McCarthys and a tough nut, Father," Venus said. "If all my sources were as tough as you, I'd never get my story."

"I am a priest, Ms. James. Keeping people's secrets is a particular skill."

Aed shook Tim's hand. "Do you remember me, Father? I had darker hair and fewer wrinkles the last time you saw me."

"And I had fewer pounds." Tim patted his belly. "Of course I remember you. You and Richard Riordan were two of my flock's most faithful members. Almost never missed a Sunday."

Aed leaned closer to the priest and lowered his voice in a conspiratorial fashion. "I have a confession, Father. We came for the post-mass tea and biscuits."

"I've a confession, Aed," Tim said. "I come for the tea and biscuits, too." He winked.

Venus had wandered off while the men reminisced. She called out from over by the euphorbia. "Is this where it happened? Where Eamon McCarthy was poisoned?"

Gethsemane raised an eyebrow. Venus knew where Eamon died. She described the scene in lurid detail in her book. So why the question? Gethsemane refused to rise to the bait. "No," she said and left it at that.

Venus's face morphed into an expression of fury as a deep frown creased her forehead. Her eyes narrowed and her red lips curled into a snarl.

Gethsemane bristled. If Venus thought she could intimidate

her...Before she could tell her where she could take her attitude, Venus stormed past her, spiked heels leaving a wake of holes in the garden's gravel path. She marched past Father Tim and Aed and stopped in front of another man—short, slim, balding, bespectacled—who'd appeared at the garden's gate. Toes touching, she glared down at him from her six-inch advantage, then drew back her arm and slapped him. His head whipped to one side, and his tortoise-shell glasses flew into a bush.

"Gethsemane, Father, meet Bernard Stoltz," Aed said. "The man who ruined my life."

Bernard scrambled after his glasses. Venus advanced toward him and drew back her foot. Gethsemane and Father Tim rushed between the author and the newcomer. Aed put an arm around Venus.

"What are you doing here, Bernard?" Venus asked. "Did someone give you a 'get out of hell free' card?"

Bernard resettled his glasses and brushed off his slacks. "Always good to see you again, Venus. As fit and feisty as ever." He prodded the red welt spreading across his cheek. "I think that's going to bruise."

Venus started for him again. Aed held her back. "What are you doing here, Stoltz?" he asked. "You're not wanted."

"I developed an urge to explore Ireland. I've heard it's a beautiful country. Wanted to see for myself. Cross it off the bucket list." His accent screamed New York.

Even if Bernard Stoltz hadn't scuttled Aed's career, Gethsemane would have disliked him. He had that effect. "I guess you have more time to travel, Mr. Stoltz," she said, "now that you've been let go from *Classical Music Today*. Something about accepting payment for reviews, wasn't it?"

Bernard's eyes narrowed and his jaw tightened for a second. Then his face relaxed. All smiles again. "Dr. Gethsemane Brown. Renowned multi-instrumentalist and conductor. Vassar and Yale graduate. First African-American winner of the Strasburg Medal, among many other accolades. Imagine meeting you out here in the back of beyond. Come down in the world?" He offered Gethsemane his hand.

She accepted it to keep herself from balling hers into a fist and punching him. He gripped like soggy bread. "No, just needed a change of venue. You know, to get away from sleazy, backstabbing, manipulative critics who know less about music than I know about the Scottish herring fishing industry."

Father Tim stepped in. "Now that you've all reacquainted yourselves, why don't we head back up to the church. I have it on good authority today's biscuits came from the new French bakery that opened near the library. We'll grab some before they're all gone."

"Thank you, Father, but," Bernard touched his reddened cheek, "I've got a bit of a toothache. Think I'll go back to Sweeney's Inn and find an ice pack."

"You're staying at Sweeney's?" Aed swore. "Could you not find any place else in the whole of the village to darken?"

"No, Aed, I couldn't. Seeing as it's the only commercial lodging in this...charming but isolated area. I heard a rumor an American hotel developer had plans to build here." Bernard paused and glanced at Gethsemane. "Maybe you picked up something on the local grapevine?"

"The deal didn't work out," she said. "Climate didn't agree with the developer."

Venus aimed a manicured digit at Bernard. "I'm not staying in the same inn as that—that creature."

"Hard to imagine you sleeping on the street, dear," Bernard said. "Maybe you'll make a local friend who'll put you up for a couple of nights." He eyed Aed. "You're good at making friends."

Venus launched at Bernard. Aed grabbed her just before she put their nemesis's eye out. Bernard advanced toward Venus, but Father Tim's hand halted his movement, if not his swearing. Gethsemane wondered how Venus managed to move so fast in those heels.

"You won't find the accommodations as luxurious as at

Sweeney's," Father Tim said, "but you're welcome to the spare
room in the parish house."

"Oh no, Father, I couldn't do that." Venus blushed and cast her
eyes downward. "Consider your reputation. What would people say
about you spending the night alone with an unmarried woman?"
Her concern for the priest's reputation seemed genuine.

Father Tim laughed. "I don't flatter myself they'd say much of
anything. Except, perhaps, accuse me of boring you to tears. But if
you'd feel more comfortable staying elsewhere, perhaps
Gethsemane..."

Could put Venus up for a night or two? The woman who wrote
those awful things about her friend? She shuddered. A nearby
oleander bush offered avoidance. She turned to examine its
leathery green leaves.

Father Tim repeated himself, drawing her name out the way
her mother did when she wanted Gethsemane to do something
Gethsemane found distasteful, like putting on a frilly dress and
playing the piano for her parents' work friends when she was a girl
or having dinner with one of the milquetoasts her mother insisted
on introducing her to when she was just out of college. She
examined the oleander more closely.

A hand touched her elbow. "Gethsemane," Father Tim said,
"there's a spare room at Carraigfaire. The back bedroom."

Gethsemane spun to face Venus. "It's tiny. Spartan. I think I
left my laundry on the bed."

"For the sake of keeping the peace," Father Tim said, "in the
name of Christian charity."

Gethsemane looked back and forth between the two
combatants. Bernard, the deceptively benign creep who poked and
prodded until his target erupted. Venus, muscles tense with
restrained rage. She pictured Bernard discovered dead in his room,
stiletto heel embedded in his skull. Guilt tickled the back of her
neck. "If Venus wants to stay at the cottage, fine with me," she
conceded.

"That's settled, then," said Aed. "Thank you. I'll help you move your things, Venus."

"Would you like to stay at the parish house, Aed?" Father Tim asked.

"I'll be all right where I am, Father. I know how to handle vermin."

Venus and Aed crossed the cemetery toward the street. Bernard started after them, ignoring Father Tim's pleas to "Use your sense, man." Bernard caught up to the duo near the wrought-iron gate that separated the church yard from the sidewalk.

"We should do something," Gethsemane said to the priest.

"Did I ever tell you I used to box at university?" He led the way to the trio now embroiled in another argument.

Gethsemane and Tim arrived as Venus grabbed Bernard's arm. Bernard's shove sent the author crashing into Gethsemane, who broke both their falls.

Aed spewed a tirade of profanity that would have made both Eamon and Captain Lochlan blush. He swung at Bernard, who dodged the blow and swung back. Soon the two men rolled on the ground amongst the tombstones as they pummeled each other. Bernard punched Aed in the ear. Aed punched Bernard in the flank and pinned him. He drew his arm back and aimed his fist at Bernard's nose.

"Enough!" Father Tim grabbed Aed's elbow and pulled him off the battered critic.

Bernard hoisted himself up and launched at Aed and Father Tim.

Gethsemane stuck out her foot and tripped Bernard. He tumbled into a tombstone and lay still. Aed collapsed onto a bench. Venus sat next to him and put her arms around him.

Bernard sat up. He spat into a nearby flower arrangement. Gethsemane thought she detected a pink tinge to the spittle as it reflected the sunlight. He pressed one hand against his side and ran his other across his comb-over. "Where are my glasses?"

Gethsemane and Father Tim searched. She spotted them a few feet away from Bernard, tortoise-shell frames twisted and broken, near an urn. She pointed. "Over there—watch out!"

She flinched as a concrete statue of a weeping angel slipped from its perch atop a marble column that stretched far above their heads. Shock transfixed her as the angel's wing caught the edge of the column and pulled it down. She willed her feet to move and pushed Father Tim out of the way. Aed grabbed Venus and dove to one side a second before the angel crashed to the ground. Bernard rolled in the opposite direction a second before the pillar landed where his head would have been. A crowd came running from the cloister to the scene.

"It's all right, everyone," Tim raised his voice above the chatter to reassure the upset parishioners. "It was just an accident. We're all okay."

Poe picked up a broken piece of angel's wing. "Maja did this."

"Oh, for Chris—" Hardy hid his face in his palm. "Don't start that again, Poe. No one wants to hear it, not now."

"Want to or not, what other explanation is there? That one," she pointed at Aed, "sticks his thumb in Maja's eye by writing an opera in direct defiance of her curse, then rubs salt in by whistling the damned tunes in a pub."

"And in a school," Gethsemane mumbled.

"What?" Poe asked.

"Nothing," Gethsemane said. "Please continue."

Hardy interrupted. "Please don't." He grabbed Poe by the arm and dragged her, still clutching the broken statuary, away. "Let's find you a drink. Someplace around here must serve on Sunday morning."

Poe protested and insisted Maja was out for Aed's blood.

Hardy spoke over her. "Mind if we raid the bar at Carraigfaire? Some of that Waddell and Dobb might shut her up."

The rest of the onlookers dispersed in various directions, whispering about mysterious accidents and blue-haired ghost hunters and the trouble Americans caused wherever they went. More than one cast a glance at Gethsemane. Father Tim helped Bernard up and Gethsemane tended to Aed and Venus.

"Is everyone all right?" the priest asked. "Do I need to run anyone to A and E?"

"We're fine, thank you, Father," Venus said.

"No serious injury, Father." Aed scowled at Bernard. "Certainly, none worse than what that bastard's done to me in the past."

Bernard lurched forward and collided with the arm Father Tim extended in his path.

"Enough!" Tim shouted. "From all of you. Aed, please escort Ms. James back to the inn. Mr. Stoltz, you'll wait." Bernard protested but Tim's grip on his arm cut him short. "You'll wait in the parish hall while I send for a taxi. The hospitality hostess will make you a cup of tea." He marched Bernard toward the church.

Venus and Aed excused themselves and left for Sweeney's.

Gethsemane knelt and examined the fallen statue. "It could have been an accident," she said to Tim as he returned.

"I'm sure it was. It's an old statue, been there for at least a hundred years. All that tumbling about Aed and Stoltz did, they probably knocked it off balance."

"Poe thinks Maja knocked it over."

"She blames everything on Maja. Or credits everything to her. What would a cursed ghost be doing in a churchyard, a sacred space?"

Eamon couldn't come into the churchyard because he'd been buried in unhallowed ground as a suicide. But did being walled up alive in a castle against your will count as being buried in unhallowed ground?

Tim continued. "And no one complained of any odd smells, pepper, grease, or otherwise."

"True." She picked up a softball-sized piece of marble and hefted it from hand to hand.

"You're skeptical."

"You're probably right. An accident caused by the fight is the most likely explanation for the statue falling. But something nags me." She aimed the marble at a nearby tree and pitched it. "Poe, even if she is a poltergeist nidus, didn't come near the statue until after it fell. Neither did Hardy. Aed, on the other hand...Do you think he could have messed with the statue? Rigged it to make it unstable so it would fall if something hit it? Something like two men having a knock-down drag out?"

"Aed couldn't have known Stoltz would pick a fight."

"Tim, a blind man could have seen that fight coming."

"Even so, Aed stood in the statue's path as much as Stoltz. Why would he put himself in jeopardy?"

"The best laid plans of mice and men, et cetera? Maybe Aed didn't think he'd be so close to ground zero. He's fitter than Bernard. Maybe he didn't think Bernard would put up such a fight. Maybe he thought he could take him down with a punch or two and get safely away. Bernard would be too busy licking his wounds to notice a ton's worth of stone angel aimed at his head."

"That would be murder. Rigging lights to fall in deserted hallways is one thing, but murder is a bit far for a publicity stunt."

"The hallway wasn't deserted. I was there, and so was the custodian."

"But, if Aed did it, he'd have had no way of knowing anyone would be there. You're suggesting he deliberately set Stoltz up."

"As you said, folks have done horrible things for money. And dropping a statue on Bernard would serve two purposes: generating buzz for the opera and getting revenge on the man who ruined his life."

"I don't know, Gethsemane. It all seems a bit much. He'd need technical know-how, opportunity, indifference to human life. He couldn't guarantee Stoltz would be the only one injured by the statue, just as he couldn't guarantee no one would be in the school hallway. And he doesn't seem sociopathic. Look at the way he protected Ms. James."

"I admit, I don't have much evidence. Any evidence. Against Aed or against Maja or against anyone to shift the blame for all that's happened away from the forces of fate. I'm not ready to run to the garda. Nor to build one of those spirit-catching devices described in your book to go after Maja. I only have suspicions. Which, with five euros, will buy you a latte at the coffeehouse. I do, however, have a solid idea of how to throw Kent and crew off Eamon's scent. Use Maja as a decoy. If Eamon will behave long enough to convince the *Ghost Hunting Adventures* boys that he's a dud—" Lucky the temperamental ghost couldn't come into the churchyard; she'd pay if he overheard that. "—maybe they'll do their stakeout in the theater, instead of up at Carraigfaire."

"A ghost is a ghost, no offense to Eamon. We don't want them to capture proof of her existence, either."

"But there hasn't been any proof. A bad smell that only a few people have noticed, one scream that might have come from anywhere, and a couple of incidents that were probably accidents but could have been staged. I'm not convinced Maja doesn't exist mostly in Poe's mind. Granted, I'm not an expert on poltergeists, but events so far have been underwhelming compared to the few attacks I've read about. No shower of stones or furniture flying around the room. Just enough for innuendo and conjecture, typical TV fare, nothing earth-shattering or faith-destroying."

"How are you going to convince Kent and crew to relocate from Carraigfaire to the Athaneum?"

"What better place for a snipe hunt, or should I say, a Maja hunt, than the opera house where Aed's tempting fate with his production? Poe should be easy enough. Going after a paranormal sociopath who kills indiscriminately is more her style than staking out a relatively sane murdered composer."

Father Tim crossed himself and mouthed a silent prayer.

"I can sell Hardy on the move by promising access to Aed. I'm sure Hardy would love to tell his mother that he's hanging out with her favorite composer. The others may take more doing. Poe's rantings might work in our favor by convincing her colleagues Maja's the real paranormal deal. Or, at least, the more interesting one."

"And Billy? He'll lose out on whatever fee that crew is paying him to investigate at Carrick Point."

"Whose side are you on? You're the one who told me I had to stop them from filming in the cottage."

"I'd be remiss if I didn't point out the flies in the ointment."

Gethsemane crossed her arms. "You think of something then."

"Actually, I like your idea. Reminds me of something I might have done in my days as a curate."

"You played bait and switch with ghost hunters when you were a curate?"

Father Tim laughed. "No. I was thinking of the priest I was assigned to. Cantankerous buzzard who demanded everything his way. Believed the only good ideas were his own. So I mastered the art of making him think my ideas were his."

Gethsemane hugged him. "I knew I liked you. Now we need to figure out the details of our plan."

"Can I help?" A blonde head popped out from behind a statue of Saint Philip Neri a few feet from where Gethsemane and Father Tim stood. The blonde hair framed a thin face and a pair of startling green eyes.

"Saoirse Nolan, listening at keyholes." Father Tim clicked his tongue.

"Hiding behind a statue, more accurately. And I wasn't eavesdropping. I already knew what you planned to do."

"No point trying to keep a secret from someone who's both prescient and precocious," Gethsemane said.

"Good thing I am. How else would I know what's going on? No one tells me anything."

"Because you're twelve, Saoirse."

"I'm a genius."

"A twelve-year-old genius," Gethsemane said. "I'm not involving a twelve-year-old in any schemes. I'm determined to the point of stubborn, but I'm not irresponsible."

"I'm very grown up and independent for my age. And I can help," Saoirse said, her voice pleading. "I helped you before, didn't I?"

The girl's parents recognized their daughter wasn't quite like other children and knew the villagers would look out for her, so they tended to give her free reign. And she had provided key information in Gethsemane's investigation of the McCarthy murders, information she might not have uncovered the killer without. She wavered.

Saoirse pushed her case. "I know every corner and cranny of the Athaneum by heart. Secret ways in and out. Places to become invisible. I come and go, silent as the wind."

"Don't oversell it, Saoirse." She told the truth, however. Gethsemane supposed the girl went home for meals once in a while, but Father Tim's library and the Athaneum were the two locales most likely to yield a Saoirse sighting. "How can you help?"

"I can pretend to see Maja's ghost. I can scream and point and swoon."

"No swooning," Father Tim said. "Swooning's so nineteenth century."

Saoirse rolled her eyes. "The rest, then. I'll put on a holy show, and they'll believe me because I'm twelve."

They probably would. Still..."I don't know."

"You're afraid I'll get hurt. It won't be dangerous. All I have to do is play act. That's not dangerous, especially in a theater. And Colm will be there."

"How do you—" Gethsemane began. "Prescient. Never mind." Colm Nolan, one of the two most talented musicians at St. Brennan's, protected his little sister like a mother bear protecting her cubs. Colm had faults—arrogance, chronic lateness—but he scored A-plus in the big brother department. "Ruairi will be there, too." Ruairi O'Brien, the other best musician, had a crush on Saoirse, two years his junior. Between him and Colm, she'd be well looked after.

Saoirse blushed and lowered her head. She looked up at Gethsemane through blonde tresses. "So I can help?"

Gethsemane looked at Father Tim.

"I think she'll be all right. She takes care of herself pretty well. Reminds me of you."

"Oh, all right. I can't think of any other way. The Saoirse Show, it is. You'll be at the Athaneum—"

"Before anyone gets there." Saoirse grabbed Gethsemane in a hug. "Thank you for letting me help. I won't let you down." She skipped off across the cemetery.

"How about a biscuit?" Tim asked.

Gethsemane followed him to the refreshment table.

"Father, Dr. Brown." The voice caught her mid-sip, sending tea out her nose. A returned Poe stood at the end of the table, one hand in her pocket.

Gethsemane grabbed a napkin and dabbed tea from the front of her dress. "I thought Hardy took you out. I mean, took you away somewhere."

"Just couldn't resist these cookies." Poe bit into one. "Bet they'd go well with that fancy bourbon," she said around a mouthful.

"You do not pair cookies with Waddell and Dobb. And you didn't come back for the cookies."

"No." Poe pulled her hand from her pocket. She clasped a small battered leather-bound book. "I came back to ask about this. What can you tell me about it, Father?"

Gethsemane recognized it as one of Tim's grimoires. She grabbed for it, but Poe snatched it out of reach.

"Where did you find that?" the priest asked.

"In the garden shed," Poe said. "On a shelf full of occult books. Odd things to find on church grounds."

Tim took the book from Poe. "I'll thank you not to poke your nose into other people's garden sheds."

"The door wasn't locked," Poe said. "Care to comment on the collection?"

"No," Tim said. "I don't."

"How about you, Dr. Brown? Anything to say?"

"Nothing I'd care to say in front of a man of the cloth."

"Don't let me stop you," Tim muttered.

Poe shrugged. "I'll mark you both down as 'no comment.'"

"Isn't Hardy waiting for you?" Gethsemane asked.

"Hardy has plenty to keep himself busy without babysitting me."

"What's with the two of you, anyway? You date, you used to date, you—"

"Used to be drinking buddies. That's all. Then Hardy got sloppy, then Hardy quit drinking."

"Then he realized you were a lot easier to tolerate when he was drunk."

Poe started to speak, then seemed to change her mind. "Now that you mention it, he probably is waiting for me. Thanks for the cookies." She grabbed another and left.

Gethsemane took the book from Tim and thumbed through it. "What're the chances she reads Latin?"

"I wouldn't think it to look at her, but I suspect she knew exactly what she had."

Faint strains of "Pathétique" played in her head. "I'm afraid you're right." She said goodbye to Tim and exited the churchyard, one eye out in case Poe put in another appearance. Eamon materialized as soon as she stepped outside the boundary of the wrought-iron fence.

"We need to do something about you not being able to enter hallowed ground," she said.

"Exhumation, reinternment, a formal exculpation by the Church." He waved away the suggestion. "Did you and the padre come up with a way to get rid of the nosy nellies?"

"No one can see you, can they?" She moved behind a nearby tree and peered around its trunk.

"At this distance? I doubt anyone could see me, even if they could see me. But if someone turns this way, I'll hide behind you."

"So not funny." Eamon towered over her by a foot. "And don't be too confident you're invisible. I suspect Hardy can see you. Or at least sense you. He raised an eyebrow a couple of times when you manifested up at the cottage."

"I don't think he can see me in all my glory. And the rest of that ghost hunting bunch wouldn't know I was there if I dumped ice water on their heads." Eamon glowed an impatient turquoise. "Clue me in on the plan."

"The plan is for you to make yourself scarce. As in, don't be here."

Eamon looked hurt. His aura shifted to a wounded umber.

"Don't," Gethsemane said. "You know I'm not wishing you away. But we can't risk these guys capturing evidence of you."

"At least you said 'we.'"

"Pouting is not a good look on you."

"What do you do while I do nothing?" Eamon leaned against the tree, his shoulder disappearing into the bark.

"Convince the crew that Carraigfaire is a waste of time, then convince them to shift operations to the Athaneum."

"Why would they do that?"

"Because they'll think the ghost of Maja, doomed Hungarian noblewoman, will show up to stop Aed's opera from being performed." She briefed him on her conversation with Father Tim and Saoirse.

"That's ridiculous."

"It's not ridiculous. It's misinformation. Misdirection. Mis— Mis—Anyway, it's a good plan. Unless you've got something better?"

"No, I don't, actually." He shone russet with grudging admiration. "What am I supposed to do while I'm doing nothing?"

Gethsemane shrugged. "What do you usually do when you're not haunting the cottage?"

"I'm never 'haunting' the cottage. I feckin' live there."

"Okay, what do you do when you're away from home?"

Eamon laughed. "Follow you around, mostly."

Her blush garnered more laughter. "Why don't you find a ghost drinking buddy to hang out with? Captain Lochlan, maybe? I think you two'd hit it off."

"And how would I find the captain? The afterlife doesn't come with GPS coordinates." His glow dimmed to yellow. "If it did, I'd have found Orla by now."

"I know." She sighed. "Just promise me you'll be careful. And quiet. Please?"

He winked and disappeared.

Screams traveled from the direction of the church. Squealing children darted back and forth among statues and shrubs as they played tag. The scream from the previous night hadn't sounded like children playing games. It had sounded desolate. She pulled out her phone and dialed Niall's number.

She disconnected the call before the first ring ended. Niall wouldn't tell her if they'd found anything remarkable. He'd tell her to stay out of it. He didn't need moonlight to be overprotective. Frankie, on the other hand, would be much easier, as long as he wasn't in curmudgeon mode. She dialed the math teacher.

"'Lo?"

"Frankie? Good morning, it's Gethsemane."

"Sissy. Good morning." His voice sounded low-pitched and sluggish.

"Is this a bad time?"

"No, it's fine. I just woke up is all. What can I do for you? Help you break into something?"

"Tell me about last night's scream. What did you and the inspector find?"

"Nothing. We couldn't find anything. No radios, no televisions, no one in distress, no mythological creatures or other paranormal entities. Nothing."

What did she hear on the other end of the line? Hoarseness? "Are you sure you're feeling all right, Frankie? You don't sound like yourself. I missed you at church this morning."

"Overslept. Right through my alarm. Must have stayed out too late chasing after our phantom screamer."

"Who do you think screamed?"

She imagined his shrug. "A banshee, like the man said?"

"Banshees are only heard when someone's going to die."

"I really can't explain it. Maybe it was a prank. Maybe Devlin hired someone to scream to get people talking about ghosts and create some publicity for his—" A yawn drowned out the end of Frankie's sentence.

"Are you coming down with something? Tell me. I can run to the pharmacy for you. Or bring over the fixings for a toddy."

"I told you, I'm fine. I just overslept. Don't fuss."

"I'm not fussing, I'm inquiring. I'm your friend. Friends inquire about each other's health. Especially when one of them doesn't sound like his usual self."

"You're usually complaining about my usual self."

"Francis Grennan, I'm serious."

"And I appreciate it. I do. But I'm not sick. I'm just knackered. I'm going back to bed. I'll see you in the morning."

"All right, the morning. But promise me you'll call if you need anything before then." Frankie lived in bachelor faculty housing and had no family in the area. Something they had in common.

"You're fussing. But I promise I'll call." The call disconnected.

"I am not fussing." Annoyed, but not fussing. Frankie had been no help. He'd seemed more curmudgeonly than usual. Was he coming down with something?

"Stop it," she said aloud to herself. The math teacher was a grown man and she was neither his wife nor his mother. She still wanted to know what that scream was about, which meant asking Niall. She put her phone away. She'd do this face to face.

She rode her bike to the village. She spotted Niall as she passed the village square, tossing what looked like the remains of lunch into a trash can. She veered toward him.

"Morning, Inspector." She leaned her bike against a nearby bench. "Early lunch?"

"'Inspector,' is it? You're still mad about last night."

"I'm not some fragile hothouse flower who needs to be protected from the Big Bad Wolf."

"That's the worst mixed metaphor I've ever heard."

"You know what I mean. I can take care of myself."

"Yes, you can. I apologize if I seemed patronizing or

chauvinistic. Blame it on fatigue."

She frowned. "You, too?"

"Me too what?"

"I just hung up with Frankie. I woke him up. He complained of fatigue. He'd slept through church."

"Late nights at the Rabbit will do that to a fella. Our enthrallment with Ms. James resulted in attendance at her pub salon-sessions every night for two weeks running."

Gethsemane smoothed the lapel of his wool-silk blend suit jacket. "I suspected the wardrobe upgrades were her influence."

A shout from across the street cut off his response. "Inspector!" Bernard, hair askew, pants grass stained, glasses missing, marched up to them. "Inspector, I want to file a complaint. I want someone arrested."

"And you are?" Niall asked.

"Bernard Stoltz. I was attacked and I want to file a complaint." He inclined his head toward Gethsemane. "She was a witness."

"I'm a terrible witness, Mr. Stoltz. I can't seem to remember my own name, let alone dishonest critics getting what they deserved."

Bernard sputtered. Niall hid a laugh.

"How did you know he was with the garda?" Gethsemane asked Bernard.

"That woman over there told me." He gestured toward the proprietor of the art supply store who leaned in the doorway of her shop, watching. "I asked her where the police station was and she told me the tall man with the hat was a cop. Or guard, or whatever you call them here."

Niall grumbled. "Remind me to thank her. Did she tell you I'm with the cold case unit? If your murder goes unsolved for more than three years, I'm your man. But for assault and battery, you need to go to the station."

"A cop's a cop."

"Except when he's a garda."

"You!" A shout from across the square drew their attention.

Aed stood on a balcony overlooking the street in front of Sweeney's. He pounded a fist on the balcony's ornate concrete rail, then disappeared inside the hotel. He reappeared a moment later at the hotel's front entrance, fists still clenched.

Bernard yelled back. "I'm warning you, Devlin, don't try anything. I've got witnesses. He's a cop."

"Garda."

"Well, Mr. Garda," Bernard said, "I demand an escort back to my hotel. That man attacked me in the church yard and she saw it. I demand protection."

"I'll walk you across the street," Gethsemane said. "If Aed takes a swing at you, I've got your back."

Niall hid his laugh less well this time.

"You think this is funny? I'm almost beaten to death by that baboon and you treat it as a joke?"

"I told you, I'm a terrible witness," Gethsemane said. "I don't remember you being beaten by a large monkey. I recall you being slapped silly by Venus James, but monkey beat down? No, don't remember that. By the way, did you get your glasses fixed?"

Bernard sputtered again and advanced toward Gethsemane.

Niall stepped between them. "Why don't we all walk over to Sweeney's together?"

They crossed the street with Niall in the lead.

Aed blocked their path at the hotel's entrance. "You're a guard, aren't you?" he asked Niall. "I remember you from the pub. Arrest that gobshite." He shook a fist under Bernard's nose. "He tried to kill me in the church yard."

"Two attempted murders on the same day in one church yard," Niall said. "What did Father preach on?"

"I'm serious, Inspector," Aed said.

"And Mr. Stoltz is serious about having you arrested for trying to kill him. So why don't we call it mutual combat and let it go?"

"I need to get inside to get to my room," Bernard said.

"Both of you staying in the same inn," Niall said, "doesn't seem like the wisest idea."

"Father Tim offered to put Aed up at the parish house."

"Maybe you should accept Father's offer," Niall said.

"I'm not leaving." Aed sneered. "Damned if I'll be run off by him."

Bernard crossed his arms. "I'm not leaving, either."

Niall wrinkled his nose. "Do you smell something?"

"No," Gethsemane said. "I don't smell anything."

"An odd smell, can't quite figure it out." He looked around the area where they stood, then craned his neck to look up at the balcony. "Restaurant's not up there, is it?"

"Inspector," Aed said, "if you're not going to take this seriously—"

"Move!" Niall shouted and shoved Bernard to one side. Gethsemane and Aed jumped back. A large, concrete finial from the balcony's rail crashed to the ground where Niall and Bernard had been standing.

"Second time today something's nearly landed on your head, Mr. Stoltz," Gethsemane said. And Poe nowhere in sight. So much for poltergeists. Aed, on the other hand...She stepped off the curb to look at the balcony. Aed had stood next to where the finial had been. Did he tamper with it?

"Step out of the street, Sissy," Niall said. "Getting hit by a car's no better than being crushed by a design feature. Is everyone all right?"

They all answered they were.

"Then you, Mr. Devlin, go on in. Mr. Stoltz, give him to a count of twenty, then you go in. I'll leave word at the station desk that if any calls come in about the two of you fighting to send a trio of the biggest, meanest uniformed guards out here to deal with the situation. Understood?"

The men nodded and went inside in the order Niall had instructed.

"Are you all right?" Gethsemane asked. "That landed pretty close to where your head was."

They moved out of the way of the hotel staff who'd come

outside to assess the damage.

"I'm fine. Takes a lot more than a chunk of balcony to stop me." Niall sniffed. "The strange smell is gone."

Gethsemane's phone rang. "Excuse me."

Kent's voice greeted her. "When are you headed back to the cottage? We'd like to start filming. Best if you were here."

"On the way." She made a face and ended the call.

"Off on a snipe—I mean, ghost—hunt?" Niall asked.

"Don't laugh."

"I'm not laughing. Well, maybe a wee bit on the inside."

"Before I go, tell me, what did you and Frankie find last night when you went searching for the source of that scream?"

"Nothing. Not a damn thing. I'm not one given to superstition, but I'm inclined to admit the fella who claimed it was a banshee's cry might have been right." He yawned. "Sorry. Must be more tired than I realized."

"Are you sure you and Frankie aren't coming down with something?"

"I can't speak for anyone but myself, but I'm healthy as an ox, as my grandda would say. I don't get sick, at least not since I was ten. It's nothing more than too many late nights for a man my age. I have to remind myself I'm not at university anymore."

"All right, I'll stop fussing."

"I didn't say you were."

"Frankie did."

"Makes us even, then. Be careful riding your bike home."

Five

Gethsemane arrived home from church to find a transformed Carraigfaire. Cameras on tripods dotted hallways upstairs and down. Black boxes studded with flashing lights crowded corners. Cables snaked along floorboards. Heat from spotlights warmed the cottage to temperatures reminiscent of Virginia summers. She inhaled. Nothing but peat and sea air. She relaxed a bit. Eamon must have taken "lay low" to heart.

"Everything all right?" Hardy poked his head into the hall from the music room. He and Poe had left Our Lady at the same time as Gethsemane, but their SUV outdistanced her Pashley bicycle without effort, bringing them to the cottage before her.

"Fine. Everything's fine. I just, uh, take a deep breath every now and then, because it aerates the lungs which, um, improves musical performance."

"You play the violin, right? That's a string instrument."

"I play the violin among other instruments." None of them wind instruments, but why nitpick? "The harmonica, for instance. Most people don't realize how much lung power it takes to play the harmonica. Do you have to be in there?" She pushed past Hardy into the music room in time to snatch her violin from a curious crew member. "It's an antique, it's not haunted."

Hardy corrected her. "Cursed. It's an object, so we'd say 'cursed' instead of 'haunted.' Unless it was a trigger object. Something familiar to the ghost that might attract it."

She placed the violin, a Villaume copy of a Stradivarius, in its case and held it tight to her chest. "It's my violin. It's not cursed, it's not haunted, it's not a trigger object. It's worth more than anyone in this room earns in a year and none of you need to touch it."

"How about this?" Hardy placed a hand on the Steinway piano that dominated the room. "This is Eamon's, isn't it? He actually played it. Composed some of his best work sitting in front of it." He ran a finger along the keyboard. "Maybe you could play something during the stake out, something that might lure the ghost. Or maybe you could get the ghost to—"

She cut him off. "You won't catch any ghostly arpeggios played by unseen hands, if that's what you're hoping for."

"Too parlor trick-y? Not McCarthy's style?"

Kent appeared in the doorway. "I'd like to interview you now, Gethsemane, if you don't mind."

Of course she minded. She'd rather be interviewed by an IRS tax auditor. She followed Kent to the study.

"Your experience living here is crucial," he explained. "You're on the front lines of the haunting, so to speak. Every day, you have the chance to encounter the paranormal. Viewers want to know what that's like."

Boy, wouldn't they? In less than a year, she'd gone from dismissing ghosts—like the folklore and family legend of her Virginia ancestors—as pure fantasy to providing her very own ghost with an alibi. Not that she intended to admit as much to Kent or his viewers. Outright denial wouldn't work. Limited admission and deflection seemed the best option. "It's probably not as exciting as they think."

"I heard you were fearless, Gethsemane." Kent gestured to the couch, set up for interviews with lights and cameras trained on it. A digital audio recorder and an EMF pod lay on the coffee table. Did Kent think he'd pick up some evidence during their talk? She bit her lip and glanced around the room. If Eamon didn't control himself and stay away, she'd kill him.

Crew surrounded them. After a flurry of microphone, makeup,

and lighting adjustments, Gethsemane and Kent arranged themselves on the couch. Kent reached out and laid a hand on her arm. "Don't be nervous."

Gethsemane patted Kent's hand. "Don't worry, I'm not." She'd performed live all over the world and she taught teenaged boys. Nothing unnerved her.

Kent signaled ready. He leaned toward her and asked, "What's it like living with a ghost?"

"Well—" Gethsemane paused and shifted on the sofa. "'Living with' might be phrasing things a bit strongly." She searched for words that sounded thoughtful, instead of like a stall. "It's not as if I come down for breakfast every morning to find a ghost sitting at the table with eggs and bacon ready." Which was true. Eamon had coffee ready for her every morning, but she ate breakfast at the school dining hall.

"But you've had experiences that can't be explained away in rational, scientific terms," Kent persisted.

She shrugged, hoping to appear noncommittal. "Some orbs, some footsteps, the odd smell or two." She waved a hand. "Cologne, you know, that sort of thing."

Kent stiffened. A muscle worked in his jaw. "But he said—I mean, I heard—there have been rumors of full-bodied apparitions, telekinesis..."

"Who said?" She didn't get the full-blown Tchaikovsky treatment, but warning bells went off. "Who's he?"

"You know, just rumors." Kent's shrug mirrored hers, but the redness of his cheeks belied its noncommittal nature. "Local gossip. Talk at the pub."

Liar. No locals would tell this brash American outsider anything about Eamon's ghost, even if they knew about him, no matter how much money he threw around. Dead or alive, Eamon remained one of their own. The only rumors coming out of the Dunmullach gossip mill would be about Kent and Ciara and the rest of the paranormal investigators. So who had Kent talked to? "Don't put too much stock in gossip, Kent. People get into trouble that way."

He pressed her. "I understand your reluctance to talk. Admitting belief in the paranormal opens one to ridicule, embarrassment. There's a stigma. You have a career to consider, a reputation. But this is your chance to help open people's eyes, their minds, to the possibility of the existence of things beyond what they can touch and taste and feel. Your experiences can help others understand that reality is so much bigger than what's right in front of them."

Therein lay the problem. Her experiences threatened to upend eons of theology and science. She leaned forward and laid a hand on Kent's arm. She locked eyes. They were simpatico, on the same wavelength. She understood what he wanted to do. She believed. "It's not shame or embarrassment, Kent." She lowered her voice and lied. "Truth is, not much happens up here at Carraigfaire. The Athaneum is the real center of activity. The action happens at the theater."

Kent ripped off his mic and stormed out of the study. "At the theater? The theater? You've got to be effing kidding me." He stormed through the cottage, tipping over camera tripods and lights, swearing at Gethsemane, Billy, and the entire Irish nation. "We waste two days up here on this godforsaken cliff setting up our gear, and now you say McCarthy's ghost haunts the theater?" Poe, Hardy, and the rest of the crew dodged equipment and watched him rant. Poe smirked. Hardy remained inscrutable.

"Problem?" Ciara, who'd been photographing outside, stepped into the room, her camera still slung over her shoulder. She calmed Kent with an arm around him.

"She," Kent jerked a thumb at Gethsemane, "tells me the paranormal activity doesn't happen up here in this hovel. She claims the theater is the focus of the haunting."

"I didn't say nothing happens up here. Some things do." Gethsemane counted off on her fingers. "Footsteps, orbs, smells. But the good stuff happens at Athaneum."

"Why didn't you tell us when we arrived instead of wasting our time?"

"I'm new to this ghost hunting stuff. Besides, I didn't think you'd believe me." She eyed Kent. "You'd heard 'rumors' from—someone—that Carraigfaire cottage was haunted. If I denied it straight away, you'd have thought I had something to hide. Now you've been up here a couple of days and you've seen for yourself not much happens in the way of paranormal activity."

"She's got a point, Kent," Hardy said. "The cottage has been kind of a dud so far. Lighthouse, too."

Kent spoke to Gethsemane. "How do I know you're telling the truth about the Athaneum? How do I know you're not hiding something now?"

"Would I lie and say Eamon's ghost haunts the theater? Or would I lie and say there's no ghost anywhere and try to get y'all to leave? Whether you set up shop in the cottage or in the village, I still have to put up with you until you get what you want. I still have to go on record saying I see spooks and shades and haints. I'm still going to be picked at and ridiculed because I admitted I believe in the boogey man. What difference does it make to me which building you take your pictures in?"

Ciara rubbed Kent's back. "Hardy's right, she has a point. And, speaking from an artistic perspective, I'd rather shoot in the theater." She turned to Gethsemane. "Don't get me wrong, the cottage and lighthouse are lovely in a picture postcard sort of way. But the Athaneum offers a more gothic setting, more in keeping with the show's atmosphere."

Poe perked up. She bounced on the balls of her feet and grinned like a kid who just learned she was going to Disney. Gethsemane half expected her to clap. "That opera guy is going to stir up Maja Zoltán's ghost at the theater. What if we captured her as well as McCarthy?"

"A two-for-one ghost special?" Hardy snorted. "Get over the Maja obsession."

"You get over yourself," Poe said. "I believe in the curse, and that's no stranger than any of the things you believe in, Mr. Holierthan-thou Hardy."

What's the term to describe a situation where two paranormal investigators debate whose beliefs are more outrageous? Surreal. Gethsemane leaned against a wall and watched them hash it out.

Poe went on. "This might be my only chance to investigate a story I've been following since I was thirteen. She," Poe jerked her head toward Gethsemane, "says McCarthy's ghost is at the Athaneum. We," her gesture included the entire ghost hunting crew, "haven't seen or heard jack up here, not so much as a light anomaly or a disembodied sneeze. The locals are happy to talk to us about the weather or sports or American politics, but when we ask them to tell us about this house or the McCarthys, they say," Poe mimicked a brogue, "'I will, yeah,' and then they don't. We only have a few more days here, and if we want enough material for an episode, we better expand our ghost hunting horizon beyond Carrick Point. Right now, we don't have enough for a podcast."

"I agree with Poe," Ciara said.

"So do I," Hardy said. "Reluctantly."

Kent surveyed his crew. "Who else thinks we ought to shift our base of operations?" One by one, the entire crew raised their hands.

"How are we going to get permission to film at the theater?" Kent asked.

"I have a couple of connections," Gethsemane said. "Including Aed Devlin. A cameo, or tiny segment, on your show would be good publicity for his opera. People might buy a ticket for the chance to see Poe's ghost."

"She's not my ghost." Poe frowned. "She just is."

"Okay, the ghost. Buy a ticket for the opera, stay for the paranormal after party."

"You can arrange access?" Kent asked. "You're sure?"

"I can." Somehow. "I am."

"All right, guys," Kent said to his crew. "Pack up the gear. We'll move it down the mountain today and rendezvous at the Athaneum—" He broke off and looked at Gethsemane.

"Tomorrow. Meet me there after lunch. But not the full crew

with all your gear. Maybe just you, Kent, and a few key people. Rehearsals start tomorrow, so you'll have to wait until after to set up." She crossed her fingers behind her back. "But don't worry, I'll take care of everything."

Kent stared at her a long moment. As the silence grew uncomfortable, he said, "Tomorrow. After lunch. But you won't mind if we leave a couple of digital audio recorders and EMF pods behind here, maybe a single full-spectrum camera." His request didn't sound like a question. "You may not hear anything more than a footstep on the stairs, but sometimes technology detects things human senses can't."

"Not a problem."

"Good." Kent smiled. "See, we both want the same thing. Proof life persists after the body dies."

Whatever. "I'm going to take a walk up to the lighthouse so I'm out of the way while you pack up."

"I left some equipment up there," Hardy said. "I'll be up in a while to get it."

Gethsemane left the *Ghost Hunting Adventures* crew to their task. Eamon joined her halfway to the lighthouse.

"Fair play, grasshopper." The green of his amused aura matched his eyes.

"You shouldn't be here. It's not safe."

"We're alone. Those fellas will be scurrying around gathering up their toys for a while."

"I'm glad you can be cavalier about the situation. We're not in the clear yet."

"I'm not being cavalier, you're being paranoid."

"I risk making a huge fool out of myself to protect you and that's what you have to say to me? Ooh, wait until I find a spell to send you to hell." She stomped ahead.

Eamon rematerialized in front of her. Her momentum carried her through him. The buzz shook them both.

"I hate it when you do that," they said simultaneously.

Gethsemane kept walking.

Eamon materialized in front of her again. The tingle of his hand on her arm stopped her. "Remind me why we're fighting. Whatever I said, I'm sorry."

An apology from Eamon McCarthy truly ranked among the rarest of events. She relented. "We're not fighting. And I'm not mad. I'm—worried."

"About?"

"You. This Maja business might be sufficient to send most of the crew on a wild ghost chase—"

Eamon laughed. "I see what you did there."

Gethsemane failed to suppress a grin. "Kent's up to something. He let slip that someone, a male, put him on to you."

"Is he triggering the Tchaikovsky treatment?"

"No, just an uneasy feeling."

"Maybe he's giving you the glad eye," Eamon said.

"Please, I'm a bit old for him."

"Not as old as Ciara. And she's got him pretty well wrapped."

"Kent is not interested in me. But he is interested in more than Ciara," she said. "I just can't figure out what."

"I think Hardy's the one who needs figuring out. That fella's agenda stretches far beyond the paranormal. The 'your man Friday, perennial designated driver, always ready to lend a hand and do the jobs no one else wants' routine is just that, a routine, a shtick."

"He's just strange. As strange as Poe in his own way."

"No one is as strange as Poe," Eamon said. "That bure's a quare header."

"Okay, you're right. Not that strange. But, well, Hardy's never come right out and said so, but I think he may have had substance abuse problems in the past. I think that's why he gave up drinking and smoking."

"You think he's just become very intense in his sobriety?" Eamon glowed a doubtful hickory. "I think that greasy dark hair covers a head full of secrets."

"Now you mention it, I did notice a trace of Irish accent beneath the Noo Yahwk."

"Brogue, darlin'. An Irish accent is a brogue."

"Seriously? You're going to nitpick while I'm warning you about—"

"Gethsemane!"

She turned in the direction of the shout. Hardy, several feet below her on the path between the cottage and lighthouse, snapped a photo. He waved and disappeared inside the house.

Six

Venus and Aed pulled up in front of Carraigfaire as the *Ghost Hunting Adventures* crew pulled out. Gethsemane offered to help carry Venus's luggage from the car, but Aed waved both women aside and hauled the bags, five of them, himself.

Gethsemane could pack for a month in a roll-aboard and a backpack. "Not a fan of traveling light?"

"I've been here for months. Some stories take longer to get than others."

"You know Dunmullach has a laundry and a dry cleaner? In the village square, next to the stationer's."

Aed squeezed between the two women, carrying the last bag. "Where should I put these?"

"Upstairs. I'll show you." Gethsemane led the way up to the back bedroom.

"It's," Venus looked around the room, "quaint."

"It's an almost-two-hundred-year-old thatched roof cottage," Gethsemane said. "Not the Ritz Hotel."

"It's charming," Aed said. "Reminds me of Gran's place in Adare." He headed back down for more luggage. A few more trips and Venus's bags crowded the small room. "It's only for a short while."

"I blame Bernard Stoltz for this," Venus said. "What's that snake doing here, anyway?"

"Good question," Gethsemane said. "He's unemployed,

officially, at least since the Cleveland Symphony scandal broke and *Classical Music Today* finally fired him."

"'Bout time." Venus sat on the foot of the bed and kicked off her shoes. "Bernard's been selling good reviews for years. They should have fired him earlier for what he did to Aed. Aed would never pay for a good review or to keep someone from publishing a negative story."

Aed must have told her about the rumors. "You just met Aed. What makes you certain he wouldn't pay?"

"I just know. Haven't you ever met someone and just known right away what they're capable of and what they're not? Aed would never pay a bribe. He should have taken Bernard to court, scandal be damned."

"He wouldn't have gotten far in court without evidence. Prior to Cleveland, Bernard was never stupid enough to let anyone record their meetings or post photos to social media."

"None of this explains what Bernard's doing in Dunmullach," Venus said. "No offense, but this is off the beaten path even for washed-up journalists."

And, by extension, washed-up musicians? Gethsemane couldn't let that one pass. "But not for true crime reporters?"

Aed, apparently sensing an argument brewing, stepped back in. "Maybe Stoltz is freelancing. Sniffing around for a story to put himself back in the game."

"Maybe hoping your return to the opera world will blow up in your face and he'll be there to trumpet the news to the world? That would be how his mind works." Venus reached for Aed's hand. "Not that your new work will be anything but brilliant."

Gethsemane, hoping to interrupt a scene, cleared her throat. "Speaking of your opera, I invited a few people to attend rehearsals."

"What have you done?" Venus's eyes narrowed.

"I convinced the *Ghost Hunting Adventures* boys to conduct their stake out at the Athaneum instead of up here."

"Is that why they were leaving when we pulled up?" Aed asked.

Gethsemane nodded.

"Why in the name of all that's holy would you do that?" Venus asked.

If she was honest, because protecting her favorite ghost took precedence over seeing Aed resurrect his career. She pushed the thought aside with a twinge of guilt. "Because I thought an appearance by Aed on a popular TV show would boost ticket sales. Poe, the one with the blue hair, is fascinated by the legend behind 'Kastély'—"

"That is one unusual girl," Venus interrupted. "She reminds me of an informant I met when I—"

Gethsemane made a face and continued. "Poe is fascinated by Maja Zoltán. The crew didn't find anything here in the way of paranormal evidence—"

"Because there is no such thing," Venus interrupted again.

Gethsemane bit back a caustic remark. Venus's skepticism was keeping ghosts out of her book revisions. Treat it as a blessing. "So I suggested, and they agreed, the Athaneum would be the perfect place to film their show. They always interview people connected to whatever case they're investigating."

"Meaning me," Aed said.

"They devote a big chunk of each episode to backstory, in this case, the legend. And since your opera's about the legend, it makes sense they'd talk about your opera. Maybe even include some of the music. It shouldn't be too hard to convince Poe that you're playing the music to test the curse for her. Consider it the operatic equivalent of a movie tie-in."

"It's risky," Aed said. "It borders on insane. It's bold, daring. Let's do it. I'm in."

Prayers of thanks filled Gethsemane's head. "A couple of the crew, Kent and I guess whoever he considers essential, will be coming to the theater tomorrow after lunch."

"You're going to put school boys and a TV crew in the same space at the same time?" Venus asked. "Fearless becomes foolhardy in the blink of an eye."

Damn. The boys. She'd scheduled honors orchestra to attend rehearsals tomorrow. Too late to change things now. She played off her concern. "I'm not worried. The boys know how to conduct themselves."

"Like boys?" Venus asked. "That would be the problem."

"Ah, don't worry about the lads," Aed said. "I'm an Oul' Boy myself. We'll have a grand time."

"You'd have a better time if you weren't staying at the same inn as Bernard Stoltz," Venus said.

"I'm sure Father Tim's offer of a room at the parish house still stands," Gethsemane said.

"Don't worry about Aed Devlin." He tapped his thumb against his chest. "I've been looking out for myself since I was fifteen. I'm comfortable at Sweeney's, and I won't give that gobshite Stoltz the satisfaction of running me out. I feel good about 'Kastély.' It's feckin' brilliant if I dare say so. This is my time for a comeback, and damn Stoltz if he thinks he can ruin it for me again."

Gethsemane studied Aed's face, distorted by passion and anger. How far would he go to deny Bernard a second chance to wreck him? Far enough to stage an accident with a statue or balcony rail? True, Niall had smelled that strange odor. And the curse decreed anyone who performed anything based on Maja's tragedy would die horribly, but the legend made a convenient cover for murder. She chewed her lip. She couldn't bluntly ask Aed if he'd tried to flatten Bernard. Maybe she could get him to whistle the overture again. No way he could have rigged the cottage so if anything happened, like the ceiling collapsed, he'd be cleared. She looked up at the wooden beams supporting the thatch. They could probably jump out of the way.

She turned to Aed. "What instrumentation are you using for the overture to 'Kastély'?"

Aed relaxed. "Flute, piccolo, English horn, bassoon, strings, of course. I included trumpets in the original instrumentation, but the result sounded too 'William Tell.' Martial instead of tragic."

"Would you—"

Aed's phone rang, cutting her off. He glanced at the screen. "It's my assistant. Excuse me." He stepped into the hall.

Gethsemane lowered her voice. "Did Aed tell you about his wife?"

Venus stiffened. "Ex-wife. He told me enough. She should have had more faith in him, should have been stronger, more loyal."

"Bernard implied Aed and a student were romantically involved."

"Implied, alleged, hinted. Never proved. The ex-Mrs. Devlin cared more for her reputation than for Aed." The ex-Mrs. Devlin came from an extremely wealthy, extremely scandal-averse family. "Do you believe rumors and accusations about people who matter to you? Without any proof?"

"You mean, like allegations of murder-suicide? No."

Aed came back into the room. "I'm sorry, ladies, I have to go. A minor crisis with the costumer." He shook Gethsemane's hand. "Thank you, again, for letting Venus stay here. Not even a Wayne hotel is big enough to house both her and Stoltz under the same roof."

"Are you sure you don't want to stay at the parish house with Father Tim, Aed?" She hesitated. "Or here? After today's row, I worry no hotel is big enough to house you and Bernard under one roof."

"I'll be all right. Damned if I let the likes of that gobshite send me packing. He better be wide or I'll claim him, yeah."

"Please, not another fight. The one in the church yard almost turned deadly."

"I wish that statue had fallen on Bernard," Venus said. "Good riddance."

"Don't worry," Aed said. "Bernard will get his due one of these days." His phone rang again. He checked the caller ID but didn't answer. "My assistant again. The crisis must have gone from minor to major. I'd better go. Until tomorrow, Gethsemane."

She shook his hand again. "Until tomorrow, school boys and

ghost hunters in tow."

Gethsemane waited in the upstairs parlor a few minutes for Venus and Aed to say goodbye, then joined her house guest in the study. "So."

Venus sank into the couch. "So."

"Do we sit here all evening pretending either of us wants to be in this awkward situation or do we," Gethsemane held up a bottle of Waddell and Dobb from the bar cart, "have a drink?"

"Drink," Venus said. "I take mine neat."

"One thing we have in common." Gethsemane poured two glasses then joined Venus on the couch. "Here's your chance. I'm a captive audience. Go ahead and ask all those probing questions so you can get the inside scoop for your book."

Venus sipped bourbon and took her time answering. "I'm not a bad person."

"If you mean you don't pull the wings off flies and tie tin cans to cats' tails, I believe you. But your books are filled with lies and innuendo and hurtful insinuations."

"They sell well."

"And public hangings used to be family entertainment."

Venus drained her glass and got up for another. "I used to be a legit journalist. An investigative reporter."

Poe had mentioned Venus's exposés. "For the *Tattler*?"

"That low-rent celebrity gossip rag? God, no. I didn't investigate anything when I wrote for the *Tattler*, and I used the term 'wrote' only in the most generic sense of the word. I usually just made stuff up. As long as I handed something in before deadline, nobody at the paper cared if what I handed in was true. If anyone I wrote about complained, the editors called it satire and paid hush money. Since we focused on D-listers, they were happy to have the rent money. A few even called me up asking me to lie about them so they could get a payout." She returned to the couch. "When I worked for the TV station, that's when I was proud of my press credentials. I seldom had enough for food and rent in the same month, I drove a beater car that was older than I was, and I always drew the crappiest assignments, but I could hold my head up then. I could say, 'I'm a reporter.'"

"Aside from wanting to eat and have shelter at the same time, why give up television reporting? If you cut the sensational parts out of your books, they'd be as short as novellas, but they'd also be well-written examples of spot-on investigations. I hate saying this, but you've got talent. You've a knack for drawing the truth out of people with vested interests in concealing the truth. You disguise it under borderline libelous gossip, but it's there. I liked chapters eight through fifteen of your book on the CEO of that pharmaceutical company that sold expired drugs in Malawi."

"That book had forty-two chapters."

Gethsemane shrugged.

"Did you like any part of my book on the McCarthy murders?"

"I didn't read most of it. But you did make one or two good points about the shoddiness of the gardaí's investigation. And I like that you're now referring to the McCarthy murders instead of the McCarthy murder-suicide."

"I do, on rare occasion, admit when I'm wrong. Especially when I'm so publicly proven wrong. You solved a twenty-five-year-old cold case. That made news on both sides of the Atlantic."

"You never answered my question. Why'd you give up television news?"

Venus fingered the pattern cut into the crystal old-fashioned glass.

"Bernard Stoltz?"

"What do you know about that?" She eyed Gethsemane sideways.

"Nothing, specifically. But you nearly killed him in front of a priest, and you moved from a luxury lodging in the village center to the spare room of an old cottage on a cliff just to get away from him. You don't know Aed that well, in the non-Biblical sense of the word, anyway. We all agree Bernard deserves a swift karmic kick in the ass for ruining Aed's career, but your reaction seems extreme."

"I need another drink."

"Help yourself. Bar cart's stocked. Will you tell me why you hate Bernard?"

"I hate him because," Venus drained a glass and poured another, "that subhumanoid POS cost me my job, broke my heart, and killed a dear, dear man whose only sin was to try and do the right thing."

The two women sat in silence. Gethsemane knew Bernard's vituperative reviews had ruined more careers than Aed's and his behavior had wrecked more than a few marriages, but she didn't know of any deaths resulting from his words or actions. Classical music's genteel veneer deceived people into believing nothing more salacious than a harpist uttering a mild epithet ever happened behind the scenes. In reality, classical music saw its fair share of vicious players and abominable acts—both on the performance and the business sides of the world—but killing? Gethsemane waited.

Venus seemed to be far away from Dunmullach, lost in the bell-like note her glass emitted as she traced her fingernail around and around its rim. Gethsemane counted thirty seconds on the clock, sixty, two minutes, three. Finally, Venus inhaled sharply and returned to the study in the cottage on the cliff. She looked around and blinked. Without being asked, she said, "Bernard Stoltz was my lover. I'd been at KXBH for two years when I met him. He was the music reviewer for the local paper, owned by the same company that owned the station. I don't remember what event we met at, but he was charming and funny and seemed more interested in what I had to say than my cup size. I was working on a story about a record label with a lucrative side business in pirating music by acts signed to competitors. Turns out, Bernard was accepting hefty bribes from several of the artists signed to that label. They paid him money, he wrote good reviews. If they refused to pay up, he'd sink them. His newspaper was small-time, but Bernard's writing was influential."

"Sounds like the same scheme that got him fired from

Classical Music Today."

"Bernard was a pro at the art of the bought-and-paid-for review by the time he landed that job. Scuttlebutt says *Classical* hired him as part of a deal he made with the managing editor, whose daughter happened to be an up-and-coming cellist. And whose first solo concert Bernard had tickets to."

"What happened with the record label?" Gethsemane asked.

"I discovered—too late—Bernard's interest lay in neither my cleavage nor my intellect. He was after my little black book. I had a contact at the record label, an informant. The one honest man in the entire company. He provided me evidence of the pirating operation. Names, dates, master tapes, everything needed to blow the ring wide open and send a lot of people to prison. They'd have done anything, including selling their firstborns to the devil, to stop my investigation."

"They paid Bernard to find out who your informant was."

"By seducing me. Me falling in love with him was my own stupidity. Long, painful story short, Bernard stole my notes and named my informant to his bosses. They gutted him—framed him for embezzlement, tricked his wife into thinking he cheated on her, called Child Protective Services to report him for nonexistent child abuse. You name it, if it was evil and a lie, they did it. He held up as long as he could, but eventually the anguish of losing his job, wife, children, and reputation got to him. He went down to the train depot one night and danced with the 8:10 to Pine Bluff."

"That's awful."

"I got off easy. All Bernard did to me was make it look as if I'd used fake quotes in a couple of my reports. The station fired me, I left town, got a job with the *Tattler*..."

"No wonder you tried to put his eye out."

"Yeah, well, I at least bounced back. And Bernard eventually got what he deserved. Public disgrace and job termination."

"What do you think he's doing here?"

"Like I said, he's here hoping to shred Aed again. I don't think he'd try to bribe Aed for a good review. A, he's got no clout as a reviewer anymore, and B, Aed would kill him. But if Aed's opera is anything short of a smash, Bernard will write some piece of disparaging tripe and sell it to someone and destroy Aed's chances to save his career. Smear jobs sell. I should know." Venus gulped the remainder of her bourbon. "Someone should stop that little creep before he hurts someone who matters again."

Seven

Gethsemane woke to the sounds of blood-curdling screams. She fell out of bed, cursed herself for leaving her shillelagh near the front door, and stumbled toward the back bedroom. She got as far as the doorway when she realized the screams emanated from the lower level. A quick glance at the bed told her Venus wasn't in it. She scrambled to the stairs. Eamon materialized without warning on the landing at the head of the stairs. She crashed into him and passed through him, her skin on fire with infinite pins and needles. She pitched forward and tumbled down the stairs. Something grabbed her pajama collar mid-somersault and hauled her back up to the upper landing.

Eamon, glowing the brightest purple-blue she'd ever seen him, stooped to stare at her eye to eye. "For the love of God, woman, make her stop!" He vanished.

Gethsemane, wide awake and smarting from both bruises and her collision with Eamon, hurried downstairs. She followed the shrieks to their source in the kitchen—Venus, in silk robe and bare feet, wide-eyed with terror, with a kitchen knife gripped in one white-knuckled hand. The other hand pointed at an empty chair at the breakfast table. A pot of coffee simmered on the stove.

Gethsemane stepped toward her terrified house guest, but the kitchen knife drove her back. "Venus, it's me. Stop screaming. What is it?"

The screams ended. Venus's mouth moved, but no words came

out. She kept pointing at the chair and kept the knife held between her and it. Either a flesh-eating demon zombie rat had run across her foot, or—

"Oh my God, you saw Eamon." Gethsemane face palmed. She didn't need this on a school morning.

Her alarm clock sounded upstairs. The shrill tone seemed to snap Venus out of her terror. She dropped the knife and collapsed into a chair. Gethsemane sprinted up to her bedroom to silence the noise, then returned to the kitchen.

Venus shook and wrapped her arms across her chest. "A man, a man, there was a man with dark curly hair and green eyes, a big man, in that chair." She nodded her head toward the chair on the opposite side of the table.

Gethsemane moved to sit.

"No, don't sit in it!" Venus shouted and half-leapt out of her seat.

"Okay, okay." Gethsemane pulled Venus back down and knelt beside her. "I believe you. There really was a man there, you're not crazy. Please trust me, I know exactly how you feel right now. Please also trust me when I tell you that you've seen a ghost."

"A ghost? A ghost?" Venus's feared turned to fury. "I have the most terrifying experience of my life and you make fun of me by telling me I saw a ghost?" She came out of her chair again.

Gethsemane wrestled her down. "I'm not making fun of you. I'm explaining what you saw. You saw the ghost of Eamon McCarthy."

"Ghosts. Don't. Exist."

"Yeah, actually, they do." Gethsemane held up a hand against Venus's sputtered protest. "I didn't believe in them, either, until I moved up here and met Eamon. His ghost convinced me to investigate his and his wife's murders."

"That's not funny. That's—that's cruel."

"I'm not lying." Gethsemane stood. "Eamon, Eamon, where are you? This would be a really good time to show yourself."

Eamon, still a frightened angry mixture of purple and blue,

materialized in a corner as far as his waist. Venus jumped up, mouth wide open. "If she screams again, so help me—"

Gethsemane clamped her hand over Venus's mouth and pushed her back into the chair. "The rest of you, please," she said to Eamon. His legs appeared. The stove and sink were clearly visible through him. "Try solid."

The appliances faded as he grew denser. "Satisfied?" He crossed his arms and leaned into the counter. "What's wrong with her?"

"Wrong with—? She's just seen her first ghost."

"You'd think she'd just peered into the very bowels of hell."

"I freaked out the first time I saw you."

"Not like that you didn't. Not screaming to shame a banshee."

"I ran from the cottage into the path of an oncoming car."

Eamon grinned. His aura took on a green tinge. "I'd forgotten that bit."

"It's not funny. Did you also forget I put a paper weight through the middle of your chest?"

"After telling me about your softball prowess. Yeah, I do remember that."

Venus gasped words between ragged breaths. "What. Is. Happening. Here?"

"Eamon McCarthy haunted this house for twenty-five years because he couldn't rest in peace after being falsely accused of killing his wife then being erroneously buried in unhallowed ground as a suicide. He disappeared after I solved his, and his wife's, murders, but came back after I recited a spell and fell off a catwalk that creaked the notes matching his sympathetic resonance. He frightened away a smarmy hotel developer, but now he's stuck. We don't know how to get him back."

"Not that I've any intention of going back to limbo. I told you."

"I heard you. I'm giving Venus the Cliff's Notes version of events."

"But, those guys, the ghost hunters, Kent and the weird one with the hair, and the others. You said you told them the theater was haunted, that there were no ghosts in the cottage."

"I lied so they'd go away and not capture proof of Eamon's existence, because Father Tim convinced me the world might fall off its axis if they did."

"The priest knows?"

"He knows. He can't see Eamon, but he knows about him."

"Shouldn't he do something? Stage an exorcism? Call the Pope?"

Gethsemane shrugged. "He's a pretty broad-minded priest. And folks around here seem laid back about the idea of the paranormal. Adds local color."

"Local color?" The blue returned. "What am I, a feckin' leprechaun?"

Gethsemane stuck out her tongue.

Venus looked back and forth between them. "Seriously? I'm witnessing firsthand tangible proof that life doesn't end with the death of the body and you two are at each other like preteen siblings in the backseat of their parents' car?"

"At least she didn't say like an old married couple." A green glow edged out the blue.

"Give her a break, Irish. You do take some getting used to. And don't laugh at her."

"How do you know he's laughing?" Venus asked.

Gethsemane pointed to his aura. "Color-coding."

Venus patted her robe. "Where's my phone? I have to call my editor. This is the biggest story since—since—the discovery of the Dead Sea scrolls."

"Sissy..." The warning came through clear.

"You can't do that." Gethsemane pinned Venus's arms at her sides. "Maybe the shock of accepting the reality of ghosts kept you from paying attention, so I'll repeat myself. I sent the *Ghost Hunting Adventures* boys to the Athaneum to keep them from finding proof of Eamon's existence. You can't call your editor and tell him Eamon exists."

"Her. My editor's a her."

"Him, her, it. I don't care. You can't broadcast this."

"Of course I will. This is news."

Gethsemane glanced at Eamon's fingertips. A large blue orb sizzled and popped. She released Venus's arms and stood. "You know what, you're right. Go ahead and call your editor. You can use the kitchen phone. It has long-distance."

"What?" Venus said.

"What?" Eamon said.

They both cocked their heads and stared at her.

"Have you taken leave of your senses?" Eamon asked.

"I am one hundred percent rational." She glanced at the clock. "And I'm going to be late for school. You call your editor, Venus, tell her you've seen a ghost and want to write about it. Not that you have any evidence. No photos. No video. Nothing you can put into a box or a bag and slip into your carry-on. Literally nothing you can hold onto. I, of course, will deny everything. I'll tell them the sea air made you a little, you know." She rotated her finger near her ear then turned to Eamon. "Not the full shilling, that's the term, isn't it?"

"Among many." The orb faded.

"Go ahead and revise your book and include a chapter on how a ghost helped solve his own murder. Then try to get a legit writing assignment. Maybe the *Tattler* will take you back."

Venus stood. Gethsemane craned her neck to maintain eye contact.

"Bitch," Venus said. "You're as bad as Bernard."

"Not quite. Bernard is willing to ruin someone for money. I'm willing to ruin someone to save a friend."

Venus glared at Gethsemane, then at Eamon, then at Gethsemane again. "Fine," she said after a moment. "I'll keep my mouth shut. Not much of a story, anyway. Ghosts are so off-trend."

Eight

Gethsemane rushed to dress for work. Coffee would have to wait until the teacher's lounge. She ran down the stairs to find Venus waiting by the door.

"I'm late for work." She tried to squeeze past her.

"I'm coming with you," Venus said.

"I did mention I'm going to work. School. To teach music classes."

"I heard you. I'm sticking with you. Number one, you're not leaving me here with a ghost."

"'Tis my house," a disembodied Eamon bellowed.

"Number two, things happen around you, Gethsemane Brown. I'm not letting you out of my sight. The price of my silence."

"Fine. If you want to spend the morning learning about music theory with a bunch of male adolescents, suit yourself. But," she looked at Venus's stiletto-clad feet, "you might want to put on some flats. It's a bit of a walk."

Venus pulled out her phone. "Call an Uber."

"You might find a ghost out here. An Uber..." She shook her head.

"A cab, then."

"Put your phone away." Gethsemane pulled out her own phone—she'd committed herself to Dunmullach and gotten one with an Irish number—and called Father Tim. A short while later, the two women rode in the back of Tim's car, headed for St.

Brennan's.

"How many people can see McCarthy's ghost?" Venus asked.

Gethsemane and Venus jerked forward against their seatbelts as the car braked to a sudden stop. Tim swiveled in the driver's seat to stare at them.

"She can see him," Gethsemane said.

"Jesus, Mary, and Joseph." The priest crossed himself and resumed driving.

Venus leaned forward over the seat and tapped Tim on the shoulder. "Why can't you see McCarthy's ghost?" She whispered to Gethsemane, "Why can't he see McCarthy's ghost?"

"I don't know," Gethsemane said. "I can't suss out any patterns or predictors. Some people both see and hear him, some only one or the other, some only sense his presence, and some can't detect him at all."

"That doesn't bother you?"

"No. I choose to view the quirks in the system as endearing. And no stranger than my grandparents' stories."

"But those were just stories."

"Maybe not."

They stopped first at the headmaster's office, where Gethsemane convinced Riordan that Venus was there to research a book on the role of progressive education methods in a classical educational environment. With Riordan's blessing, she escorted Venus to class. She soon discovered Venus had a working knowledge of music and an expert knowledge of how to keep a roomful of boys under control. They ate lunch—fish fingers, carrot batons, and steamed rice—which prompted Venus to threaten to write an exposé on cafeteria food. Afterwards, Gethsemane took her to meet the honors orchestra.

She opened the door to the music room and stopped short. Colm, Feargus, Aengus, Ruairi, and the other boys sat in their assigned seats, hands folded. No one ran, shouted, threw anything, or otherwise acted the maggot. Gethsemane checked the brass name plaque by the door. Yes, she'd come to the right classroom.

"Check for snakes, frogs, and booby traps before you sit on anything," she warned Venus as she surveyed her chair for hazards. Venus took an empty chair near the windows.

"Good afternoon, Dr. Brown," the boys said in unison.

"Okay, who are you people and what have you done with my students?" she asked them.

"Is a TV crew really going to be at the theater this afternoon?" a boy in the back row asked.

"Can we be on TV?" another asked.

"Is there really an evil ghost who rips people's hearts out?" a third asked.

"Ah." News of the TV crew and the curse must have gone out on the rumor mill. "Best behavior so you can be on TV or meet a killer ghost." Both options probably appealed equally to her adolescent charges. She introduced them to Venus. "Ms. James is coming with us this afternoon. I want you to treat her with the respect you'd show to any one of your instructors." She spotted the grin on Colm's face and corrected herself. "No, I want you to show her more respect than you'd show to any one of your instructors."

"Are you going to write a book about the opera ghost, Ms. James?" Ruairi asked.

Venus glanced at Gethsemane before answering. "Um, no, ghost stories aren't my specialty."

"Are you going to write about us in the revised edition of your book about the McCarthys, Ms. James?" Colm asked.

"You know about that?" Venus asked.

"Of course, Miss," Colm said. "We all do. We follow the *True Crime Writes* podcast. We listened to your episode."

Gethsemane addressed the class. "All right, guys, time to go. The van should be here to take us to the Athaneum."

Monday afternoon's crowd at the Athaneum threatened to outdo Friday night's crowd at the Rabbit: Aed, the theater owner, the *Ghost Hunting Adventures* team, musicians, and dozens of people she didn't recognize milling about onstage and in the wings—crew, she assumed. If as many people bought a ticket to the premiere as crowded the theater now, the show would be a sell-out performance.

Gethsemane marveled at the set design. The proscenium stage had been transformed into a menacing forest with an unfinished castle tower to one side. Piles of stones and gleaming steel trowels hinted at Maja's fate. The familiar rows of blue velvet seats faced an alternate universe convincingly constructed of plywood and canvas to evoke the sense of dread and desperation that would drive a duchess to murder her own daughter-in-law. The orchestra pit yawned between the seats and the set, the audience's only protection from the forest perils.

She paused just inside the entrance as Tchaikovsky's "Pathétique" rushed at her out of nowhere. A couple of boys bumped into her.

"Are you all right, Dr. Brown?" one asked. "Have you seen a ghost?"

"What? No, no ghost." She reassured the two students. "I'm fine." She ushered the boys inside, then shook her head to clear away the unwanted music. Damn, damn, and damn. Something awful was going to happen. What? When? And why did it have to be when the boys were around?

Aed separated from the crowd and greeted the new arrivals. "Welcome, welcome, to opening rehearsals for 'Kastély.' And Venus, so happy to see you here." He shook the women's hands. Venus stepped toward Aed, glanced at the boys, then stepped back.

"Meet the honors orchestra, Aed." Gethsemane began the introductions. "Colm Nolan, Head Boy and one of the finest young violinists anywhere."

"And nephew of the great Peter Nolan. Pleased to meet you, young man."

"It's an honor, sir."

"Ruairi O'Brien. Another of the best young violinists around."

Aed shook the boy's hand. "I heard about your virtuoso

performance in the All-County. Fair play, lad, fair play."

"Thank you, sir."

The twins came next. "Feargus Toibin, deputy head boy, and Aengus Toibin. Both percussion."

"Which of you is the oldest?" Aed asked the redheads.

"I am, sir," Feargus said. "By fifteen minutes."

Gethsemane introduced the rest of the boys, then escorted them to seats in the center orchestra section near the stage. Venus declined Aed's offer to join him in the wings and sat near Gethsemane. Kent, Hardy, Poe, Ciara, and the rest of the paranormal team claimed the grand tier.

Hardy stopped as they passed by. "I wanted to show you something." He pulled a phone from his hip pocket.

"Is that the new Samsung?" Gethsemane asked. She thought of her own low-end phone with a jealous twinge. She should have let the sales clerk talk her into the upgrade.

"No. This isn't available on the market. We," he gestured to the rest of the investigators, "work with an engineer who custom designs a lot of our equipment. She's an inventor. She's come up with a way to combine FLIR, thermal, and full-spectrum technologies in a single smartphone camera." He lowered his voice. "She also incorporated some space telescope technology developed by MIT."

Venus leaned across Gethsemane to get a better look at the phone. "How would your engineer get her hands on MIT technology? I suspect it's not open source."

Hardy smiled and slipped the phone back in his pocket. "That would be telling. But if anything can capture a ghost on camera, this will."

A stingy-brimmed fedora, balanced on a knee, connected to a leg that led to a well-shod foot tapping a beat in the right orchestra section caught her eye. Inspector O'Reilly chatted with a brunette in paint-stained overalls seated in a middle row.

Gethsemane called to him. "Niall?"

He looked up from his conversation and raised his hat in

greeting. "Sissy, good to see you."

She sighed. Apparently that stupid nickname had stuck. She'd be "Sissy" as long as she remained in Dunmullach. She'd be sending her brother-in-law a strongly worded note offering the opposite of thanks for revealing it. She made her way across the rows of seats to where Niall introduced his friend. "She's the set designer. We know each other from our art history days at university."

Gethsemane shook the woman's hand. "You've done an amazing job with the stage. I felt the dread all the way to the door." She wished the creepy set had been the only cause of her unease. But she couldn't forget the Tchaikovsky.

She found a redheaded math teacher chatting with Venus and a dozen math students occupying the rows behind her boys when she returned to her seat. "Frankie, what are you doing here?"

"Teaching, Sissy. School-sanctioned field trip. We're having class on the relationship between music and mathematics. They are related, you know."

"I do know. My father was a mathematician, remember?" She added a reflexive, feeble, "And stop calling me Sissy," as she accepted the futility of further resistance.

Three raps on the stage drew everyone's attention. Aed stepped into the center, arms spread, and welcomed them as they settled into their seats. He sat next to Venus.

Eamon's voice spoke near her ear. "About time we get this hooley started."

Good thing he couldn't read minds. He'd launch a blue orb for sure if he knew what she thought right now. So much for staying away.

Venus glanced at Eamon, then turned back to the stage, slightly pale.

Aed's voice boomed. "Friends, colleagues, future performers. Today we begin rehearsals for my new opera, 'Kastély,' the tragic story of the sacrifice one woman makes—the daughter she loves for the people she's sworn to protect. As both librettist and composer, I believe this opera is the piece that will stand as the greatest work of my career." He swept an arm toward the wings. "Now, please allow me to introduce Mademoiselle Sylvie Babin, world-famous soprano, who will sing the role of Maja." A smattering of applause greeted a striking, almond-eyed beauty arrayed in layers of iridescent organza that trailed behind her like peacock finery as she crossed the stage to stand next to Aed. "Many of you may remember Mademoiselle Babin from—"

The theater door banged open. Heads turned. Bernard Stoltz strolled down the aisle to an empty seat in the left orchestra section. The room grew silent. Almost silent. Onstage, Sylvie said, "Merde." Kent shouted the same thing, in English, from the grand tier.

"Carry on," Bernard said. "Far be it from me to interrupt art."

"What the hell are you doing here, Bernard?" Venus asked.

"I'm here by authorization of the theater owner." Bernard waved at the man, who tried to shrink into the theater wings. "I'm not leaving."

Venus gripped the arms of her chair and pushed herself up. Niall also rose, his eyes on Venus. Aed stepped toward the edge of the stage.

"Children present," Gethsemane hissed and pulled her back down.

"As I was saying," Aed shot an angry glance at Bernard, then resumed his previous position and his speech, "many of you may remember Mademoiselle Babin from her recent performances in 'Lucia di Lammermoor' and 'Ruslan and Lyudmila.' This afternoon, as a special treat for the lads," Aed nodded toward the students, "Mademoiselle will perform Maja's final aria from 'Kastély.' Sung in Italian, it describes the moment Maja realizes she's been tricked and left to die, walled up inside the castle. She expresses her despair, her anger at being given no choice in her fate. It ends with her cursing future generations of the Zoltán family with her dying breath. I, myself, shall perform the ritornello on the piano. Of course," he again addressed his remarks to the students, "during the actual performance, the ritornello would be performed by the entire orchestra."

As Aed made his way down into the orchestra pit, Gethsemane got up and peered over the edge. She first met Saoirse down there. No sign of the girl now. Had she made it to the theater? Gethsemane looked up at the ghost hunters. Cameras and microphones lined the grand tier, all aimed at the stage. Mademoiselle Babin's aria wasn't the performance they hoped to record. Gethsemane moved to a seat in an empty row behind the students with a good view of the balconies as well as the stage and the rest of the orchestra. Eamon materialized next to her.

The music began. Aed played an eerie introduction—dark, moody, desperate notes. Saint-Saëns's "Danse Macabre" seemed a cheerful nursery rhyme in comparison. Several of the younger boys huddled small in their seats, knees hugged to their chests. The final note of the ritornello became the first note of the sung portion of the aria. The diva sang, in a clear, pure voice, lyrics evocative of the terror and fury of a young woman suffering a miserable, slow death at the hands of people she loved and trusted. Entranced by the performance, Gethsemane forced herself to look away from the stage and scan the theater for Saoirse. Blanched knuckles gripped seats. Frankie comforted a boy who hid his face against the math teacher's shoulder. Even Niall sat low in his seat, his eyes fixed on the soprano, muscles tense as if ready to spring into action to save her from her fate. Venus and Bernard had disappeared from their seats. Poe bit her thumb and leaned far out over the grand tier's railing. Hardy pulled her back. No blonde head peeked from behind any curtains or pillars. Gethsemane focused on the stage. The soprano held a high note. Theater windows rattled. Still she held it. Glass cracked. Gethsemane turned to see Kent holding up a damaged EMF pod. Mademoiselle Babin paused for breath but the note lingered. No one moved. As the note faded, a new sound ripped the air. An ear-splitting scream shot down from the rear balcony. Everyone in the theater turned in unison.

Saoirse stood in the rear balcony's front row and pointed to a spot just above the on-stage castle. "She's there!" the girl screamed,

"She's there! Maja's ghost, I see her, she's there."

Eamon materialized next to Gethsemane. "The girl may be coddin' but she's not wrong. Maja is there and she's pissed."

Gethsemane whispered, hoping Saoirse's commotion would keep anyone from noticing her talking to what appeared to them to be an empty chair. She squinted in the direction Saoirse pointed. "Where? I don't see anything."

"Not there." He pointed to a spot at the base of the castle, several feet below where Saoirse pointed.

"That blue haze? That's Maja?"

"Give her a moment," Eamon said. "It's been a few centuries since she materialized. This ghost business isn't as easy as folks think." He gestured to the balcony. "Girl's a bit melodramatic. Maybe you ought to give her a signal to stop bogarting the scene."

Saoirse kept screaming and pointing at the empty corner. Kent, Hardy, and the other *Ghost Hunting Adventures* crew jockeyed for space as they focused their cameras on Saoirse, the corner, and the crowd. Colm leapt over seats to get to the balcony stairs with Ruairi not far behind him. Colm took the stairs two at a time, burst onto the balcony, and grabbed his sister.

"Saoirse, hush, it's okay." He held her close and smoothed her hair. "I'm here. It's all right."

"There, in the corner." Her gestures grew more frantic. "Can't you see?"

"See what, Saoirse?" Ruairi asked. "There's nothing there."

"It's Maja, the ghost, the one who kills the firstborn."

"Shh, it's nothing. Nobody's there." Colm tried to hold his sister tighter, but she wriggled from his grasp enough to peer over the balcony rail. Gethsemane caught her eye and drew her index finger across her throat.

Saoirse stopped screaming. She broke free of her brother and smoothed her skirt. "I'm fine, Colm. Don't be such an old woman." She kissed his cheek. "Cook's making pandy tonight. Don't be late like last time." She hugged Ruairi and skipped downstairs.

"What the hell's wrong with the girl?" Aed had climbed out of the orchestra pit and stood on the orchestra level with the others, staring up at the source of excitement. All eyes watched her leave the theater. Colm ran after her.

"She saw a ghost, Mr. Devlin," Poe shouted down at him from the grand tier. "The ghost you conjured with your opera." She held up her camera. "The ghost I caught on film."

Gethsemane looked at the castle again. The blue haze had morphed slightly into a shape recognizable as a figure—a head, shoulders, maybe an arm—but far from anything recognizable as any specific person. Had Poe and the crew actually captured anything? "There wasn't supposed to be a real ghost," she hissed. "Manky smells, yes. Actual manifestations, no."

"Don't look at me, darlin'," Eamon said. "I didn't call her. This was your idea."

"I didn't call her. I'm nowhere near an instrument, and I haven't recited any incantations since—Damn it. Poe."

"What did she do?"

"She found Tim's occult books and took a grimoire. Not by accident, I'd bet money. She must have used a conjuring spell."

"A spell alone isn't enough."

She and Eamon fell silent for a moment.

"The overture," Gethsemane said.

"The aria," Eamon said.

"Weirdness has been happening since Aed whistled the overture at school."

"Smells, like you said, and the accidents. They weren't publicity stunts, they were the opening act. Aed triggered the curse with his whistle. Sylvie's high notes brought on the full-scale production."

"Sylvie did sing a nasty curse. The words of the aria might have acted as their own spell, even without Poe's interference."

"What about the aria?" Aed approached from the direction of the stage. He gave no indication of seeing Eamon.

"It was so powerful," she said. "Overwhelming. I wondered if it stirred more than the audience's emotions."

"You're not giving credence to this curse rubbish, are you? This ghost nonsense. That poor girl's obviously touched in the head."

"Don't be too hasty to dismiss her sighting." Gethsemane glanced over her shoulder. The blue haze still hovered on the stage. It had grown denser, more shadow than haze now, and had a distinctly female shape. "We should see if the paranormal crew caught something on camera."

"I agreed to have those fellas here because I wanted some free publicity, not so I'd become a laughing stock. You know how important this is to me."

Sylvie rushed up the aisle from the stage, sheer layers in full flutter behind her. She slipped between Gethsemane and Aed and fanned herself with a hand. "Aed, I must lie down. The shock. The shock is so bad for the voice." Her impossibly French accent reminded Gethsemane of Pepé Le Pew from the old cartoons.

"A diva in every sense of the word," Eamon said. "Wans like her are the reason I stayed away from operas."

Aed assisted her into one of the blue velvet seats. "Has anyone seen Venus?" he asked.

Sylvie harrumphed and stood. "I shall find someplace to lie down on my own. Y'all driving me fou."

Y'all? Gethsemane raised an eyebrow. The expression was more South Carolina than southern France.

Venus called to Aed from the far side of the auditorium. He excused himself and went to her.

The paranormal investigators came down from the grand tier to the orchestra level. Sylvie moved off to try her luck with one of the camera men.

Kent came over and grabbed Gethsemane in a bear hug. "That was a-maz-ing. Amazing. Gorgeous. It couldn't have been more prefect if you staged it. The little girl? Is she psychic?"

Ciara walked up to Kent and laid her hand on his back. "We should get back to ops base and analyze our footage."

"We can't leave yet." Poe joined the group. "Something else is going to happen. Something huge. Can't you feel it?"

Hardy walked up behind her. "Something bigger than a poor kid being terrified out of her mind?"

Poe didn't seem to catch the distaste in his voice. "Way bigger than that. Something tremendous."

"I'm going to check on the boys," Gethsemane said. She headed back to the front of the orchestra.

Colm returned without Saoirse and plopped into a seat near Feargus. "May we go now, Dr. Brown? I don't like this place. I don't feel well."

"Nor do I," Feargus said. "I think I may gawk."

Gethsemane studied the boys. They looked pale and feverish. Much different than the hale and hearty youth they'd been when they climbed into the van to come to the theater. Several of the other boys looked just as ill as Colm and Feargus. What could have come over them so fast? "We'll go. You wait here. I'm going to ask Mr. Grennan to help me round up the others, then we'll leave."

Aengus ambled up and punched his brother in the shoulder. "Some hooley, huh? With the French lady shattering glass and Colm's little sis screaming to raise the dead and that blue-haired bure with the camera going on about blood and guts. Pure fun, that's what it is."

Feargus pushed Aengus away. "Not now. Can't you see I've got a bad dose?" He sniffed. "Do you smell something?"

"Not me," Aengus said.

"I do," Colm said. "Smells like pepper and grease."

Seeing Feargus and Aengus together made Feargus seem even worse. The twins looked like before and after pictures in one of her mother's medical texts: Feargus, the before treatment, Aengus, the after recovery. "Aengus, keep an eye on your brother and Colm." Time to gather her flock and go. She waded into the crowd gathered near the stage.

"Have you seen Bernard Stoltz?" Niall appeared at her elbow. He scanned the room over her head.

"No, but I haven't looked for him."

"I have. I've accounted for everyone except him. All the boys, you, Frankie, Devlin and Venus, Mam'selle diva, the ghost crew. Everyone's here except Stoltz and Saoirse. And Father Tim just texted me to say Saoirse's fine, enjoying tea over at the rectory. Where's Stoltz?"

"Maybe we should look for him."

"Maybe I should look for him. Certainly, you should stay here and help Frankie with these kids. And don't argue."

"I didn't say anything."

"You would have." He tipped his hat and headed for the stage.

"Psst."

Gethsemane turned. Eamon balanced on the orchestra pit rail. His feet disappeared into the brass. "Your guard friend is going the wrong way." He pointed down into the pit.

Gethsemane leaned over the rail. Venus joined her. "Does your ghost friend always pop up out of the blue like that?"

"Yeah, it's a habit. You get used to it."

"I can hear you both," Eamon said.

Both women leaned over the rail. Gethsemane saw it first. "Inspector O'Reilly?"

Niall came out of the wings. "Nothing good ever follows when you address me by my rank and family name."

Gethsemane pointed.

Niall swore. "Get those lads away from here, will ya? Now."

"I'll do it," Venus said. She clapped her hands until all attention was on her. "Guys, I'm getting ready to Skype Angie Morocco." Audible gasps greeted the name of Hollywood's hottest "it" girl. "Who wants to be on the call?"

Every boy in the auditorium raised their hand. Even the sick ones rallied. Venus fished her phone from her purse and led the boys out to the lobby.

"You," Niall pointed at Gethsemane, "stay here."

"Of course I won't. I found him."

Eamon interjected. "You mean I found him."

Gethsemane mouthed, "Shut up" behind Niall's back. He'd

already started down the steps into the orchestra pit. She hurried to catch up.

"I thought I—" He closed his eyes for several seconds. "Never mind. Since you're determined to interfere, make yourself useful and call the garda station. Tell them to send a crime scene unit and someone from homicide." He handed her his smartphone. "The station number's programmed in favorites."

"Me call? How's that going to work? They'll think it's some crank."

"Oh, no. They all know who you are. Just tell the dispatcher Gethsemane Brown found another body and they'll send help right out."

She said something rude.

Niall knelt by the piano, a Steinway grand that looked much like Eamon's. She watched over his shoulder as he reached under the cabinet, past splayed legs, past the gleaming steel trowel protruding from a motionless back, past broken tortoise shell glasses, to the neck of what used to be Bernard Stoltz. He pressed his fingers against flesh for a moment, then dropped his hand and sat back on his heels.

Gethsemane's call connected. "Dunmullach Garda," the voice on the other end said. "How may I help you?"

Nine

The inspector from the homicide unit glared at Gethsemane. She leaned back in the box seat where she'd been kept waiting for twenty minutes and glared back.

"What is it with her?" the inspector whispered to Niall, loudly enough for her to hear. "She cursed or something? Some kind of jinx?"

"Lay off, Bill. Dr. Brown has an alibi for this one. Me. She never left the auditorium. She couldn't have killed Stoltz. She's about the only one who couldn't have. Her and Grennan and the students. Can't vouch for the rest of them. They were all in and out at various points."

"I'm not saying she drove that trowel into his back with her own hands. But people do have a habit of turning up dead when she's around." He cast a nasty glance in her direction. "I'd make some new friends if I was you."

Gethsemane spoke up. "Excuse me, since your colleague just assured you I'm one of the few people in this building who couldn't have committed murder today, may I go? I need to get the boys back to school. Some of them aren't feeling well and they're all upset." To put it mildly. A half dozen had taken ill since the blue haze—now clearly the transparent outline of a dark-haired woman—appeared. The wraith had moved from the stage and popped up in various places around the periphery of the auditorium. She didn't speak, and her facial features remained indistinct, but she radiated anger from the corner where she now lurked. Eamon had vanished right after pointing out Bernard's body. Gethsemane wished he'd come back. She didn't know what Maja could do but sensed she'd be less likely to do it in the presence of another ghost. Maja unnerved her, even more than Bernard's corpse. Corpses were predictable, rational, heartbreaking but harmless. And she was getting used to them. She repeated her request to the homicide inspector.

"Answer a couple of questions first." He pulled out a notebook. "You knew this Stoltz?"

"I'd met him. And I knew of him. He was a miserable jerk who made his living by bribing musicians and ruining their careers if they didn't pay. Until he went after the wrong person and his misdeeds caught up with him. I doubt he'll be missed."

"Do you know what he was doing here? Who invited him?"

Gethsemane shook her head. "I assumed he'd come as a freelancer to review Aed's opera. He's a talented—was a talented writer. A horrible human being, but still talented. If he'd sold a review—especially a bad one—he might have been offered a permanent position with a magazine or paper. That's guessing on my part. Bernard never told us what he was up to."

"Fair to say many people wanted him dead?"

She admitted it was. "But there's a huge leap between 'wanted him dead' and 'grabbed a sharp construction tool, lured him into the orchestra pit, and stabbed him in the back.'"

"One more question. The girl who did the screaming," he consulted his notebook, "Saoirse Nolan. Where's she?"

"She's twelve. Surely, you don't suspect her of stabbing a grown man in the back."

"I asked where she was."

"At Our Lady of Perpetual Sorrows with Father Tim. Last I heard."

He snapped his notebook shut. "She's all yours, Niall. Do me a favor and keep her out of my way." He glared at her again. "Some of us don't need any help from school marms." He moved off to question one of the theater employees.

She looked down at the orchestra level. The boys clustered around Frankie, some stretched out as best they could over the seats. Gardaí, uniformed and plainclothes, stood scattered among Venus, Aed, Sylvie, Kent, Hardy, Poe and the other paranormal investigators, preventing them from talking to each other. More officers and a crime scene unit made noise down in the orchestra pit. She couldn't see what they were doing. "I think I should—" She broke off. "Niall, what's wrong?"

Niall, pale and clammy, had slumped in a seat. His prized hat lay on the floor near his foot.

Gethsemane scooped up the fedora and laid her fingers on his wrist in a single, swift movement. "Are you having chest pain? Can you breathe?" His pulse beat a steady, if fast, thump, thump, thump. "I'll call 999."

He reclaimed his hat and waved away the suggestion of an ambulance. "I'll be all right. Must've just got a dose of what the boys got." He jerked his head toward the orchestra level. "Better stay back, it must be contagious."

"Are you sure you don't want me to call an ambulance?"

"Positive. A, I don't need one. B, I'd never live it down. You can do me a favor. Send one of the uniforms up to give me a ride home. I'll come back for my car later."

"I can drop your car off. Or get your set designer friend to do it."

"She's happily married with three wee ones, if you're curious." He made a face as he handed her his car key.

"If you'd rather I left it in the parking lot—"

"It's not that." He sniffed. "Do you smell pepper and grease?"

The same thing the boys complained they smelled. Maja hung in a corner, brighter and more solid than before.

"Go home, Niall," Gethsemane said. "I think there's something bad in the air here."

She whistled down to the orchestra level for Frankie. They'd get the kids together and—

He looked up at her. Even from the distance between the box seats and the main floor she could see he was sallow and feverish.

"Jeez, Frankie," she said. "You've got it, too."

She waited in the box until a uniformed garda collected Niall and escorted him out. Then she went down to check on Frankie.

"Why don't you head back to school? I'll manage the boys."

"Manage this lot?" Frankie spread his arms. Boys, all pale and clammy, sprawled on seats and on the floor. "You're going to carry them all out to the vans yourself?"

"Someone's going to have to carry you out if you don't sit down. You look awful."

"Don't I always?"

"No, you usually look scruffy." Even that was no longer the case, since Venus arrived in town. "Not sick. Bernard has better color than you. Please go home. I already sent Niall out."

"Now you're that kind of doctor?"

"It doesn't take a physician to see you're sicker than sh—"

"Language." Frankie gestured to the boys.

"To see how sick you are. Go home. Stop being a martyr."

"And if I don't do as I'm told?"

"Have you ever won an argument with me when you're well?"

"No," he admitted.

"What makes you think you can win one now?"

He held up a trembling hand. "I concede. I need some fresh air anyway. Can you not smell that?"

"Pepper and grease?"

Frankie nodded. "Worse than casserole night at the dining hall." He excused himself.

A commotion near the stage interrupted them. Sylvie, as short as Gethsemane, stood on tiptoe to stare a young uniformed garda in the eye. She puffed like an angry pea hen and blasted the officer with the full force of her magnificent voice. "I. Am. Ma-de-moi-selle Ba-bin." She accentuated every syllable like a slap in the face. "I am not used to being treated this way. I am not une criminelle!"

The garda cast about for someone to save him.

Why pass up an opportunity? "Excuse me," Gethsemane said. "May I help?"

Sylvie gestured. "Can you make this petit garçon go away? Can you make them release me from this maison du mort?"

"I do have experience with the local law enforcement." More than she'd ever imagined she'd have. "The best way I've found to get them to let you go home is to answer their questions."

"But I have no answers. I don't know anything. I have nothing to do with murder. I am Mademoiselle Babin!"

Eamon was right. A diva in every sense of the word. Gethsemane imagined the look on Niall's face if he ever had to interview Sylvie. Then she remembered the look on his face a few minutes ago. Nothing to laugh at. "All the more reason to cooperate, Mademoiselle. As an uninterested party—you are uninterested, aren't you? You didn't know Bernard, did you?"

Sylvie deflated. "Know? Know? Who really knows anyone?"

The garda slipped a notebook from his pocket and mouthed "Keep going."

Gethsemane invited Sylvie to sit on the edge of the stage. "People are a mystery, aren't they?" she asked. "Did you ever meet someone and wonder what went on inside them?"

"Of course."

"Did you ever meet Bernard and wonder what motivated him?"

"Batard. That was no mystery. Greed and self-interest were the only things that creature cared for."

"You did know him, then. In the sense of met, encountered, had dealings with?"

Sylvie hesitated. "Well, yes, once or twice. In Paris."

Gethsemane pressed her hand to her chest and fluttered her eyelashes. "Paris. I adore Paris. But who doesn't adore Paris? Did you meet Bernard at the opera?"

"That philistine knows nothing about l'opera. Gilbert and Sullivan are too deep for him, he said. I don't know why he's here to review this one. He should stick to write-ups of food trucks."

Food trucks? "You lost me. Bernard wrote music reviews."

Sylvie snorted. "If that's what you want to call them. He wouldn't have gotten his first assignment if not for me. I introduced him to the editor of La Musique. And what did it get me? Phfft."

"You introduced Bernard to the editor of *La Musique*?" Gethsemane knew the magazine. Not large, but once-upon-a-time a topnotch publication in the classical music world. And very particular about who they hired. Winning a Pulitzer Prize was rumored to be easier than getting a meeting with an editor if a writer didn't have connections. Subscriptions had dropped off ever since a scandal over reviewers receiving improper compensation for reviews, however, and financial trouble plagued the magazine. "You must have met him more than once if you helped his career. Or are you just that nice of a person?"

"Bah. No one is that nice," Sylvie said. "Perhaps I did meet Bernard more often. We may have had, how you say—"

"A fling? A hookup?"

"L'affaire. Y'all Americans make everything sound tawdry."

"How'd you two meet?"

"At a restaurant. Josephine's. Bernard was writing a review for the opening. It was not a very good restaurant. Much hype, little substance. Bernard seemed unimpressed. I was equally unimpressed. We bonded over our mutual dislike. Later, after we got to know each other better, he complained of wanting to get out of the restaurant review world. That is why I introduced him to my friend, the music magazine editor."

"What happened?"

"Bernard abandoned me as soon as my friend hired him as a, how you say, freelancer? Then, of course, he abandoned her once he'd used her connections to land a job as a staff writer at a rival music magazine, *Classical Music Today*. Un chien. Good riddance."

The garda leaned closer.

"Just to reassure the young man," Gethsemane jerked her head toward the officer, "where were you when, you know..." She glanced at the orchestra pit.

"How can I say?" Sylvie shrugged. "I do not know exactly when Bernard got what he deserved. I was on stage singing, then I was," she shrugged again, "around." She stood. "Now, I will go. I have cooperated, and these," she waved a dismissive hand at the garda, "will not keep Mademoiselle Babin when she does not wish to be kept. I must go and rest my voice."

"One question. What do you think of us here in Dunmullach as far as our appreciation of opera?"

Sylvie looked blank.

"Are we rustics? Hopeless rubes? Sophisticates? Ripe with potential?"

"Y'all have le potentiel."

There it was again. Y'all. Sylvie had Frenchified her speech but the tell-tale y'all hung on. You could take the girl out of the southern United States, but you couldn't take the south out of the girl. Not completely.

"Dunmullach is far from New York or Paris, but your youth shows promise." Sylvie gestured to the boys. "I do hope they feel better. The promise of youth is hope for the future. Au revoir." She swept from the stage.

"Good luck with that one," Gethsemane said to the garda as he slipped his notebook away.

"So—" Eamon materialized beside her. "It seems Mademoiselle is more of a Miz. What other secrets is she hiding?"

"A motive for her killing Bernard isn't so secret. He seduced her and used her, then threw her over for his next conquest." The same way he'd treated Venus.

"She may have wanted him dead, may even be glad he's dead. But did she have time to run from the stage to the pit, stab him, then come back upstairs?"

"As she, herself, pointed out, we don't know exactly when Bernard was stabbed. I don't suppose you caught that?"

"Sorry," Eamon said. "I was paying attention to our girl." He pointed at Maja. She hovered in the rear of the auditorium, distinct—and angry—facial features visible.

"She's getting stronger, isn't she?"

"And the fellas are getting sicker. She's feeding off them."

"Got any idea how to stop her?"

"We could ask Poe. She seems to be the resident Maja expert."

"Poe wouldn't tell us if she knew. I'm pretty sure she's on Maja's side. She doesn't seem to be too good with humans." Did she hate humans enough to shove a trowel into one's back?

"I'll do some digging, see what I can come up with."

"Digging?"

"You're not the only one who can conduct an investigation." He vanished. His head reappeared. "Sissy." He vanished again.

She didn't get the chance to remind him what she thought of him for calling her Sissy. A garda ran up to the homicide inspector who'd questioned her earlier. She held a camera. Gethsemane recognized it as one of the tech crew's.

"Sir, I think you'll want to see this." She turned the camera's view screen so her superior could see it.

He watched silently for a moment, then turned the camera off. "Where is he?" He scanned the room then nodded toward Aed. The two guards closest to Aed moved to stand on either side of him.

"Aed Devlin?" the inspector asked as he approached the composer.

"You know I am."

"Aed Devlin, you're under arrest for the murder of Bernard Stoltz. You do not have to say anything." He advised Aed of his remaining rights.

Venus grabbed Aed's arm and tried to pull him away from the officer putting cuffs on him. "Murder? No, he wouldn't. You can't." She looked about the auditorium. "Somebody stop them."

"You have some evidence, Inspector?" Gethsemane asked.

He frowned at her. "Niall may let you poke your nose in his business—"

"It's just a question. What's on the camera?"

"A crystal-clear shot of your man Devlin pulling a trowel out of a bucket of stones."

Ten

Gethsemane stared at Headmaster Riordan's office door. All the boys and Frankie had been transported back to St Brennan's and the sick sorted from the well. Now she wondered how to explain to the headmaster why one teacher and a couple dozen students looked like plague victims and his old friend faced a murder charge.

She didn't have to explain. Riordan almost ran her down as he rushed from his office.

"Excuse me." He stopped an inch short of her foot. "I'm in a terrible hurry. A cadre of panicked parents has descended on the school campus. I have to head them off before they reach the infirmary."

"The infirmary? You had to put boys in the infirmary?" True, the students had looked bad, but bad enough to be put in sick bed...

"Grennan, too. Ward's full. We called in extra duty nurses. Transferred one boy to the hospital. You were at the theater. Do you have any idea what's happened? How to explain this? What's caused this, this," he searched for a word, "epidemic?"

Not any ideas she could share with a skeptical administrator about to have his head handed to him by angry, frightened parents. "Some of the boys complained of smelling an odd scent in the auditorium. Pepper and grease. Frank—Mr. Grennan smelled it, too. And Inspector O'Reilly."

"An odd smell. And you say the adults, as well as the boys, smelled it? Not their imaginations, then. A gas? A fungus? Did you smell anything?"

"Only the ones who got sick smelled it."

"Thank you for that." Riordan consulted his watch. "I have time to grab the chemistry teacher. Maybe he can come up with a story to mollify the parents. Allay their fears, I mean, at least until we have some official word. The health department investigators are already here."

"I wish I could help more." She would help, just not in any way she could talk about. "And I'm sorry about Aed."

"There is something you can do. Go to the garda station for me." He fished in a pocket and pulled out a business card. "Tell Aed I've got a solicitor coming from Cork and not to say anything until she gets here."

"You want me to go now? Not that I mind, but class starts in ten minutes. Introduction to Western Music."

"No, class doesn't start. I've canceled all classes until further notice. Activities, too. I don't want this thing to spread any further than it already has. St. Brennan's is under quarantine."

Gethsemane approached the information desk at the garda station and laid Niall's car key on the countertop. "Excuse me, I'm returning Inspector O'Reilly's car."

The officer at the desk didn't look up from her computer. "Leave the key."

"May I speak to the inspector?"

The guard still didn't look up. "He's not here."

Gethsemane's throat tightened. Workaholic Niall must be bad off to miss work. "Where is he?" The officer ignored her. Gethsemane raised her voice and repeated the question.

"Home sick." The officer answered without looking at her.

Gethsemane took a deep breath and remembered Riordan's request. "I'd like to see Aed Devlin. Please." She'd give him the information about the lawyer then go check on Niall.

The officer tapped at her keyboard. "I'd like to win

Eurovision."

Gethsemane closed her eyes, counted to five, and willed the snark away. "Let's try this again. My name is—"

"Gethsemane Brown." The officer's eyes remained on her screen. "The American living up at that old cottage on Carrick Point, the one who keeps finding dead bodies and interfering with official investigations."

Had they written a standard response and inserted it in the police instruction manuals? "Be that as it may, I'd like to see Aed Devlin."

"Well, you can't."

Gethsemane held the solicitor's business card in front of the garda's computer screen. The guard tried to look around it, but Gethsemane moved the card where she couldn't avoid it. "I'd like to tell Aed Devlin that his lawyer's on the way. If you prefer, I can stay here, right by your desk, until his lawyer arrives and explain how you tried to deny Mr. Devlin access to counsel."

"I never did."

Gethsemane waggled the card.

The garda huffed. "Fine." She pushed a buzzer and another officer appeared.

"Not her again," he said when he saw Gethsemane.

"Take her to see Devlin."

They passed through security screening and into the visiting room, where she waited for guards to escort Devlin to her booth. He dropped heavily onto the seat opposite. His age appeared to have caught up with him all at once. He registered surprise at seeing her.

"Headmaster Riordan sent me. He's hired a lawyer—a solicitor—who'll be here from Cork soon. He gave me her card but they," she indicated the guards, "wouldn't let me give it to you."

"Rick's my only man. Tell him fair play when you see him. Have you seen Venus?"

"Not since the theater. Getting the boys back to school preoccupied me."

"The poor fellas. I can't understand what happened to them. We worked in that theater for a couple of weeks building the set, breathing in paint and glue and dust, and no one took ill."

"Had anyone sung Maja's aria before this afternoon?"

"No. Not all the way through, anyway. I just finished writing it a few days ago. Why?"

"Its power hasn't diminished. I'm still awed. Did you adapt the words or are they completely original?"

"I adapted them from a Hungarian text I found in a cathedral library."

"And Sylvie's voice—wow. Is she a native French speaker?"

"As far as I know. You do ask odd questions."

"Habit. How are you holding up? Headmaster will want to know."

"They're not beating me or starving me. That's about the best I can say for this place. Tell Rick I didn't kill Bernard."

"I'm sure he doesn't believe you did." She chewed the inside of her cheek for a moment. "Did you?"

"I just said—"

"You said tell headmaster you didn't kill him. That's not quite the same as denying you did it."

"I'm not a murderer. I didn't kill Bernard. I hated him, yes. I wanted to rub his nose in my renewed success. I did not want to rub him out."

"Did you invite him to come see the performance?"

"No. I'd never stoop to asking him to review me. I assumed he was freelancing and came on his own. Or that he seduced some bure into hiring him."

"I'll concede you didn't kill him."

"Thank you."

"Any idea who did?"

"Anybody else at the theater. Excluding the kids."

"Can you narrow that?"

Aed shook his head. "Bernard was a nasty piece of work. To know him was to loathe him. Whoever did it might have killed him on general principle. Even you."

"I didn't do it. I have an alibi witness." An ill alibi witness. "I assume you'd have noticed a body under the piano during the ritornello."

"Of course."

"Then he must have been killed during the confusion after Saoirse screamed. Which also doesn't narrow it down. Why did you move the trowel from the bucket?"

"A lighting tech told me there was glare from the metal. I set it down behind the castle."

"Where anyone could have lifted it."

"You sound like a detective."

"I'm not. I just have a way of getting drawn into situations that seem wrong on the surface. I ask questions to sort things out. Wrongness activates my social justice warrior tendencies. Wrongs should be righted. I feel compelled to right them."

Aed leaned closer to the divider. "If you believe that, please keep asking questions. I swear I've killed no one."

A guard approached. "You have to go now."

"Can't she stay another minute?"

The guard stepped closer.

"That means no," Gethsemane said. "I have to leave, anyway. I need to check on Inspector O'Reilly."

"The guard who got sick? Tell him I wish him well. He seems like a decent fella."

"He is."

Eleven

Gethsemane halted her bike on a street corner in the quiet residential area south of the library. The Eurovision-wannabe officer had refused to give her Niall's address, but Murphy—the barman knew where almost everyone lived in the village—had obliged. She walked her bike and scanned the row of neat brick townhouses. Third from the end. Manicured topiaries in planters at the foot of the front steps gave the entrance a stately air. Drawn curtains with no lights on behind them gave her pause.

She rang the bell. When no one answered after half a minute, she knocked. Still no answer. She balled up her fist and pounded.

"Meow." A black cat's face appeared in a front window. She'd forgotten Niall had a cat. Nero, after Rex Stout's detective.

She tapped on the window. "Hey, kitty, go wake up your person."

The cat yowled and jumped away.

She pounded on the door again and shouted. "Niall! Inspector!"

"Are you puttin' on a holy show," a voice said behind her. Gethsemane spun. An elderly lady with a shopping cart stood on the sidewalk. "Where's the fire?"

"Niall, Inspector O'Reilly, took ill earlier today."

The woman put a hand to her throat. "Not that dose that's going round the school?"

"That one. It started at the Athaneum. Niall was there and he caught it, too. He said he was going home to rest, but he won't answer the door."

"Maybe because he's resting."

"He looked awful, ma'am. I just want to make sure he's—" She couldn't say it.

"Don't break the door down. Or break your hand." The woman dug into a coat pocket. "I've got a key." She pulled out a ring full of keys and hunted. "I live down the way. I look after Nero and the plants when Niall's out of town. Do as much for most of the neighbors." She found the key she wanted. "Neighbors hardly look out for each other anymore these days."

Gethsemane tuned out the story of how neighbors used to be neighborly. She pushed past the woman as soon as the door swung open. She met Niall coming down the stairs.

His cat clung to his shoulder. He pulled Nero free and held him out to Gethsemane. "Look after the cat for me?"

Before she could answer, he collapsed.

"Jimmy Binden, two-ninety-six; George Britt, five hundred; Ameal Brooks, three-sixty-two; Ray Brown, two hundred." Gethsemane recited Negro League batting averages as she counted Niall's respirations. She tapped rhythm with her finger on the arm of the hard plastic chair next to his hospital bed. He looked almost as pale as his sheets. She'd reached the end of the 1933 Homestead Grays roster by the time he woke up.

She had to lean close to hear him, his baritone just above a whisper. "What happened?"

"You fainted."

"I've never fainted in my life."

"Until today." She stared at him, unsure what to say.

"Don't look at me that way." He closed his eyes. "Next, you'll be telling me Father Keating's on the way to give me last rites."

She remained silent.

Niall opened one eye. "He's not, is he?"

She dug her nails into her palm until she was sure she could speak without her voice breaking. "Your neighbor's looking after your cat."

"That's not what I asked." Niall pushed himself up against his pillows. Sweat dotted his forehead with the effort. "What do you know, Gethsemane Brown, that you're not telling me?"

That an evil spirit is sucking the life from half the males in the village out of revenge for her murder five hundred years ago. "Nothing, Niall, really."

"I look that bad, then?" He managed a wan smile. "You don't have to answer. I see it in your expression. What have the doctors said?"

"They haven't said anything to me. I'm not your next of kin."

"You and I both know you've no trouble ferreting out information that's none of your business."

She couldn't suppress a grin. She had, in fact, convinced a doctor, the one who'd stitched her up when she'd been brought to A&E with a head wound, to talk to her. "They're stumped. They know you've got the same thing that's hit St. Brennan's but nothing more than that. They called your eldest sister. She's on the way down."

"Bloody hell, what's she doing that for?"

"Because she's your sister and she loves you and she's worried about you? If I had to guess."

"I don't want her around whatever this is." He gestured toward himself. "She's expecting her third. She needs to look after herself and the baby, not worry about me."

"That's the price you pay for being a good brother. Sisters who care."

"Who fuss, you mean."

"Fuss, care. Same thing in sister-speak. Anyway, 'this,'" she waved a hand over him, "has only affected males. So your sister should be okay." Especially since she's working on baby number three and not number one.

"Only males, you're sure?"

"I'm not sick, neither is Venus. Nor Poe, nor Sylvie. Not a single female who was at the theater has fallen ill. For that matter, no males who weren't at the theater have fallen ill."

"Does that make sense, medically speaking?"

Medically, no. Supernaturally, yes. She shrugged.

"Your ma's a doctor, isn't she? Can't you call her, ask her what she thinks?"

"She's a psychiatrist, Niall, not an infectious disease specialist." And she knows nothing about curses. "Besides, she's on a different continent. The doctors here will consult their own specialists, I'm sure." They won't be of any help, but they'll consult them.

A nurse appeared in the doorway. "I'm sorry to run you off," she said to Gethsemane, "but the doctor's on her way to examine Mr. O'Reilly."

Gethsemane rose. "Inspector O'Reilly."

Niall squeezed her hand. "Thanks, Sissy, for everything."

She smiled down at him. "Aren't you going to warn me to keep my nose out of Bernard's murder investigation?"

"Would you listen?"

"No."

"Good. If I was dying, you'd treat that as my last request and say yes."

Gravel crunched as worry and exhaustion won out over proper bicycle maintenance, and Gethsemane let her Pashley fall onto the drive. The moon drifted behind a cloud as she dragged herself up the steps and into the cottage.

She froze with her arms half out of her jacket. Did she hear—crying? She followed the quiet sobs to the study. Venus lay face down on the couch. A throw pillow held tight against her face muffled her tears.

"Venus?" Gethsemane laid a hand on her shoulder.

Venus jumped up, wiped at her face, and tried to look as if she hadn't been crying. "I'm sorry. I don't cry. I hate tears. Tears mean you're weak."

Gethsemane handed her a box of tissue. "Or that you're having a shite day." Gethsemane rarely cried herself—tears didn't solve problems—but she didn't begrudge others the experience.

"No excuse in my business." Venus blew her nose. "I interview drug dealers, gun runners, and wives with knives. Never let your guard down."

"Be sober, be vigilant, your adversary the devil walketh about as a roaring lion, seeking whom he may devour."

"One Peter Five Eight. The favorite Bible verse of true crime writers and investigative reporters." Venus smiled and sank into the couch cushions with a sniffle. "I hope you don't mind that I came back here. I just...The inn..."

"I don't mind. Glad of some female company." She meant it. Her Dunmullach circle consisted of men: Eamon, Father Tim, Frankie, Niall, ninety-eight percent of the school faculty, her students, and a twelve-year-old girl. Her social circle when she toured with the symphony had consisted largely of men, as well. She didn't mind—she could talk baseball and whiskey for hours. But she'd grown up the third of three sisters and, despite a sometimes-cantankerous relationship with her older siblings and mother, she appreciated hearing the female perspective from time to time.

"How's your day been?" Venus blushed and giggled. "I know that's a ridiculous question, given the circumstances, but I'm not good at small talk. Drug dealers, gun runners, and wives with knives aren't big on chitchat."

"No such thing as a ridiculous question. Let's see. Aside from the dead body? Niall's in the hospital, Frankie and half the school are in the infirmary, the school's shut down, and an evil ghost is rampaging in the village opera hall. Oh, and I saw Aed."

"You did?" Venus sat up straight and grabbed Gethsemane's arm. "How is he?"

"He's in jail, but otherwise he's doing all right. He has a

lawyer. He says he didn't do it."

"Of course he didn't do it. That was never in question." Venus released Gethsemane's arm. "I'm glad you saw him."

"He asked about you."

Venus smiled, then the tears flowed again. "I can't stand this helpless feeling. I know Aed's innocent, but I can't do anything for him." She punched a couch cushion.

"Who says you can't? Who says we can't? Not the woman who uncovered a cult in the Harper Valley PTA. Not the woman who exposed a counterfeit sex toy ring operating out of adult video stores."

"Damn, my work is sordid." Venus dabbed her eyes. "Would you believe I used to write about government corruption, consumer protection, and fraud, waste, and abuse?"

"Whether you're investigating white-collar crime, street crime, or weirdness in the suburbs, you ask questions. Which is what Aed wants me to do. Ask questions."

Venus fixed herself a drink and offered Gethsemane one. "What questions can we ask? Who stabbed Bernard? One of the many people at the Athaneum. Who had access to the murder weapon? Everybody at the Athaneum. Who had motive to kill that little POS? Who didn't?"

Gethsemane declined the drink. She paced in front of the bookshelves. "Why did Bernard change from restaurant reviews to music reviews?"

"Where'd you hear that?"

"From Sylvie. Speaking of whom, why does she pretend she's French?"

"Isn't she French?"

"Has 'y'all' entered the French lexicon?"

Venus pursed her lips and tapped a finger on her whiskey glass. "Huh. Odd."

"Who invited Bernard to Dunmullach to hear Aed's opera? He could have picked any one of a zillion performances in the US or the rest of the world. Why come to Dunmullach for this one? Just to provoke Aed?"

"I like your questions." Venus swigged bourbon, then set her glass down. She propped her feet on the coffee table and tapped on her phone. Reporter mode. Was this how she'd looked when she researched the first edition of her book about Eamon? "Let's start with Mam'zelle Sylvie. She might be putting on the French act for career reasons. A name like Mary Sue Buttersby or Ella Mae Schifflet wouldn't look good on an opera marquee."

"Did you find anything?" Gethsemane moved behind Venus and read the phone over her shoulder.

"Nothing yet. Basic web search turns up bubkes. Do you still have any music world contacts? Maybe they could tell us something."

She kept in touch with a few people from her former career trajectory. Her old maestro, an executive director of fundraising, a couple of symphony league presidents. "Let me make some calls. You want to tackle the restaurant review issue?"

"No. Bernard's travel arrangements. My sister-in-law is a travel agent with a background in intelligence gathering."

"She books trips for spies?"

"No, she has a master's in library science. She thought she wanted to work for the CIA until she discovered booking cruises and amusement park dream vacations was fun and less dangerous."

"One thing before we head off down the rabbit hole. I'll state up front this is none of my business, but I'll ask anyway. Why so weepy for Aed? I like him, too, and I don't want to see him take the fall for a crime he didn't commit, but anguished sobs?"

"You like him. I love him."

"You met him once at a premiere years ago and didn't see him again until the pub a couple of days ago."

"Haven't you ever met someone and known instantly they were the person you'd waited your whole life for?"

"Love at first sight? Call me a cynic but that's strictly for rom coms."

"Cynic."

Twelve

Gethsemane retreated to the kitchen. She scrolled through her contact list. Mother, sisters, brothers, friends from Vassar and Yale. She'd scrubbed her list when she bought a new phone. But she'd saved one or two numbers whose acquaintance she wouldn't mind renewing. She'd start with Xavier Herren. As head of a major fundraising organization, he kept tabs on countless people.

He answered on the third ring.

"X? Gethsemane."

No response.

"X, are you there?"

"Gethsemane Brown?"

She confirmed her identity.

"My God, I thought you'd been kidnapped by leprechauns and taken away over the rainbow. How are you, love?"

"Fantastic. Irish village life agrees with me." Except for the murders. "How's Stephen, the kids?"

"Great and great. Steve's taken Gloria to a father-daughter art camp, so I'm batching it here with Zach." He paused. "But you didn't call me out of the blue after a year of radio silence to catch up on my social life, did you? Need some funds raised?"

"No, only some questions answered. Easy peasy. No banquet halls, silent auctions, or celebrity endorsements required. Do you know Sylvie Babin?"

"Not personally. She's...shall we say, not on my Christmas card list? We tried to get her to perform at a fundraiser for an inner-city youth orchestra. She offered to sell us her time at an exorbitant price. For a fundraiser. Why?"

Gethsemane briefed him on recent events.

"Good lord, girl, you may as well come live with us in Chicagoland. Bodies don't turn up beneath Steinways out here."

"If I lived in Chicago I wouldn't have found out that Sylvie's not really French. She hails from somewhere in the southeastern US is my guess. Can you find out for me?"

"Uncover potentially salacious details about the probably unsavory past of a snob who tried to highjack funds from poor kids who want to play music? Absolutely. Let me make some calls."

Gethsemane went back to the study to check on Venus's progress. "Any luck?"

"Tons. You?"

"Working on it. What did you find?"

"Have a seat. Or a drink. You'll need one or both."

She sat. Second thoughts sent her to the bar cart. She poured Waddell and Dobb. She'd already done a lot of sitting that day.

"Bernard didn't just turn up in the village on a spiteful whim. His plane ticket and his lodging were paid for by Verschreken Productions."

"Which is?"

"The company that produces *Ghost Hunting Adventures*."

Gethsemane spat bourbon. She blotted her dress with a cocktail napkin. "The paranormal investigators paid to fly Bernard out here and put him up at the inn? Why? Does he work for the show? Did he work for the show, I mean?"

"I don't think so. The travel arrangements for the entire crew were made as a package deal. Bernard's were separate and went on a different company credit card."

"In other words, by someone in the production company who didn't want the whole team to know Bernard was traveling on the company dime. Who'd have access to a separate credit card?"

"An owner, most likely. Kent is one of the owners of the

production company. Guess who's another."

"Hardy?"

Venus shook her head. "Poe. Turns out Anti-social Annie is actually quite the entrepreneur. This is the third production company she's bought into. Helped turn them all around with a hit new show or project."

"Why would either of them want to sponsor Bernard?"

"We'll have to track them down tomorrow and ask."

The first measure of "The Carnival of the Animals" played on Gethsemane's phone. A text from Xavier. "That was fast." The message read, *Call me back.*

"Anything?" Venus asked.

"Let's find out." She dialed Xavier. He answered on the first ring this time. "Were you sitting on the phone?"

"I could not wait to tell you this."

"How'd you find something so quickly?"

"Because the heavens are smiling upon me."

"What's he saying?" Venus asked.

"Who's with you?" Xavier asked.

"Venus James."

"The true crime author? Tell her I loved the piece she did on the PTA."

Gethsemane relayed the message, then turned back to the phone. "Go on."

"Put me on speaker, I'll tell you both." Gethsemane tapped the button. Xavier's voice sounded distant through the phone's speaker. "Since this is about murder, I decided to start with the security firm we use to do background checks on our potential event headliners and celebrity endorsers."

"You do background checks on people you're asking to volunteer their time and talent?" Venus sounded incredulous.

"Of course," Xavier replied. "Famous is not a synonym for decent human. You should know that given your line of work. Can't risk the owner of a dog-fighting ring raising funds for an animal shelter or a pedophile's face on a poster for a children's hospital benefit."

"Sylvie's not, is she? The owner of a dog-fighting ring or a—"

"Don't even try to guess," Xavier interjected. "You never will."

"Then tell me. Tell us."

"The security firm had already done the background check but never gave us the report after the deal with Sylvie fell through. Now that I know what's in the report, I'm over the moon about not getting mixed up with her. Saved us all from serious embarrassment."

"What?" Gethsemane and Venus asked simultaneously.

"Sylvie Babin was christened Sadie Burns. She was born and grew up in the teeny, tiny town of Attapulgus, Georgia. Where there's a warrant for her arrest for—ready for this? For pandering." Xavier's claps replaced his voice on the speaker.

"Mam'zelle Nose-in-the-Air is a pimp?" Venus doubled over laughing. "Classic."

"That would be Mam'zelle Le-nez-en-l'air," Xavier corrected before joining Venus in her laughter.

"I'd like to point something out," Gethsemane said, "but I don't want to kill your buzz, so I'll wait 'til you're done." The peals died down and she continued. "As amusing as the idea of Sylvie's criminal past is, it doesn't connect to Bernard. She'd become Sylvie before she met him."

"Maybe he discovered her real name, blackmailed her," Xavier said, "threatened to out her as a hick fugitive."

"He seduced her to get what he wanted," Venus explained. "His usual modus operandi with women."

"Seduced or blackmailed," Xavier said, "she had motive to kill him."

"She admitted she had motive when I spoke to her," Gethsemane said. "I think she was kind of proud of wanting Bernard dead."

"You don't think she did it," Xavier said. "I hear the doubt in your voice."

Gethsemane shook her head. "No, not really. I think we ought to pursue finding out who funded his trip. Someone went to considerable expense to get him here. They had a reason."

"What are you talking about?" Xavier asked. Gethsemane explained about the company credit card. "That doesn't sound like Sylvie or Sadie or whatever her name is," he added when she finished. "She wants people to spend money on her, not the other way around. Sorry I couldn't be of more help."

"You were a huge help, X. Thanks. Love to Stephen and the kids."

"Back at you. And if you ever need me—No, on second thought, I take that back. Please don't make a habit of chasing murderers. Try bungee jumping. Or smoking. They're less hazardous to your health."

Venus stared at her after she ended the call. Neither woman spoke for several seconds then Venus asked, "What about me? Do I make the top ten list of most likely to stab a double-crossing creep?"

"No," Gethsemane said, "I don't think you did it. Which is good, since I'm letting you stay under my roof."

Sleep eluded Gethsemane. She turned on her right. She turned on her left. Covers on. Covers off. One pillow. Two pillows. No pillows. Pillow thrown across the room.

"Give it up, darlin'." Eamon materialized at the foot of her bed. A pillow sailed through his chest and landed against the chifferobe. "Go downstairs and have a drink. Or go for a walk in the night air. That always helped Orla."

She pulled the covers up to her chest. "How long have you been watching me?"

"Not long." He laughed and glowed green and covered his eyes. "I didn't see anything." He dematerialized then rematerialized, seated next to her on the bed. "What's got you so twisted up, anyway?"

"You mean besides my friends and my students being

horrifically sick with a supernatural illness I don't know how to fight? Nothing much. Just a dead body, a man I believe to be innocent sitting in jail charged with the crime, and a woman, who isn't the harpie I thought she was and who I'm starting to like, heartbroken because of it."

"Why don't you do something about it? You've a knack for clearing innocent men's names." He winked.

"Do what? I found out Sylvie's not Sylvie, but I don't see how that gets me anywhere."

"Don't be so quick to let her off the hook. She lied about her identity, she may be lying about other things."

"I just can't see Ms. Diva stabbing someone in the back and hiding their body under a piano. Breaking a magnum of champagne over someone's head in a room full of people? That's dramatic. But a discrete murder deep down in an orchestra pit?" She shrugged.

"You've got the stuff Venus turned up about Bernard's travel arrangements. Find out who funded him."

"Would someone pay all that money and go to all that trouble just to kill him?"

"Sure. If they needed to lure him someplace where no one knew either of them well enough to connect them to each other."

"Why would someone hate him that much?" She drew her knees up to her chest. "What could he have done to earn that level of wrath?"

"Some people hold tight to grudges. Look at Maja."

"Yeah, she does elevate that whole 'revenge is a dish best served cold' thing to a new level."

"At least with Bernard you won't have to go back five hundred years to find a motive. Twenty or thirty should do."

"Sounds like you've got a knack for investigating, too."

"Comes from hanging around you."

"Say, how'd you know about Sylvie's alias and Bernard's secret travel agent? You weren't there when—"

He disappeared. "Just because you can't see me," his disembodied voice said, "doesn't mean I'm not there."

"I can smell you. Gaeltacht, Mrs. Leary's. Your cologne and soap."

He materialized. "You only smell me when I'm as close as I am now."

"Thank goodness you don't smell like grease and peppers." She wrinkled her nose. "Speaking of Maja, have you uncovered a way to get rid of her? Soon?" Poe's gory details of the wasting sickness's end state flashed through her head. "Before Niall, Frankie, and the boys slip past the point of no return?"

"I may be on to something." He radiated a hopeful salmon pink. "I popped into that bookstore, the one run by the bure who stepped out on her fella at the pub the other night."

"Arcana Arcanora." The occult shop.

"I found a lad visiting from uni over in Cork browsing the shelves. He got to chatting with the clerk. Turns out he's studying folklore, Eastern European folklore, specifically."

Gethsemane gasped. "Did he say something about Maja?"

"Well, no, he didn't come right out and mention her by name or state he had a surefire way to defeat evil ghosts. He did let slip his plans to head over to the library tomorrow." He glanced at the bedside clock. "Today. Turns out the library owns several volumes on Eastern European folklore and legend. A St. Brennan's alum married a Ukrainian anthropologist way back when. They willed their private library to the public library. I'll head over there as soon as it opens."

"Eamon McCarthy, I'm impressed. You can investigate with me anytime."

He blushed and affected an American accent. "Aw shucks, ma'am."

She read the clock. "A few hours until daylight. I think I can get to sleep, thanks to you helping me sort things out. No school since Riordan's quarantined the place. I'll talk to Venus and we'll hammer out a plan of attack. Kent, Poe, and Bernard's past."

"And Sylvie's," Eamon added.

"And Sylvie's." She stretched out a hand. "Hand me my pillow, please."

A pillow levitated across the room and landed on her head.

She snatched it away. "Hand it to me. This—" she waved a hand under his nose, "is my hand."

He kissed it, sending tingles up her arm as his lips passed through her skin. "And a lovely hand it is. Get some sleep. And be wide while you're out snooping—"

"Investigating," she interjected.

"Whoever stabbed Bernard is probably a pretty nasty piece of work."

"You be careful, too. Maja is definitely a nasty piece of work."

Thirteen

Gethsemane briefed Venus over breakfast on her conversation with Eamon.

Venus frowned. "How come he didn't wake me up to tell me any of this himself? I can see him, too."

Her stomach tightened. Why should Eamon wake Venus? He was her ghost. "Maybe he figured you needed your sleep."

Venus raised an eyebrow then hid a smile behind her coffee cup. Gethsemane forced the pout from her face.

Venus sipped coffee, winced, and reached for the sugar bowl. "You made the coffee this morning?"

"I make it a little stronger than Eamon. I like strong coffee."

"I've met arms dealers who don't take their coffee this strong."

"Speaking of criminals—potential criminals—we need a plan if we're going to look into Bernard's murder. Divide and conquer. I'll take Kent and Poe. You tackle Sylvie. We can meet at the library after and see if we can dig up some of Bernard's old reviews. They've got back issues of some American newspapers on microfiche. We know he wrote about Aed. Let's see if he wrote anything about Poe or Kent or someone connected to them." She added, "Or if he wrote about Sylvie."

"I've got a better idea. Why don't I pay a visit to the local paper and give them my 'I'm a journalist, you're a journalist, let's help each other' routine and see if I can't get access to their WorldNews Archive database?"

"What's a WorldNews Archive database and why would the Dispatch have one?"

"It's what it sounds like, an electronic archive of newspapers from all over the world dating back to about 1850. Almost every newspaper subscribes to it. Much cheaper than having to fly reporters and fact checkers to Timbuktu or Outer Mongolia to research a piece."

"I'll search with you. We can meet at the newspaper office after we finish with Kent, Poe, and Sylvie."

Doubt played across Venus's face.

"Two sets of eyes are better than one," Gethsemane said. "Besides, you need a better cover story than Brotherhood of the Fourth Estate. Tell them that I've decided to cooperate so you're going to include more about me in the book revision—Please don't, by the way, this is just for cover—and you need some reviews from the Dallas Morning News from my time with the orchestra there. Or articles from the Poughkeepsie Journal about the youth orchestra I volunteered with when I was at Vassar. Then you'll have a reason to look at New York papers. They get my vote for most likely to contain Bernard's old reviews."

Venus clattered her cup against the table. "Most people would love a chance to be in one of my books."

"I'm not most people."

Venus harrumphed.

Gethsemane held out her hand. "Okay, truce. Sniping at each other won't accomplish anything."

"Truce." Venus accepted the handshake.

"Then we have a plan?"

"We have a plan. See you at the Dispatch."

Gethsemane reviewed her options as she rode her bike down to the village. Poe, seldom cooperative, even when not being accused of murder, would be the tougher interview. Would she talk about anything other than Maja's ghost? Would she talk at all? Buying her a drink or three might help, but it was still a bit early in the day for the pub. She'd pay Kent a visit first.

She slowed as she pedaled past the Athaneum. Gardaí posted at the door meant the theater was still off-limits. Poe argued in the parking lot with a garda. Probably demanding to be let in so she could commune with Maja. Why did Poe idolize a ghost devoted to killing innocent people? Maybe she championed Maja because she saw something of herself in the tragic Hungarian. Maybe Maja's terrorism gave Poe vicarious satisfaction. Or maybe Maja inspired her to stab Bernard.

The parking lot argument turned against Poe. She flipped the garda her middle finger and stormed off. She wouldn't be in any mood to cooperate. Best save her for last. Gethsemane turned the Pashley toward Sweeney's. Maybe Kent hadn't gone out yet.

She glanced over her shoulder at the Athaneum. A faint blue glow surrounded the theater.

Sweeney's Inn, constructed in 1902, prided its status as a historic luxury small hotel. Flower arrangements as big as a toddler graced the lobby. Uniformed employees manned the registration desk and front door. Tasteful furniture arranged in seating clusters invited guests to linger and read one of the English or Irish papers displayed on a sideboard. Silver candy dishes offered an assortment of hard candies. Gethsemane helped herself to a strawberry-flavored treat.

"Good morning," the chipper young woman at the registration desk greeted her. "How may I assist you?"

"Kent Danger's room, please."

The clerk consulted something hidden below eye level behind the desk. Gethsemane slid an oversized guest book to one side and, on tiptoe, peered over the marble and brass countertop. A computer.

Lists of names scrolled by as the clerk navigated the screen. "I'm sorry, no one's registered under that name."

Could the room be listed under Ciara? This was the twenty-first century. Maybe she paid. "Ciara Tierney, then."

More names scrolled by. "I'm sorry."

"They're two of the paranormal investigators. The good-looking blond man, the lead investigator, and the photographer with silver hair."

She stopped scrolling and looked up. "Oh, yes, I know who you mean. They're hard to miss." She reflexively glanced at her computer.

Gethsemane followed her gaze. The clerk's finger obscured most of a name about a third of the way from the top of the screen. Gethsemane strained to read upside down without tipping off the clerk. She deciphered Konra—Konrad? Who was Konrad? A pseudonym Kent used to travel? Or, more likely, his real name? "Kent Danger" was the stagiest of stage names. Aliases seemed to be the order of the day.

"They're out," the clerk said. "I saw them leave a while ago. Would you like to leave a message?"

"Can you tell me what room they're in? I'd like to go up."

The clerk lowered her eyes and shook her head. "I'm sorry, I really can't say."

A perk of staying at an exclusive hotel—discretion. She'd have to wait in the lobby until Kent came back from wherever.

"What's it like?" the clerk asked in a lowered voice.

"What's what like?"

"Living in a haunted house." The clerk giggled at Gethsemane's surprise. "I recognize you. I've seen you at the Rabbit. And my cousin's in your music theory class." Good old Dunmullach, where everybody knows everybody's face by sight and everybody's business by heart. Just like her hometown, Bayview.

"Is it scary?" the clerk continued. "I'd be scared, but I'm a coward. Anyone will tell you."

Gethsemane lowered her voice to match the clerk's. "There are worse things than ghosts." Murderers, for example. "Can't you give me a teeny hint about what room they're in? Just tell me which floor."

"I shouldn't, but..." The clerk looked from side to side then leaned closer and whispered. "You're not just anyone. Room twenty-eight. Second floor."

"Thank you."

"Boo." The clerk giggled again.

Gethsemane excused herself from the desk. She jogged up two flights of stairs and walked the entire length of the corridor. All the room numbers began with three. Then she remembered the ground floor counted as the first. She turned back and ran into Ciara on the landing, coffee cup in hand.

"Good morning," Ciara said.

Gethsemane returned the greeting. The rich aroma of coffee coming off the steam wafting from Ciara's cup reminded her a refill was due. The morning's first cup would wear off soon. "Not a tea drinker? I thought all Irish liked Bewley's."

Ciara sipped black liquid. "I picked up the coffee habit during my travels. Haven't been able to shake it."

"Being a paranormal photographer must take you to exotic places. Do you feel like a nomad, traveling from town to town, country to country, chasing the next assignment?"

"No more so than I imagine a concert musician would."

"I do miss interacting with a wide variety of people and the rush you feel stepping off the airplane after landing in a new city," Gethsemane said. "Although, some of my trips lasted barely long enough for me to pick up a souvenir magnet in the airport gift shop. No time to sightsee. I don't miss bad hotels and worse food. Sweeney's is top notch. Your team sleeps in style."

"Not always. We stay at our fair share of ratty hotels with banjaxed plumbing and paper-thin walls. It helped that Dunmullach lacks another hotel. We were able to justify the budget to the producers."

An opening. "I thought Kent owned the production company."

If her knowing this information surprised Ciara, Ciara didn't show it. "Co-owns. He answers to others. Poe, for example. She owns a share of the company. Imagine negotiating with her."

No secret about the company's management. Kent's and Poe's business partnership was public knowledge. Or known among the show's crew. Or known by Kent's girlfriend. Best not to assume. Who else knew? Enough people to create difficulties for someone buying secret plane tickets and hotels? They had been put on a separate card.

Ciara's laugh brought Gethsemane back to the present. "Congratulations," Ciara said.

"I'm sorry, what? My mind went someplace else." What had she done to prompt the outburst?

"You've broken the record." Ciara showed Gethsemane her watch. "Longest conversation held without asking me where I met Kent in a moderately judgmental tone."

"Where did you meet him?" Since she brought it up.

"Tone kept neutral. Nice job. A routine question asked in the course of chatting. Fair play. I always feel like yelling, 'Of course I know he's young enough to be my son, you wish you were so lucky,' when people ask the question in that certain way they ask to telegraph their disapproval of my life choices."

"You're both grown and neither of you are related to me, so it's none of my business." Southern code for "but if you want to talk about it..."

"Thank you for that. Kent and I met in New York. I photographed people then, not ghosts."

"You're not a native New Yorker."

"My accent give me away, did it?" Ciara winked. "I don't consider myself native of any place. I drifted around, among continents, among jobs. Until I stumbled into a photography class in a university extension program. I turned out to be good at it and it suited my, what was your term, nomadic lifestyle."

"You've no family ties? Regardless of how far I travel or how long I'm gone, I know I've got a big old family tree rooted in Virginia, keeping me connected to home. Sometimes I'd like to shake the tree and several of the nuts are cracked, but I wouldn't ever cut the tree down."

"Not me." Ciara sipped her coffee and kept her eyes on her cup when she answered. "Family tree got chopped for firewood eons ago. I've learned it's best not to stick with any particular tribe for too long. Seldom ends well."

Was Kent in for a letdown? Or brush off? "Speaking of your tribe, where is Kent? I wanted to speak with him." Gethsemane pointed to the steps. "Got off on the wrong floor."

"That ground floor-first floor thing does seem to trip you Americans up. Kent's always getting off at the wrong place," Ciara said. "He's still down at breakfast."

"Back to the, wait, don't tell me, ground floor again." She paused at the lower landing and spoke to Ciara still on the landing above her. "Were any of your pre-photography jobs in the music field?"

"Nah. Have a tin ear. Why?"

"No reason." No reason to have run across Bernard. "Another question. How well do you know Hardy and Poe?"

"You sound a right regular detective."

"I was Nancy Drew in a past life. Can't help it."

Ciara shrugged. "No matter. I told the guards, I'll tell you. I met both of them through Kent. Poe hates me because Kent made me lead photographer. Because of my talent. I'm demonstrably better than Poe. She, of course, won't accept that."

"You're also more stable than Poe. She gets a little, uh..."

"You noticed. How could you not? Everybody notices. I'm not sure what Poe's issues are, but they run deep. Hardy, on the other hand..." Ciara shrugged again. "Not much to see or say."

"You're closer to him than to Poe."

"Not close, exactly. Cordial. Hardy's all right. Too young for a true friendship. The younger generation is fun at night, but what do you have to talk about during the day?"

"But you don't dislike him."

"No one dislikes Hardy. Except Poe, but she dislikes her own shadow. I like him in a general 'here's a guy I work with' sort of way. Truthfully, I seldom think about him. He's just there. You look up and you see Hardy and you wonder how long he's been standing in front of you."

Convenient to have around in case you need a designated driver or designated church-goer. "He and Poe seem to have an odd relationship. Odder than usual for Poe."

"They both used to drink a lot and smoke like fiends. Something happened, before my time with the team, and Hardy cut back. Poe didn't. Kent won't allow smoking on set—on location shoots or in the production booth, I mean—but off-duty, I've seen Poe tear through a pack of smokes and a fifth of whiskey single-handed and still come out swinging the next morning. I gathered she didn't want Hardy to come on this trip, but Kent overruled her."

"If Poe owns part of the production company, doesn't she have some say in who's on the team?"

"*Ghost Hunting Adventures* is Kent's show and no one else's," Ciara said. "He conceived it, nurtured it, turned it into the phenomenon it is. He controls it. He may have to negotiate funding, but when it comes to creative decisions, his word is law."

"He's the boss of all bosses."

"About the only place where he is." Ciara winked and continued up the stairs.

Fourteen

Sweeney's served the best breakfast in Dunmullach. Locals as well as guests crowded the lobby area around the entrance waiting for a spot at the bar or a coveted table. Gethsemane found Kent seated near a window with his back to the other diners. He read a newspaper. A waiter swept away an empty plate and crumpled napkin from the place opposite.

"Morning." Gethsemane slid into the vacant chair. People lined up gave her the side-eye.

"Jumping the queue." Kent didn't look up from his reading. "Poor form."

Gethsemane waved away a menu proffered by the waiter. "Nothing for me. Oh, except a cup of coffee. Cream and sugar."

Kent folded the paper and laid it aside. He crossed his arms and waited.

"I, um..." Want to know if you flew Bernard Stoltz all the way to Ireland so you could kill him. "Wondered if you guys planned to film anymore up at Carraigfaire."

"After you convinced us the activity centered on the Athaneum? After you said—"

"The activity does center on the theater. You were there. You saw for yourself."

"I grant that murder counts as activity. I meant the paranormal variety, however."

"I referred to Maja's ghost. Saoirse saw it. Saw her."

Kent frowned. "Saoirse?"

"The little girl who screamed from the balcony?"

"Oh, right, that Saoirse. Impressive show. A little hammy, but not bad for a kid. It was all for show, wasn't it? Histrionic displays by pretty girls make for good television, right?"

She'd underestimated Kent. He'd known Saoirse faked her sighting. A sharp mind lurked under that perfectly messy blond hair. "What about Poe?"

"What about her? Poe saw nothing. Poe never sees anything. She just rants on about blood and gore and evil. Children clutch their mothers tighter when Poe's in the room. She's kind of psycho."

"Why not fire her?"

"Why not tell me what you're after? You don't give a damn about my staff model. If you want my promise we won't invade your precious cottage, you've got it. I wish I'd never heard of this damned village. I wanted to do a stakeout in Portugal. 'S what I get for doing a favor."

"Favor? Favor for whom? Billy?"

Kent gathered his newspaper. "We're tying up a table."

Gethsemane followed him from the restaurant. She called after him, "Konrad!"

He stopped, hesitated, kept walking.

Gethsemane cursed his leg length advantage as she hurried to catch up. She caught him at the foot of the stairs. "Who's the favor for, Konrad? I assume Konrad is the correct name to use. I mean your legal one. Kent Danger sounds a bit like a comic book superhero."

"It fits the theme of the show." He stepped around her.

She blocked him. "C'mon, Konrad. Who set you on to me? My landlord?"

Kent's shoulders slumped. He leaned against a wall. "What the hell, it doesn't matter now. No, not Billy McCarthy. Although he bought into the concept pretty quick."

"Bought in or was sold on? You paid him."

"Quite a lot of money. Usually, our location owners give us free access. They want the publicity."

"Who funded this stake out? I won't let up until you tell me, so you may as well tell me now."

"My uncle."

"Bernard Stoltz?"

"No, not Bernard. You think I'd admit to being related to that tick? There's a reason no one's sad he's dead."

"What's your reason?"

"Stoltz used to stay at my uncle's hotel when he visited New York. He seduced the concierge, sweet woman, too trusting. Also, my godmother. She believed Stoltz loved her. He used her to get access to personal information on some of the VIP hotel guests, information that later ended up in his reviews. As soon as he got what he wanted from my godmother, he dumped her. Broke her heart and sent her into depression. She had to quit work. Was even hospitalized for a while."

"Who's your uncle?"

"An acquaintance of yours. Hank Wayne."

"Bloody hell. Hank Wayne who tried to destroy Carraigfaire? Hank Wayne who's the reason my landlord is making me put up with you guys? That one?"

"Hank Wayne who made a legit deal to own Carraigfaire only to have the piss scared out of him and years frightened off his life by a music teacher and her pet ghost. Uncle Hank's my dad's brother."

"Making you Konrad Wayne." No wonder he hadn't told her his real name. "And I don't have a pet ghost. I do have a gorgeous historic cottage that your uncle would have ruined in the name of money. A lot of money, but still..."

"Uncle Hank and I don't agree on everything. Turning that cottage into a hotel would have bordered on criminal. But what you did to him—"

"He had it coming. I won't apologize."

"Nor will I. Hank's family, and when someone goes after

family—"

Gethsemane finished his sentence. "Family gets even. What was the plan? To make me look like a raving lunatic on camera, a lonely, unstable spinster who talks to nonexistent ghosts? Or to convince the world that Carraigfaire is a paranormal paradise and leave me overrun with tourists? Or was the plan just to annoy the hell out of me by being underfoot and in my face everywhere I turned?"

"The last two. Uncle Hank knew the ghost was real." Eamon had shown Hank, up close, just how real. "And I believe in ghosts," Kent said, "though I've never personally seen one. I wanted to find proof, incontrovertible proof, of the persistence of life after the physical body dies." He smacked the stair rail.

"Once the gardaí clear out, you can go back to the Athaneum, try to collect your proof there."

"We both know the theater was a decoy to get us away from Carraigfaire. The girl—what's her name?—Saoirse didn't see a ghost.

"Just because she didn't see one doesn't mean none were there."

"You saw something? Honest?"

"You saw it, too. Tangible evidence of it, at least."

"What did I see?"

"The sickness. You saw how many boys fell ill. My friends, too."

"The cop and the teacher."

"And Hardy, your own crew member. You heard the guys who got sick all complain of smelling pepper and grease, didn't you?"

"I thought it was a gas leak or something."

"Then why didn't you get sick? You weren't holding your breath the whole time. Why didn't I get sick or any of the other women?"

Kent said nothing for a moment. "You're right. It just hit me. No women got ill and only some men? How could I miss the significance of that?"

"How many older brothers do you have, Konrad?"

"Kent, please. I have two. How'd you guess I had older brothers?"

"Niall, Inspector O'Reilly, the garda who got sick, has three younger sisters. Frankie Grennan, the math teacher, has no siblings. Saoirse is Colm Nolan's little sister. Colm's one of the sick students."

"All sick, all firstborn sons." He drummed his fingers on the stair rail. "I'll put Ciara and Poe on it. They'll hate working together, especially Poe, but Maja might communicate more with women than men." He started up the stairs. "I have to go. Arrangements to make."

Gethsemane called up after him. "Where does Bernard fit into this? Was he going to write an article on the investigation?"

"I told you I had nothing to do with Bernard."

"But you called him a tick. You must have some reason to think that."

"Public knowledge."

"The public Bernard is a—was a—music critic. Merciless but fun to read. Bernard kept his tickhood private. What'd he do, write a scathing review of the show?"

"I doubt he ever saw our show. I know what he did to other people, what he did to Aed. Scant room in the reporting business, or the human race, for jerks like that."

"If that's how you feel about him, why pay his way here?"

Kent rejoined Gethsemane at the foot of the stairs. "I didn't. Why do you think otherwise?"

"Someone purchased Bernard's plane tickets with a credit card issued to your company, Verschreken Productions. They used the same card to secure a hotel room."

Kent swore. "Poe. That little—"

"Why would Poe pay for Bernard's trip?"

"Who knows? Did I mention she's psycho?"

"Regardless, bringing Bernard to Dunmullach seems random. She must have had a reason, even if it only made sense to her."

"It's one of her power plays. Pay Bernard to write an excoriating review of the show. He's talented, even if he is a jerk, and he still has connections, people who don't care what he did in the classical music world, people with secrets he can leverage. Post his venom on some blog or social media account and watch our ratings tank. Push me out the door, fire me from my own show—my own show—and reboot it with her as host and she can take it in any direction she wants. That's what she thinks." He took the stairs two at a time and paused on the upper landing. "She thinks wrong."

Gethsemane debated. Stay and wait to see if Poe arrived at the inn or go try to track her down? Either way, she'd be riled up. Kent would call or text her. Tell her off or warn her. The "Poe's a psycho" routine could be as phony as Saoirse's ghost spotting. Maybe Kent and Poe were in it together. Maybe Bernard explained Poe's bitterness. He devastated as many women as he had careers. Maybe Poe convinced her business partner to partner up in killing him.

A dark cloud cover followed by steady rain convinced Gethsemane to choose option A, stay and wait. She sat in an oversized club chair, so deep her feet dangled if she sat back, and tried to read a paper. She glanced at the door so often the words failed to register, so she quit and got up to read captions on historic photos of the inn.

A mail carrier walked up to the front desk and handed a bundle of letters to the desk clerk. The clerk's yell halted the mail carrier at the door. "You can take this one back."

The carrier examined the envelope. "Says room forty-two, don't it?"

"Yeah, but he's not in room forty-two anymore." The clerk lowered her voice. "He's the one who got murdered."

"No concern of mine," the carrier said. "Envelope says room forty-two so I delivered it."

Fifteen

Room forty-two. It had to be Bernard's room. How many of Sweeney's guests got murdered? Gethsemane chewed her lip. Should she do it? One last survey of the lobby revealed no signs of Poe. This might be her only chance.

A large American couple with large American children and loud American voices stopped at the front desk to ask for maps and dinner recommendations more suitable for "young people" than the hotel's three-star offering. Gethsemane took it as a sign. While her countrymen monopolized the clerk, she stole upstairs.

The fourth-floor hallway sat deserted except for a maid's cart at one end. Gethsemane tried the handle of number forty-two. Locked, of course. She needed Frankie. He'd helped her break into more than one dead guy's room. She hadn't heard much about his condition. Riordan kept tight reins on information flow. "To avoid scandal," he'd said in the text he'd sent the faculty asking them not to talk to the press. Who cared about scandal when Frankie might—

She pinched herself. No time for that thinking now. Now was the time to figure out how to get into Bernard's room. Had scandal, or the fear of it, gotten him killed? Ruining lives seemed to be Bernard's stock and trade. People had killed for less.

She moved along the hallway, trying to think of a way to get past Bernard's locked door. Fingers crossed his stuff remained where he'd left it. The gardaí didn't concern her. They'd arrested Aed, a man with a known motive and opportunity to kill, so they had little reason to confiscate Bernard's effects as evidence. The inn, however, might have decided they needed room forty-two and moved Bernard's things to storage while they located his next of kin. Go in now and hope for the best. She wouldn't get another chance.

Luck struck near the elevator. A blue plastic keycard, decorated only with the hotel name, lay partially obscured by a planter. Someone must have dropped it. It might open any room. Even forty-two. She scooped it up.

She'd tried the key in the lock a half-dozen times before the maid noticed her.

"May I help you, miss?" the young woman asked.

"Yes," Gethsemane said. "I seem to have demagnetized my key. I'm sure this is my room." She pointed to the brass plaque engraved with "42." "I knew I shouldn't have put it so close to my cell phone." She inserted the key into the lock a seventh time and turned the handle. Nothing.

"It happens, miss." The maid took out her pass key and opened the door. "They'll make a new one for you at the front desk."

"Thank you so much," Gethsemane said. "I feel quite stupid."

"No worries, miss. Like I said, happens all the time."

Gethsemane closed the door behind the maid. She flipped the deadbolt as an afterthought. No reason to risk being caught. Bernard's room revealed him to be a pig in more than one sense of the word. Clothes draped over furniture and hung out of suitcases. Newspapers and takeout containers littered any convenient surface. No laptop. Had someone taken it? Or did Bernard not have one? Maybe he used a tablet or his phone. Or maybe he'd left it in the car he drove to the Athaneum, in which case, the gardaí had it now. Probably password protected, even if she found it. The drawers. She opened them to find socks, underwear, ties. Then she pulled open the small drawer in the bedside table. No Gideon Bible or phone directory. Much better. Better than a laptop. Papers. Not password protected. Receipts for restaurants, sundries, laundry—had he planned to expense them? Would O'Zamboni's Irish-Italian

Pizzeria have shown up as a charge on Verschreken's account?

She sifted further. A brochure of Cork city attractions. A couple of postcards, both unsigned and blank. Didn't he have anyone to write to?

Someone had written to him. She held up a letter.

Dear Mr. Stoltz,

Rare opportunity to review Aed Devlin's new opera. Pays top rates to freelancers.

The letter head looked legit, but the letter bore no signature. It purported to be from Aria magazine, a small but respected publication that specialized in operas. She held the letter to the light. A faint, almost imperceptible black line marched across the top of the paper, between the masthead and the body of the letter. A tell for a photocopy. A cut and paste job. A good one. If she hadn't been looking, she wouldn't have noticed the line. Someone lured Bernard to Dunmullach under pretext of reviewing Aed's opera. A lot of trouble to go to in order to kill him. Who'd done it? She examined the letter again. Venus's contact who helped people reinvent themselves might do this kind of work. When you helped people create new lives, you probably did a lot of cutting, pasting, and photocopying. She shoved the letter in her pocket. It wasn't theft, it was evidence gathering. She'd turn it over to the guards. Eventually. Maybe Niall would be—Don't go there, not now.

Something caught her eye as she returned the other papers to the drawer. A strip from a photo booth, its corner caught under one of the drawer's side panels. Four photos, not much larger than postage stamps. Bernard, with his tortoise shell glasses perched on his head. Perched on his lap? Poe. She sported pink hair, but no mistake. The world's angriest photographer and the world's sleaziest reporter. His hand on her thigh, her arm around his neck.

*   *   *

Hardy bumped into her as they crossed the lobby in opposite directions. The rain had kept up. Hardy's wet hair left damp spots on the back of his t-shirt. He looked terrible. Sunken eyes, pale skin, sunken cheeks, giving his head a skeletal appearance. Niall had looked better when the emergency technicians had loaded him into the ambulance.

"Should you be in the hospital, Hardy? Or at least in bed?"

"I have things to do."

"Hardy, you look bad. Worse than bad. If you auditioned for a part in a zombie movie, they'd turn you down for being too realistic. Whatever you have to do, delegate." Riordan shut down an entire school over this outbreak. What could be important enough for Hardy to risk his health?

Hardy only shrugged and ambled listlessly to the front desk. Gethsemane overheard him ask for messages. No point in trying to talk to him. She'd get nothing of any use if he managed to remain conscious long enough to speak. Poe, on the other hand, promised to yield more substance. Assuming she didn't literally rip Gethsemane's head off. Or impale her or beat her to death with a camera tripod. She checked with the desk clerk after Hardy stumbled away. Poe hadn't returned to the hotel. That narrowed down her probable locations to two: the Rabbit or the Athaneum.

Hardy called her back as she reached the front door. "Hey, how are the boys doing?"

"Still breathing." But, if they were as ill as Hardy, for how long?

"I'm sorry they got mixed up in all this. Sucks when kids get dragged into things. When they get hurt."

"Tragic." Was Hardy thinking of any specific kids? Gethsemane waited to see if he'd go on, but he just stared at the floor. She prompted him. "Have you seen anything like this before? If you know something that might help..."

"I've never seen anything like this before. Not ever. I was

thinking of some other kids."

"Kids who got sick?" Hardy nodded. "Kids who died?"

"One did."

"Was it your child, Hardy?"

"I don't have any kids." He grinned. "At least none that I know of." The grin faded, replaced by an expression Gethsemane couldn't read.

"Who died?"

"My little brother."

"I'm sorry."

"It happened a long time ago. He was four. An outbreak of a stomach bug at the pool. E. coli H-something."

E. Coli O157:H7. Gethsemane remembered helping her brother prepare an epidemiology report for his infectious disease rotation. E. Coli O157:H7 produced toxins that caused gastrointestinal bleeding. Infection could be fatal. A dangerous bacterium, especially for young children.

"A bunch of kids got sick, and my brother didn't make it. I blamed myself. Mom blamed me, too, I think, although she never said so to my face."

"How is an infectious disease outbreak at a swimming pool your fault?"

"I was supposed to take my brother to the movies. One of my friends got some new video games, so I weaseled out of going to the Cineplex. I promised him we'd go for ice cream later, figuring he'd just forget. Turns out he was pretty bummed about the movies, so Mom took him to the pool instead."

"I'm really sorry, Hardy. How awful."

He didn't seem to hear her. "The worst of it is, the pool knew. There'd been a couple of cases a month earlier. The pool operators claimed they increased the amount of chlorine or whatever in the water and it was safe. They lied. The real problem was they needed a new pump or filter or something. An expensive part. They didn't want to spend the money."

"That's beyond awful," she said. "That's criminal."

"I can almost understand the pool operators. They cared more about money than some stupid kids from poor neighborhoods. What I don't get, who I'd really like to grill, are the newspaper reporters who covered the story after the first incidents. The reporters just took the pool's word for it that the problem was solved. They didn't investigate. They didn't ask for water quality reports to see if the water was safe, they even implied the parents who expressed doubt were just angling to file lawsuits against the pool. One reporter even said he'd let his own kids swim there. Of course, he didn't. He had a country club membership. His kids used that pool."

"I don't get it. Why would a newspaper—"

"Let's just say no one in the neighborhood thought it was a coincidence when it came out that the pool operator's daughter played soccer on the same team as the newspaper's senior editor. This was a top-tier paper. A lot of people read those articles and thought the pool was safe. Mom believed the water was safe." Hardy gasped and collapsed into a club chair. He wiped his face on the hem of his t-shirt. His color had worsened since he'd first bumped into her.

"Okay, Hardy, enough. I'm calling an ambulance."

"No, don't. I hate hospitals. My brother—I hate hospitals. I'll go to my room and lie down. I promise." He hoisted himself from the chair and staggered more than walked to the stairs.

"The elevator's back that way." Gethsemane pointed.

He changed direction then turned back to face her. "The reporters. That's who I'd like to kill."

Sixteen

The rain showed no sign of letting up, so Gethsemane called a cab.

"Where to, miss?" the cab driver asked.

She played a hunch. "Drop me near the Athaneum theater, please. Not right at the front entrance. About a block away."

The cab driver stared at her. "You and your bike will get a soaking."

"The bike needs a good cleaning and the dress is wash-and-wear."

The driver left her where instructed. She left the bike near a tree and crept around the rear of the building to the stage door. She borrowed a key during rehearsals for the All-County and had neglected to return it. She found it on her keyring. Only one garda stood watch at the entrance. She walked up to him.

"Excuse me, sir."

He looked her up and down and back again. His expression held more suspicion than lechery.

Gethsemane smoothed her wet skirt, pulled her jacket tighter, and pretended the rain had no impact on her natural hair. "I got caught out while riding my bike."

"We're no taxi service. Don't give rides home."

"I don't want a ride. I was waiting across the street for the rain to stop when I saw a woman with blue hair and cargo pants trying to climb in through a window."

"Where?" The garda craned his neck back and forth, trying to see the windows.

"On the other side." Gethsemane pointed off in the distance.

"Damn manky gobshite weirdo," the guard muttered as he headed around the building. His radio crackled as he warned his colleagues.

As soon as he rounded a corner, Gethsemane slipped inside. She had no trouble finding the stage. She'd led St. Brennan's to triumph on that stage four months ago. She could find her way in the dark. But she didn't have to. Maja's blue glow illuminated the theater like emergency path lighting in an airplane. Gethsemane kept an eye out for the entity but saw only the glow.

Then she found Poe. The photographer, intent on adjusting equipment, didn't notice her. Gethsemane called up to the grand tier. "The guards are looking for you."

Poe's hands stopped moving, but she didn't take her eyes off the machine she'd been calibrating. "I'm right here, let's see if they're smart enough to find me." She resumed her work. "I'm not worried."

"Subtlety" and "Poe" didn't belong in the same sentence. Best use the direct approach. "How long have you been in love with Bernard Stoltz?"

Poe dropped a camera lens. "What? I'm not—In love with? Who told you—What the—" She sputtered.

"Don't deny it. I have proof. Isn't that what *Ghost Hunting Adventures* is all about? Proof on film?" She held up the photo booth strip.

Poe came down from the grand tier and looked at the pictures. And laughed. She tried to grab the strip, but Gethsemane snatched it away.

"Keep it," Poe said. "Hang it on your fridge. It means nothing."

"It means you had an affair with a man who's lying in the morgue."

"That's not me."

Gethsemane looked at the photos, at Poe, and back at the photos. "It's you. Different hair color but—"

"That's my sister, J. Sheridan. Yes, I'm a twin. Sickening thought, huh? Two of me."

Kind of sickening, yeah. Mildly nauseating, at least. Two Poes. An identical twin sister.

Poe went back to her gear. "We got tired of people mixing us up so we decided to color our hair. We drew straws. J. lost and had to go with pink."

Her sister. Hard to imagine Poe with a family. Easier to picture her in a cave being raised by wolves. "How long's she been with Bernard?"

"A few months. Long enough to fall for his B.S. Get it? B.S. Bernard Stoltz. His name describes him. Whole family hates him. So, natch, J. Sheridan sticks that much tighter."

Family dinners with Poe and J. Sheridan must be a riot. "Did he love her?"

Poe snorted. "What do you think? Still, my sister's convinced she loves him and can save him. She'll be the one to turn him around and make him want to be a better man." Poe made a retching motion. "Makes me glad I'm Ace."

"Ace?"

"Asexual. One of the plus signs after LGBT."

Gethsemane studied the photo again. "That's really not you in the picture?"

"Look closely. See J. Sheridan's left forearm?"

A tattoo. "Is that a dagger piercing an alien?"

"See my left forearm?" Poe pushed up her sleeve. A teddy bear with a dagger in his belly surrounded by a heart adorned the front. A long scar adorned the back. "Punched through a window."

Gethsemane put the picture away. "But you did buy Bernard's plane ticket? Arranged for the hotel? Unless your sister pretended to be you and swiped the company credit card."

Poe frowned. "How did you—Never mind. Yeah, I paid Bernard's way. I did it for J. Bernard, got a letter from some rinky-dink music magazine offering to buy a piece on Aed Devlin. I don't know Aed from Zed so I wasn't impressed, but Bernard convinced

J. this was his big break, his comeback. He was broke, as usual. He always mooched off J. He claimed poor mouth until time to buy himself a new suit or new shoes. Then he managed to 'scrape some change together.' He begged J. to pay his way to Dunmullach, and she begged me once she found out we were coming for the investigation."

"And you paid with the company credit card."

"My money."

"Company money."

"Same thing." Poe turned on an EMF pod and cranked up the energy level. Gethsemane's head throbbed and she felt queasy. "For Maja," Poe explained. "Anyway, as they say in the theater, 'All's well that ends well.'"

"It didn't end well for Bernard." Gethsemane massaged her temples. The blue glow brightened. "He got stabbed."

Poe shrugged. "I'm good with that. Now he'll leave my sister alone." She cranked up another pod. "You might want to leave. High doses of electromagnetic energy make some people sick. Headaches, nausea, hallucinations."

An angry blue face hovered just beyond Poe's shoulder. A ghost, not a hallucination. "I bet you and Maja would get on real well."

Poe smiled the first genuine smile Gethsemane had seen her give. "You think so? Or are you just being nice?"

Gethsemane cocked her head and studied the photographer. "I don't get you, Poe. What makes you so, so—"

"Devoted to my cause."

"Mean. And hostile. Anger radiates off you like the blue aura off your paranormal idol. Did something happen to you? Did some trauma leave you this way?"

"What? The only possible explanation for a woman not being nice," she spat the word, "is because a traumatic experience scarred her for life, damaged her beyond redemption? She must have suffered abuse or abandonment or lost a child. Why else would she behave this way? Her husband must have dumped her for the nanny. She must have been abducted by a cult. Otherwise, she'd be sweet and meek and mild. I expect that crap from guys, but from you?"

"No one said you have to be 'nice' just because you're a woman. I'm not nice. Competent, confident, intelligent, and driven, but not 'nice.' All I ask of life is to be taken seriously, not to be 'likeable.' I'd rather be the respected one than the nice one-slash-doormat. But, Poe, c'mon. An ocean exists between 'not nice' and 'vicious, misanthropic, sadistic champion of an evil, child-killing spirit.'"

"I'm in an industry dominated by men. They show up, do their jobs, no one gives them grief as long as they do those jobs well. Performance is the only standard they're measured on. If they're high performers everyone's cool with them. If they succeed, it's just normal. Of course, they succeed, that's what men do. I show up and get gobsmacked with expectations. It's not enough for me to do my job well. My behavior's up for discussion. My attitude matters more than the outcome of my work. Would you have even noticed my behavior if I was a man?"

"In your case, yes. Attitude's hard to miss, female or male, when the person with it beats everyone else over the head with it."

Distant voices echoed through the theater. Angry voices. "Where are you?" "Over this way." "No, over there." "Damn them." "What's that smell? Peppers and grease?"

"The gardaí," Gethsemane said. "My plans for the evening don't include being arrested, so I'll leave you to your—spectral bonding or whatever. I'm going."

Gethsemane raced to her Pashley. Rain or not, the gardaí on her heels nixed thoughts of calling a cab. She pedaled to the Dunmullach Dispatch office and pulled to a stop in front of an oversized red umbrella canopy.

The canopy tipped back and Venus peered at her. "Drowned rat is not a good look."

Gethsemane secured her bike. "Thanks for the fashion tip." She shook rain from her hair. "Have you been inside yet?"

"I have." Venus shared her umbrella. "I chatted up the crime reporter, told some war stories, swapped some lies. You know, became BFFs."

"And?" Gethsemane tucked her hands in her armpits and huddled as close to the center of the umbrella as she could.

"And we're in. He'll give us access to the WorldNews database for fifteen minutes."

"Let's get to it, then." She held the door while Venus folded her umbrella. "Where'd you get that?"

"I brought it with me. It's Ireland. It rains."

Inside, Venus introduced Gethsemane to the crime reporter, Pete Donovan. They followed him to a small office at the back of the building. They squeezed through a maze of file cabinets and boxes and crowded around a computer perched on a small desk. Donovan logged on and turned the desk chair over to Venus. Gethsemane read over her shoulder. A few keystrokes and mouse clicks later, front pages of newspapers from London, Paris, New York, Washington, D.C., places from all over the world, dating back ten, twenty, fifty years...

"Not that far," Gethsemane said. "Bernard wasn't wielding a poisoned pen as a toddler."

Venus scanned the available titles. "Where do we start?"

"How about with the search box?" She pointed over Venus's shoulder to a box in the upper corner of the computer screen.

"Step back," Venus said. "You're dripping on me." She typed Bernard's name and clicked "go." A list of links to newspaper articles popped up on screen. "Bingo."

Gethsemane read the titles. "Sour Sibelius. Chopped Tchaikovsky. Massacred Mozart. Concert reviews. With titles that would fail a third grade English course."

Venus selected the Sibelius review and read, "The composer surely spins in his grave after tonight's criminal performance of his 'Violin Concerto in D Minor, Op. 47.' Vinegar tastes sweeter than the maestro's interpretation of Sibelius's masterpiece."

"An alliterative hatchet job. Are the others just as blistering?"

They were.

"If this is typical of Bernard's work," Venus said, "I'm amazed someone waited this long to kill him."

Gethsemane pointed to a link. "Josephine's Joke. I don't know of any composers named Josephine."

"Maybe it's a musician." Venus clicked the link. "'When one enters a Parisian dining establishment...' It's a restaurant review."

"Must be the one he wrote when he met Sylvie in Paris."

"Look at these others," Venus said. "Marco's Mashup Marvels Marry Two Cuisines. Tara's Truffle Triumph. Petra's Perfect Pastry. Louie's Lamb Shanks Suck Lemons. How did the headlines sneak past an editor?"

"Maybe the editor wrote the headlines. A print version of click bait."

"A print version of cringe bait."

"At least he wrote one or two favorable ones." Gethsemane pointed at a title. "I assume Tara's Truffle Triumph is positive."

"Positive crap." Venus wrinkled her nose. "Confection Confidential voted Tara's truffles the worst in Westchester County. Tasted like dirt and mouthwash. Customers sued Tara's to get refunds, alleging the candy was so bad it made them physically ill. And Petra's pastries? Far from perfect. Her bakery closed after outbreaks of salmonella poisoning from tainted eggs and listeria from under-pasteurized milk. They didn't cook the pastries all the way through. Raw dough in the middle of the muffins."

"Then why would—? Oh, they paid Bernard for the good reviews. Guess Louie refused to pay?"

"Louie started over and opened up a new restaurant about two years after that review ruined him. Same recipes. Won a James Beard award."

"Bernard honed his graft skills on chefs before taking aim at musicians."

"There are so many. More good than bad." Venus scrolled

through the list. "If these were all paid for, Bernard must have made a nice living. He was as prolific as he was crooked."

"Maybe he had some expensive habits to support. Gambling, a secret family."

"If you think Bernard would have been stand up enough to support a child or the child's mother, don't. Bernard looked after Bernard." Venus slammed a finger on the left mouse button. The list of articles vanished.

Gethsemane protested. "Hey, wait, we need those."

"Why? We've proved Bernard was a two-genre jerk."

"Names. We need people's names. There's a good chance someone he knifed on paper repaid the favor by knifing him in the back."

Donovan stuck his head into the office.

"Five more minutes," Venus said. "Maybe ten."

"What is it you're searching for?" he asked.

"Off the record or on?" Venus countered.

"Depends on what you tell me," he said.

Venus looked at Gethsemane, who shrugged. Her suggested cover story of finding old articles about her career suddenly seemed unnecessarily complicated and somewhat unbelievable.

"Background on Bernard Stoltz," Venus said. "His past reviews."

"Stoltz? The murdered man? From the Athaneum?"

"You have another murdered man?"

"Not this week." Donovan leaned against a file cabinet. His eyes darted back and forth between the two women with an alertness that suggested his casual pose was anything but casual. "What are you working on? A book?"

Venus demurred. "Still at the poking around stage."

"C'mon, I won't scoop you."

"A book," Gethsemane said. "She's looking into the, er, rumors that Stoltz may have accepted bribes to write good reviews." Just in case Donovan did decide to "scoop" Venus, better to have that end up on the front page of the Dispatch than the fact they were investigating Bernard's murder.

Donovan glanced at his watch. "I can give you ten more minutes. Someone has dibs on the office after that."

Gethsemane and Venus thanked him. He lingered by the cabinets. The two women stared at him without saying anything. Seconds passed. Donovan finally left. Gethsemane shut the door behind him.

"Thought he'd never take the hint." Venus pulled up Bernard's search results again.

Gethsemane pointed to a hyperlink at the end of the list. "'See similar articles.' What's that?"

"Let's find out." Venus clicked the link. Another list popped up. "Sato's Sashimi Scores. Sarah's Sabayon Success. More of the same."

"Except for that." Gethsemane pointed. "Look at the byline. 'Ben Schlossberg.' Who's Ben Schlossberg and why are his headlines as execrable as Bernard's? Could he be a protégé? Bernard's attempt to keep his toxic legacy alive?"

Venus pulled up the sabayon article. "Look at the date of the review."

"Three years before Bernard's first. Almost twenty years ago. Could Bernard be the protégé?"

"Ben's writing style is the same as Bernard's." Venus scanned more Schlossberg articles. "Same with these. The style's identical."

"Identical, meaning the same person wrote all of them?"

Venus did another search. "The bylines don't overlap. Ben Schlossberg disappeared after Sarah succeeded with her sabayon, and Bernard Stoltz didn't appear until Marco marveled with his mashup."

"So Schlossberg and Stolz are the same person. Were the same person. Why the name change? I could understand if he used a pen name to write novels or something, but these are all reviews. I'd think a name change would be detrimental to a reviewer. Gimmicky headlines and mean-spiritedness aside, Bernard—Ben—showed real writing talent. The kind that would generate name recognition.

Change your name, lose your clout."

"People change their names for lots of reasons," Venus said. "Reasons that have nothing to do with writing. People change their names when they want to escape their lives, reinvent themselves, hide from someone..."

"Avoid arrest. Hence, Sadie becomes Sylvie. Think Ben had a warrant? For pandering?"

"He'd be more likely to have a warrant for selling himself than for selling someone else."

"How do we find out? I could ask Niall—" Gethsemane stopped. She couldn't ask Niall to use his law enforcement contacts to see if Bernard had any criminal charges. And she couldn't ask Frankie to help her break into Bernard's hotel room to do another search. She sat on the edge of the desk and adjusted a skirt pleat.

"What is it?" Venus asked.

"Just thinking of my friends."

"Niall and Frankie? I'm sorry about them. They're a couple of the good ones. I hope they get better."

"Yeah, me too."

No one spoke. Gethsemane said a silent prayer for Niall, Frankie, and her students.

Venus smacked her forehead. "Duh. I'm an idiot. Of course we can find out if criminal charges prompted Ben Schlossberg's name change."

"How?"

"You're not the only one with contacts in law enforcement." Venus pulled out her smart phone. "Back in the day when I reported hard news I met a CI—"

"CI?"

"Confidential informant who has extensive, let's call it 'experience,' in the field of disappearance and reappearance of people and objects."

"Someone in law enforcement?"

"Technically anti-law enforcement but why split hairs?" Her thumbs flew across her phone's virtual keyboard. "He's based in

Dublin now, but he's got a multinational resource network."

"I would love to see your Rolodex from back in the day."

"I burned it." She put the phone away. "I'll let you know when I hear something."

"Let's take one more look at the reviews," Gethsemane glanced at the wall clock, "before Donovan boots us for real. Can we print these to study later?"

"I think so." Venus clicked the mouse a few times and a printer underneath the desk whirred to life. The machine ejected a sheet a moment later. She yielded the mouse to Gethsemane. "Click away."

Gethsemane made her way through the links. She printed Bernard's negative music reviews and his restaurant reviews. She started on the reviews published under Ben Schlossberg's byline. Two headlines jumped out at her. "Take a look at these. Hexacomp Recalls Infant Sleepwear. Concerns about Ponyfield Food's Safety Record Overblown."

Venus leaned closer. "Those sound like consumer safety reports. I've never heard of Hexacomp, but Ponyfield I know. They defended themselves in a class action lawsuit in Manhattan after several families sued them, alleging their children suffered lead poisoning after eating green beans imported by Ponyfield. Turns out, the cans Ponyfield's supplier used contained unsafe levels of lead, and Ponyfield knew it. They settled out of court for an undisclosed sum. A year later, the feds investigated Ponyfield for trying to re-export those same tainted canned goods overseas. They donated them to charities that provide food for children in underdeveloped countries. 60 Minutes did a segment on it."

"Guess the concerns weren't so overblown after all." Gethsemane read some of the article while waiting for the printer to finish spitting out sheets. "Same writing style as the reviews, dated earlier than the flowery headlines. Why'd Schlossberg switch from consumer safety to restaurant reviews?"

Venus tapped the computer screen. "Maybe because he was a crap judge of product safety."

"Or maybe chefs pay higher rates for positive reviews than

import-export companies. Who's to say Ben or Bernard or whatever his name is didn't cut his crooked teeth on Ponyfield? He probably cost less than the lawsuit settlement."

"Yeah, but Bernard's article didn't help. They still got sued."

"They settled. They came through the storm well enough to be able to dump their poisonous cans on unsuspecting consumers outside the U.S. Maybe without Bernard's article they would have out and out lost. Or faced criminal charges."

"True. He might have helped mitigate their damages. And then switched to restaurants because complaints were less likely to end up in court."

Donovan appeared in the doorway. "Sorry, ladies..."

Gethsemane grabbed the articles off the printer. "Just leaving."

She and Venus waited in the Dispatch lobby for a cab. The rain had picked up.

"Why don't you get a car?" Venus asked. "Since you're sticking around."

"Because getting an Irish driver's license is a serious pain. Wait twelve months, then go through the full licensing procedure, including taking driving lessons, the written test, and the road test. Never mind actually buying a car and getting it insured. The Pashley's easier."

"Except when it rains."

"Nothing's perfect."

The Addams Family theme chirped from Venus's purse. She checked the messages. "My Dublin buddy wants to talk to me. By phone, not by text."

"Because if it's not in writing it didn't happen?"

Venus pointed from her nose to Gethsemane. "Something like that. No offense, but I'll take this in private." A cab pulled up in front of the building. "You can take this one. I'll call another."

A cab dropped Gethsemane and her Pashley in front of Carraigfaire as the dim, cloud-covered daylight gave way to dim, cloud-covered twilight. The rain had increased in intensity and she dripped by the time Eamon opened the door. A towel hovered for her near the hall bench.

She snatched it from the air and toweled her face.

"Where've you been all day?" Eamon, a bright yellow-orange, scolded her as she hung up her coat and took off her wet shoes. "Folks, meaning me, worry. Why'd you even get a mobile phone if you're not going to use it?"

"Am I hearing this? You're kidding, right? You can't talk on the phone. Can you?"

"You could leave a message. I can hear the machine."

"I'm sorry I worried you." She looked up at him, six feet of brown curls, green eyes, and angst. "You're not usually like this." A poke set his saffron aura shimmying. "What can I do to make this turn green?"

"I don't know. It's not you. This Maja business has me on edge. You haven't had any 'Pathétique' warnings, have you?"

"No," she shook her head, "Tchaikovsky's been strangely quiet."

"I'm frustrated as well as worried."

"No fruit born from your snooping?"

"Ghosts don't snoop." He bristled an offended burnt umber.

"Who said to whom," she mimicked his brogue, "'You're not the only one who knows how to conduct an investigation'?"

"Ghosts investigate. They do not snoop."

"Well, I snoop. I spent the day snooping into Bernard's past and uncovered some interesting evidence."

"'Interesting' being code for 'I should hand it over to the guards straight away, but I'm going to hang onto it for my own reasons.'"

"Have you been talking to Inspector O'Reilly?"

"You're being facetious, but I'll answer you anyway. Your inspector is well and truly a skeptic. No room in that logical head for ghosts and goblins. I can't talk to him. He'll never see or hear me. I checked on him, by the way. He's stable. Frankie Grennan, too."

"You checked on them how?"

Eamon chuckled. "You may not be able to get past gardaí and school nurses, but I can."

She smiled. "Thank you for the status update. Stable is hopeful. And thank you for the towel." She passed him into the study and opened the roll top desk, where she removed the contents of one of the small drawers and replaced them with the photos of Poe's sister and the letter luring Bernard to Dunmullach. She'd hardly closed the drawer behind them when it flew open and the items floated out.

"Would these be pieces of your interesting evidence?" Eamon asked. "What is it?"

"Bernard's killer set him up. He, or she, sent that bogus letter inviting Bernard to review Aed's opera. And Poe has a once-removed connection to Bernard. Through her twin sister."

"Twins? A double portion of strangeness or is sister the normal one?"

"Sister's in love with Bernard. You decide if that's normal. Put those back."

The items nestled themselves back in the drawer and the drawer shut.

"As I said, you don't have to fret over Bernard's murder. Venus and I have it covered."

"What if Venus did it?"

"You don't believe that."

"I've been wrong." He paused. "Once or twice."

"If she'd murdered Bernard, she would have tried to kill me already."

"That is why I worry. And why you need me to look after you."

"I'm nearly forty. I'm a big girl. I can tie my shoes and cross the street all by myself."

"Don't forget coshed on the head, nearly burned alive, almost shot, almost drowned, poisoned—"

She held up a hand. "Stop. I'm not backing off this investigation."

"I'm not telling you to stop. You wouldn't listen if I did. I'm only telling you to be wide."

"What happened today to get you so worked up? No luck with your Eastern European scholar?"

"Plenty of luck. With a side order of dread. I spent the day reading over his shoulder about murder and revenge. I underestimated Maja. I shouldn't have. You know those hazardous weather alerts you Americans broadcast on your weather channels? Between a tornado watch and a tornado warning, Maja is a tornado ripping off the roof of your house and sending your bathtub into the neighbor's front yard."

Not what she wanted to hear from Mr. "Send a ghost to do a ghost's job."

"Don't look that way, darlin'," Eamon said. "We're not down and out yet. I haven't given up. I've learned a few things from you about persistence." He vanished.

A hot shower and change of clothes buoyed her mood a fraction. She resolved the debate between whiskey in the study or coffee in the kitchen by the time she hit the stairs lower landing. Sharp knocking at the front door halted her progress through the entry way.

"Who is it?" She kept a hand on the shillelagh by the door.

"Open up," the reply came. "It's life or death."

Seventeen

Hardy shivered on the porch. The rain plastered his stringy hair to his skull and his t-shirt to his thin frame. His fair complexion had turned sallow and taken on a translucent quality. He looked even worse than he had when she'd run into him at Sweeney's. No drowned rat ever looked as pitiful.

"Hardy, what's wrong?" Gethsemane showed him inside. "I told you before you looked awful. I take it back. Death warmed over would be an improvement. No coat? No umbrella? If you're trying to prove you're macho enough to brave Ireland's elements—"

He cut her off. "You have to help Aed. He didn't kill anyone."

"I'm going to attribute the randomness of that statement to delirium." She pulled him into the study. "Stand by the fire and try to reverse the hypothermia. I'll bring you a towel."

She paused on a stair on her way up to the linen cabinet. Had it really been almost a year since she was the one who stood soaking wet in front of a peat fire waiting for someone to bring her a towel?

She returned with the towel and offered Hardy a drink.

"No, thanks," he said as he sopped up drips and rivulets. After a few moments' work, he pronounced himself as dry as he was going to get and sat on the hearth. "Don't want to wreck your couch."

"Hardy, what's going on?" He still shivered, despite sitting only inches from the fire.

"I told you. You have to help Aed."

"You need to see a doctor. I'll call—"

Hardy sprang from the hearth and grabbed her arm before she could move from where she stood by the bar cart. For a guy apparently one step ahead of the grim reaper, he moved fast. And still had strength in his grip. He released her arm. "I'm sorry. I— Please just listen."

Gethsemane sat on the couch.

Hardy resumed his spot on the hearth across from her. "Aed Devlin didn't kill Bernard Stoltz."

She didn't believe Aed was a murderer, either, because she liked him and didn't think him capable, and a bunch of other people had just as much reason to want Bernard dead. But Hardy's claim sounded more like a statement of fact than of faith in the composer's character. "How do you know he didn't?"

"Because I know who did kill him. Maja Zoltán."

That clinched it. Delirium. She'd get Hardy to a doctor even if she had to knock him out to do it. She stood.

Hardy held up a shaky hand. "Did you build this fire or did Eamon?"

Gethsemane gawped. Words refused to order themselves in any fashion that resembled English.

"Yes, I can see him. But you already knew that. You caught me looking at him over your shoulder a few times."

She sat down again. She had noticed some strange glances. "I suspected—something. I knew you weren't just an easy-going tech guy. The day you snapped a photo of me near the cottage..."

"Saw the ghost with my eyes but got nothing on camera. That's usually how it works. Ghosts are so unpredictable. Ordinary technology's seldom up to the task of capturing documentation solid enough to convince skeptics. Despite Kent's show time histrionics, no one's really excited about a light anomaly or a blur in the background. Too easily dismissed as dust or bugs."

"Hence the mad scientist with the secret MIT technology cooking up exotic toys for you to test."

Hardy's laugh disintegrated into a coughing spasm. When he

could speak again, he said, "She's not mad. Maybe a little eccentric as far as middle-aged mom's go. Brilliant, definitely. Turned down jobs at NASA and Stanford after she left MIT so she could open her own lab."

"With MIT's blessing, no doubt, since she's using their stuff."

Hardy smiled. "What MIT can't prove won't hurt her. Besides, MIT can't honestly lay claim to having invented any of it. The ancient alchemists were on to this stuff ages ago."

"Yeah, the historical record's chock-a-block full of ancient smartphones and handy-cams." Her sarcasm was palpable.

"That stuff's just window dressing. The important part, the bits she's putting inside the phones and recorders and cameras are based on devices the alchemists designed from copper and crystal, silver and gold. Things we still use to make lenses and sensors and data storage devices."

"What were these alchemists doing with their precious metals and stones?"

"Building ghost catchers."

Gethsemane studied him. He shook less and he breathed better. "You're pretty calm about seeing Eamon's ghost, going on about the history of ghost hunting as if nothing more remarkable has happened than finding a penny on the street." She recalled Venus's hysterics and her own heavy-object-throwing reaction the first time she met Eamon.

Hardy shrugged. "I'm used to it. I've been able to see ghosts since I was a kid. Ironically, I'm the only one of the entire *Ghost Hunting Adventures* team who can."

"Shouldn't you be the one leading the stakeouts?"

A mixture of sadness and resignation filled Hardy's laugh. "Kent has something more important than second sight. He has on-screen personality and drop-dead good looks. And a controlling interest in the production company." He waved away her sympathy. "I don't care. Kent can have the fame. I do this for them."

"Them?"

"The ghosts. So they know they've been heard. So they have a chance to tell their story. Most of the time, that's the only thing keeping them from passing over peacefully. They want to tell their side of things. Once they share their version of events, they can go."

"And you've never told your colleagues that you can actually see what they only pretend to capture with their fancy toys?"

"My 'colleagues,'" he snorted, "do this for the glory. They don't deserve to know. They'd find some way to exploit the spirits. Hell, look at Poe's reaction to Maja. She'd set the woman up with her own social media accounts if she could. Instagrammable revenge killings, that kind of thing. That's not what the ghosts want." He pulled out his phone. "By the way, some of us—meaning me—aren't pretending when we claim we caught something on tape or camera. At least not all the time. Remember this?"

Gethsemane nodded recognition at the phone with the multi-modal spectral vision his engineer friend had given him.

"The SD card was developed with her secret technology, too." He tapped the screen and turned the phone so Gethsemane could see.

She watched video of herself at the Athaneum, leaning over the rail of the orchestra pit, looking at something in its depths. The moment she discovered Bernard's body. Or, more precisely, the moment the other entity in the video discovered Bernard's body. The ghost of Eamon McCarthy, balancing on the pit rail, glowing in high-definition.

Gethsemane lunged for the phone. Hardy snatched it out of reach. She earned nothing but a sore knee and banged elbow for the trouble.

"What are you going to do with that? Broadcast it on *Ghost Hunting Adventures*? Sell it on the internet for the equivalent of the gross domestic product of Germany?" Guarantee Carraigfaire a never-ending stream of curiosity seekers and devotees? Ruin the peace of the village, Eamon's afterlife, and untold numbers of people's beliefs about life and death?

"I could," he said. "The coolest thing about this card is that it plays back on any device with an SD card slot. These images could be viewed on every webcam and streaming service on the planet in the time it takes to say boo. But whether or not that happens depends on you," he said.

"I don't understand." She rubbed her knee.

"Aed didn't kill Bernard. He couldn't have done it because Maja killed him. Prove Maja did it. You're good at clearing innocent people's names. You've got a gift."

Gift, curse, same thing, right? "Hardy, I'm going to assume your illness is speaking. You know I can't prove a ghost killed a man. You know as well as I do that most people don't believe ghosts exist. They think ghosts are like imaginary friends. Imaginary friends can't kill people. Or be arrested. Or put on trial. You see where I'm going with this."

"Fine, then just prove Aed didn't kill him. Like you proved Eamon didn't kill his wife."

Exonerate Aed. She and Venus had a head start on Hardy. A day spent tracking down motives for Bernard's murder. A list of people, besides Aed, who wanted Bernard dead uncovered: Poe, Kent. Sylvie and Venus, if she was honest. Hardy himself. Is that why Hardy insisted she help Aed? Because he was a decent guy who couldn't live with the thought of an innocent man doing life in prison for his crime? Is that why he agreed to settle for Aed's exoneration instead of asking her to find Bernard's killer? Because he'd done it himself? She chuckled.

"A man's life's in jeopardy and you laugh?"

"What? No. I wasn't laughing at that. I just—never mind." She'd keep Hardy in the dark about what she'd been up to, just in case the harmless, nonthreatening, never-hurt-a-fly routine was phony. No need to enlighten a killer. Asking a suspect questions, on the other hand...

"Have you heard if the guards established Bernard's exact time of death?" She tried to look coy but decided she probably only looked constipated so stopped.

"No," Hardy said. "Why does the exact time matter?"

"If the time of death could be narrowed down to when Aed was nowhere near Bernard, that would prove he couldn't have killed him. And there were a lot of people in the Athaneum when the murder occurred—the opera company and crew, spectators, theater employees. That expands the suspect list by dozens. An exact time of death could make it easier to figure out who was close enough to Bernard to shove a trowel in him. If the guards knew exactly when Bernard was killed and pinpointed everyone's location, they could eliminate suspects by virtue of proximity. For instance, if they knew you were—where were you around the time of the murder?"

"I just said I haven't heard when the murder occurred. No one has. Or have you?"

"Not me." She hoped she was better at feigning surprise than coyness. "I meant, where were you when the body was discovered?"

Hardy shrugged. "Here and there. The crew moved around a lot getting equipment set up, framing shots." He shrugged again.

She'd practically accused him of murder. Why did he seem so cool about it? Not even a hint of offense. He was pretty good at feigning nonchalant. If only she could take this to Niall. His eyes would darken to storm gray. He'd rant and rave about civilian interference. But he'd take her seriously and, most important, he'd act. She pictured him spinning his hat on his finger or buffing a scuff mark from his latest designer shoe acquisition. He'd let you think he was just another useless garda then home in for the kill. Colombo without the rain coat.

But what if he didn't get better? What if Frankie didn't either? Who among the living would she aggravate, talk to, rope into schemes? She had Eamon but few others she called friends. How would she manage with two fewer?

She shook her head. No despair allowed. Gloom and doom didn't help. Self-pity accomplished nothing. Action achieved results. She narrowed her eyes at Hardy. "Tell me why you're so certain Maja killed Bernard. Did you see her do it? I assume you can see her."

He nodded. "I can. I didn't see her kill Bernard, though."

"Then how can you be sure she's his murderer?"

"Because she's killing me."

A week ago, Gethsemane would have dismissed Hardy's statement as delusional and paranoid. Now, of course, a sociopathic ghost really was trying to kill several men, present company included. However, Maja chose contagion as her weapon of choice. Cement trowels seemed out of character. And she only attacked the firstborns. Did anyone know Bernard's birth order? Mental note to check.

"Poe's version of the Maja curse is colorful and embellished almost to the point of being unrecognizable, but it holds the seeds of truth," Hardy said. "A mysterious illness fell over firstborn sons. Doctors and scientists will scratch their heads and run their tests, and write it off as an unexplained plague that passed over some and cut others down, then vanished without a backward glance. Just like a hundred other epidemics relegated to an interesting epidemiological footnote in some virology class." He broke off in a spasm of coughs.

"Hardy, stop talking. You're just making yourself worse. And we don't need poetry right now, we need a plan. We've got to break this curse."

"The plan is to clear Aed—"

"After we stop Maja. Aed's not a firstborn son, and he's a long way from convicted. He's got time. You, and a lot of guys I care about, don't, if your appearance is anything to judge by. First, we stop Maja from wiping out a large swath of the local population, including the only garda in Dunmullach who I might convince to listen to claims of Aed's innocence, then prove Bernard's death wasn't Aed's fault. Agreed?"

"I'm not really in a condition to put up much argument," Hardy said.

"Then we do this my way. Now all we have to do is figure out how to break a six-hundred-year-old curse and send a vengeful ghost packing."

A third voice entered the conversation. "I can help with that." Eamon materialized next to Hardy. "You look bate, fella. I've got more life in me, and I've been dead a quarter century."

"You can stop Maja?" Gethsemane asked.

"Don't sound so surprised, darlin'. Send a ghost to do a ghost's work."

"You're going to, what, politely ask her to go away and not come back again?"

"I'm going to use my insider knowledge to beat her at her own game."

"Insider knowledge? You can't figure out how to get out of this village."

His aura turned yellow. "Don't be mean."

"That did sound mean. I apologize. But I'm trying to be realistic. No one in this room knows jack about ghost curses from the fourteenth through sixteenth centuries."

Hardy barked a laugh. "Sounds like a college elective."

"Two of you in this room don't know anything about curses. One of us," Eamon jerked a thumb at his chest, "has been hanging out at the local library with his scholarly expert, reading through musty, dusty books."

Hardy rubbed his temples. "Has anyone ever told you two you sound like an old married couple?"

Gethsemane and Eamon both rolled their eyes. Eamon continued. "I—well, he—found a seventeenth-century treatise hidden away in the basement stacks that explained the situation. Apparently, murdered daughters-in-law uttering dying curses then coming back from the dead to carry them out is a thing. Maja draws energy from the grief generated by this sickness she's created. The worse the fellas get, the more despondent people who care about them get, and the stronger she gets. I discovered that if I can gather enough energy, I can blast her to hell before she grows too strong to stop."

"Too strong? That's a possibility? That she becomes unstoppable?" Shite. She hadn't considered Maja never going away.

"There's always a worst-case scenario when you're dealing with curses."

"And where do you get this extra energy?" Hardy asked. "I assume not from a protein shake or sticking your finger in a socket."

"Leave the snark to Sissy." Royal blue flickered around the edge of Eamon's aura. "She's better at it than you."

"Will you two shut up, and will you," she pointed at Eamon, "tell us the plan?" Gethsemane apologized. She started to sound like Poe. Worry made her snarkier than usual.

"I need another ghost," Eamon said. "One plus one equals too much energy for Maja to absorb. If another ghost and I combine energy, we overload her circuits."

"Where am I supposed to find a second ghost?" Gethsemane asked. "It's not like I can order you one online. And my track record with grimoires..." She waggled her hand back and forth in a comme çi, comme ça gesture.

"Fortunately, one of us knows what he's doing." Eamon apologized. "You know what I mean." The situation seemed to make him snarkier than usual, too. At least, she hoped it was only situational.

"Okay, you and this second ghost activate your Wonder Twin powers and blast Maja into the outer reaches of the universe. That breaks the curse and everyone recovers?"

"Yes," Eamon said. "I think so. I hope so."

He hoped. Not the iron-clad assurance she wanted to hear, but if that was the best they had to go on, she'd take it. "All right, we go for it. Double up our ghost quotient and blast Maja to the back of beyond. First step, we, you, somebody finds a spell to phone a friend from beyond the veil. That gets us started. But finding the words is only half the answer. Riddle me this, how do we find out what notes this second ghost resonates to?"

"Excuse me," Hardy said. "I was tagging along for the ride, but you lost me at the last curve. Resonates?"

"I learned the hard way," Gethsemane said, "that reciting a spell isn't sufficient to conjure a ghost. You need to combine it with notes or tones that set up a sympathetic vibration, the way Sylvie's high notes made the glass at the theater shake. Sympathetic vibration's like the key that unlocks the spell."

"Sylvie's high notes during the aria built on the energy triggered by Aed's overture and set up the resonance that brought Maja over. La Diva's as French as a corn dog at the county fair but her singing's legit. And powerful."

"But there was no spell," Hardy said.

"I'm not so sure about that. Father Keating, Tim, inherited an impressive collection of occult books, including grimoires, from his older brother, also Father Keating." Gethsemane told him about Poe's invasion of the occult collection. "Tim took the book back, but Poe had plenty of time to find a spell and photograph it, or write it down or memorize it."

Hardy closed his eyes. "That idiot."

"We need our own spell," Eamon said. "And a resonance."

"Let's start with the easy part. Which means a trip to the Father Keating memorial occult library. I can usually find a spell to fit the occasion somewhere on the bookshelves."

"Let's get over there." Hardy tried to stand but collapsed back onto the couch.

Gethsemane propped him up. "No, Hardy, you can't come with us." She flashed an understanding smile at yellow-auraed Eamon. No church grounds for him. "With me."

"But I can help," Hardy said. "You need me. I'm one of the only other people in this village who can see and hear ghosts."

She assisted him up from the couch. "You need to lie down before you fall down. You're sick. Pushing yourself won't help you, me, Aed, or anybody except Maja. Go back to the inn. Rest."

He stared at her for a long moment, apparently trying to come to a decision. He decided and pulled out his phone. He opened the back and pried out the microSD card. "Here." He handed the card to Gethsemane. "You win. I'll go back to the inn."

"Why are you giving me this?"

"My half of our bargain. Before you convinced me to listen to reason and to trust you—I do trust you—I was going to offer you that in exchange for your promise to clear Aed. But I don't want to expose Eamon, and I know you'll do your best to save Aed. And me."

Gethsemane slipped the tiny card in her pocket. She'd put it with the pictures of Poe's sister and Bernard's letter later. After Hardy left. As much as she wanted to, she couldn't trust him completely. Not yet. "Thank you, Hardy. Now, please go take care of yourself." She followed him to the door.

It struck her as he reached for the door knob. Something about his profile. He reminded her of someone. Who? She caught her breath. "Hardy, whose first born are you?"

He froze with one foot over the threshold. Several seconds passed, then he answered without turning around. "Aed's."

Gethsemane put a hand on his arm. He continued speaking as she led him back inside. "I've never seen him that I can remember. He and mom met in Dublin. Mom's from New York. She was backpacking around Europe, taking a year off before starting college. Aed was a musician with ambition to compose great works. When Mom met him, though, he earned a living by playing a fiddle on a street corner for change and doing odd jobs." He swayed.

"Sit here." Gethsemane led him to the hall bench. "Let me get you some water."

He waved the offer away.

Gethsemane sat next to him. "Will you tell me more?"

"You can guess the rest. Fodder for countless soap operas and daytime talk shows. I came along, and Aed took off. A baby struck a wrong chord in his grand plan. Mom stayed in Dublin for years, hoping he'd come back."

"Which is why you have traces of a brogue."

"You noticed. Most don't. Mom gave up waiting when I was six and moved me back to New York."

"You haven't told Aed who you are."

"I keep waiting to find the right time. I don't imagine he'll list my sudden appearance in the good news column. He's so wrapped up in this opera. And Venus James. And now the murder charge."

"Have you told anyone?"

"A couple of people on the team know. I told them to convince them to let me come on this investigation."

"Why would they not?"

"You saw how Poe treats me. Always making little remarks, taking jabs at me."

"Poe treats everyone like that."

"She didn't used to treat me that way. Back when we were drinking and smoking buddies. I ran into some trouble, had some, um, difficulties, messed up on a stake out." Who'd alluded to Hardy having trouble on the show? Kent? Ciara? "We were investigating a haunting in an abandoned hotel. A guest investigator's night vision bodycam cut out as he walked down a hall. I was drunk and stepped—staggered—away from the operations center to go for a smoke. If I'd been sober enough to pay attention to the night vision still cam, I'd have seen the elevator shaft before the investigator stepped into it. Luckily, he only fell one floor, but he busted his arm and a kneecap."

"After which you cut out the smoking and cut back on the drinking, and you're trying to make your life right again."

"And I begged to get my job back. A job on the team, any job. I wasn't totally honest about being okay with Kent getting all the camera time. Before I screwed up, I was next in line to become an on-screen investigator. Now, I'm not even sure I want to keep doing paranormal. But when I found out Aed would be in Dunmullach, I couldn't pass up what might be my only chance to meet him." He reached into his back pocket and pulled out a folded envelope. He handed it to Gethsemane. "Will you do me a favor? If Maja kills me, will you give this to Aed?"

A reflexive protest died on her lips. The way Hardy looked..."Sure."

"You can open it."

She shook her head. "It's between you and Aed." She hesitated. Hardy looked so weak and ill it was hard to imagine him going for a cup of water, let alone going for Bernard. But she had to ask. "Did you kill Bernard, Hardy? To get even with him for ruining your father's career?"

"Risk life in prison for my absentee dad who doesn't know I'm alive—alive for the time being, anyway?" He chuckled. "No, I didn't. But thank you for thinking I'm capable of it. Plenty of people take me for granted. Don't notice me even when I'm standing right in front of them."

"Where were you standing when Bernard was killed?"

"I stayed up in the grand tier the whole time. You'll see if you watch the video again. It's shot from high up."

"I'm sorry things aren't working out for you, Hardy." She squeezed his hand. "May I borrow your phone? Mine's upstairs."

He handed it to her. "Who're you calling?"

"A cab. For you. To make sure you make it all the way to the inn."

A cab pulled into Carraigfaire's drive as Hardy's cab pulled out. Venus climbed from the rear seat then turned to assist someone. "Look who I found wandering in the rain."

A bedraggled Saoirse clutched a book to her chest. "I've got it."

"Come inside before pneumonia gets you," Gethsemane said.

Eamon's voice whispered in her ear. "Once upon a time, a stubborn woman told me weather didn't cause pneumonia when I tried to convince her to come in out of the rain."

She ignored him and led Saoirse to the fireplace.

Venus followed. "Was that Hardy I saw leaving?"

"He came to ask me to help clear Aed. He thinks Maja killed Bernard. Is Bernard the eldest?"

"Bernard has two older brothers."

"Not a firstborn. Couldn't have been one of Maja's kills."

"Why does Hardy care whether Aed goes down for Bernard's murder?"

A towel floated in from the hall. Gethsemane handed it to Saoirse. To Venus she said, "He doesn't want his father to go to prison."

"His father?" Venus sank to the couch. "Aed never said—"

"Aed doesn't know yet. He hasn't seen Hardy since he was an infant."

"Aed abandoned his son? I have no words." Venus stared into the fire, her expression far away.

Saoirse dropped the towel and picked up the book. "I have words." She blew towel-tangled hair from her face. "Latin ones."

Gethsemane took the book—a grimoire—and turned to Eamon, perched on the roll top desk over near a window. "I thought you were 'digging' into a way to call up reinforcements. Why is she—" She pointed at Saoirse. "—here with this?" She held up the book.

"Because that—" Eamon pointed at the book "—belongs to Father Tim's collection. Housed in the rectory. On church property."

And, therefore, off-limits to Eamon. "Sorry. I meant to talk to Father Tim about absolving you."

Venus's head snapped up. "What? Excuse me, I was miles away."

"We were discussing Eamon's dilemma—"

"Dilemma? A dilemma is which socks to wear, black or navy. A dilemma is red or white with spaghetti." His aura turned blue. "I can set neither hide nor hair on church grounds because I was buried as a suicide in unhallowed ground. My mortal remains will spend eternity miles apart from my wife's."

"That must be difficult," Venus said.

"That must be an understatement." Eamon vanished.

"Were you talking to Mr. McCarthy?" Saoirse couldn't see ghosts.

Gethsemane smoothed her hair. "Yes. He's gone now."

"He'll be back, yeah? We need him."

Calling Eamon mercurial was like calling a diamond hard. She supposed he'd return, eventually, but when? She handed the book back to Saoirse. "How did you find that? How did you know what to look for?"

"I went to the library to see if I could find something to help Colm and the others. They keep herbariums in the basement stacks. I hoped I could find a recipe I could use with some of the plants in Our Lady's poison garden." Venus made a noise. Saoirse explained. "The plants are medicinal, too."

"Saoirse's studied botany."

"Anyway," Saoirse said, "a book kept falling off the shelf and landing on my foot."

"Let me guess, a seventeenth-century treatise on acts of revenge committed by the ghosts of walled-up daughters-in-law," Gethsemane said. Eamon had found a way to communicate with Saoirse despite her not being able to see him. He'd improved at the haunting business.

Saoirse nodded. "It explained about two ghosts being able to combine forces and break a curse. So I went through Father Tim's books and found this."

Gethsemane examined the title again. Not the same book she'd used to inadvertently conjure Captain Lochlan when she first tried to bring Eamon back from limbo. Who knew what they might bring across with this one? "We'll wait for Eamon." She wanted him there, just in case.

A leathery, soapy blast interrupted the discussion. "All right." Eamon materialized in front of the fireplace, his aura a calmer ochre-tinged robin's egg blue. "Let's do this. Every minute Maja's here, the stronger she gets, all the worse for the fellas."

Gethsemane looked at Saoirse. "Maybe you should—"

Saoirse crossed her arms and planted her feet. "I found the book."

"Oh, all right." Gethsemane recognized world-class stubbornness when she saw it.

"What do we do?" Venus asked.

"I'll read the spell," Saoirse said, "then Dr. Brown will need to play the right song."

"What song?" Venus asked. "Why a song?"

"Ghosts sympathetically vibrate to certain tones," Gethsemane explained. "A conjuring spell combined with the proper notes will bring one across from the other side."

"How do you know what noise to make?"

Gethsemane shrugged. "You don't. That's the problem."

"That's the safety valve," Eamon said. "Keeps humans from creating havoc by wantonly summoning ghosts back. Imagine the damage you'd do if you knew the key to conjuring a bank robber or mad bomber or axe murderer."

"So you don't know what note will set up the right resonance," Venus said to Gethsemane.

She shook her head.

"Then how will you figure out what to play tonight?"

"I'll start with one of Eamon's pieces and go from there." She tried to keep her face neutral as she remembered the pain and swelling in her hands after her futile attempt at the piano to guess Eamon's resonance. She gestured toward the hall. "Shall we retire to the music room?"

Venus led the way. "Let the ghost music begin."

Eighteen

Eamon, Saoirse, and Venus crowded around Gethsemane. She stared at the Steinway. She'd performed in front of hundreds in packed auditoriums with less anxiety than she felt now. She breathed measured breaths in through her nose and out through her mouth. She clenched and unclenched her fists. Stats for the 1938 Atlanta Black Crackers marched through her head. Mel Carter, two thirty-seven, Bill Cooper, three oh four, Felix Evans, three seventy-five. The mathematical precision of the Negro League numbers calmed her down.

The electric shock of Eamon's hand on her shoulder zipped down her back. "I have faith in you," he said.

With a final deep breath and round of batting averages, she sat at the piano and nodded as Saoirse recited the incantation.

Gethsemane closed her eyes and concentrated. She imagined a ghost materializing to the notes of Eamon's "Jewel of Carraigfaire." Her fingers hovered over the Steinway's keys then pressed them, gently at first, then with more confidence. The lush romantic tones of the work he'd composed to celebrate his love for Orla filled the music room.

The music's last reverberation died away. Gethsemane, Venus, and Saoirse held their breaths. No one moved. Even Eamon seemed frozen. A silence as dreadful as the music was beautiful surrounded them. Audible ticking of the clock penetrated the hush and increased the angst.

"Try another," Eamon said after a few minutes.

She closed her eyes again. What kind of ghost did they need? One willing to help Eamon defeat a dark force. A ghost both willing and strong enough to help. A hero. Play something heroic. She played Tchaikovsky's "1812 Overture."

Nothing.

John Williams's Star Wars theme.

Nothing.

Williams's "The Imperial March."

"Darth Vader's theme?" Venus whispered. "Seriously?"

Eamon and Saoirse shushed her.

No ghost.

Verdi's "Gloria all'Egitto." Something as dread-filled as she felt: Barber's "Adagio for Strings."

Nothing again. She slammed the keyboard in frustration.

"Easy, darlin'," Eamon said.

She massaged her fingers. "It could be anything. Literally any sound. You came back in response to some rusted metal twisting in the wind."

"We can't give up," Saoirse said. "Maybe you should try the violin instead.

Gethsemane pressed the heels of her hands against her eyes and recited another round of baseball stats, then rose and retrieved her violin. "Someone suggest something."

Eamon spoke up. "'The Irish Rover.'"

Everyone stared.

Eamon shrugged. "It was Orla's favorite."

Gethsemane shouldered her violin and let the song's jolly notes fly.

"Nothing's hap—" Venus said.

Gethsemane silenced her with a raised hand. The aroma, the merest trace of white roses and vetiver, drifted in. Eamon's aura shown bright red.

The smell intensified to an almost palpable fragrance. A fragrance Gethsemane recognized. The twenty-five-year-old bottle with the gilt script still sat on her dresser. Maywinds.

"Orla," she said.

A flash exploded in a far corner. Gethsemane closed her eyes against the spotty after-image. She opened them and saw an elegant blonde with soulful brown eyes standing at the opposite side of the Steinway's cabinet. She saw details of pictures hung on the distant wall through the woman's torso.

"Orla McCarthy," she repeated.

"My heart," Eamon said. His voice choked.

"My love," Orla said to Eamon. She passed through the piano, the black wood bisecting her. Gethsemane jumped from her path as she exited the other side. She embraced her husband. Another flash filled the room. When Gethsemane opened her eyes, both ghosts were gone.

Gethsemane stretched out on the couch. Her head throbbed and after-images from the flashes in the music room still marred her vision. She squeezed her eyes shut.

Venus had taken Saoirse home in a cab. She planned to try to see Aed at the jail or get drunk at the Rabbit if she couldn't. She'd promised not to betray Hardy's secret.

Tonight's events stirred emotions Gethsemane struggled to decipher. Shock. King Tut's appearance would have startled her less than Orla's. Did not see that coming. Jealousy? She chewed on that. No. She liked Orla or, at least, Eamon's memory of her. His wife's loss had gutted her friend, and Gethsemane's heart ached for his sake. Worry. Worry floated through her mind looking for someplace to attach itself. Why worry? Because, what if...? Eamon must be over the moon about his wife's return. What if he and Orla were so happy together after so long apart that they forgot why Orla had been called over? Or decided they didn't care? Maja wasn't their problem. She couldn't hurt them, only the living.

The fragrance struck first. Powder, white roses, vetiver.

"Hello." Orla sat in an armchair across from the couch. She

appeared as solid as Gethsemane. She leaned back in the chair, long legs crossed at the knee. Her elbow disappeared into the chair's leather upholstery where she rested it. "Eamon told me about you." Her voice rang high and clear, as elegant as the rest of her.

"Slander, I'm sure," Gethsemane said.

"He described you as stubborn, willful, hard-headed, sarcastic, and utterly maddening."

What a way to endear her to the wife. "Thanks?"

"High praise coming from my husband. He never could abide weak, wishy-washy gowls. 'If you won't stand up for yourself, don't be surprised when someone knocks you down,' he used to say. He thought pushovers were unreliable and untrustworthy."

Maybe it wasn't such a backhanded compliment.

Orla continued. "He also described you as highly intelligent, attractive, dedicated, determined, and one of the most talented musicians he's ever known. And he said not to call you Sissy because you hate it."

"He described you to me," Gethsemane said.

"I can imagine. Stubborn, willful, and maddening?"

"His everything."

Silence reigned for a moment. Orla broke it. "Are you in love with him?"

"In love with Eamon? No. We're friends. But he's, you know."

Orla shook her head.

"Well, dead. And he doesn't have a body. Not a solid one, anyway."

Orla laughed. Gethsemane thought of songbirds. "He might be a little bit in love with you. I think I can see why."

Gethsemane blushed. "I've no intention of trying to come between you. I'm happy, for his sake, you're back. He missed you the way you'd miss your heart if someone cut it out."

Orla's turn to blush. Her embarrassed pink aura sparkled around its edges. "I didn't mean—I wasn't—really, I just wanted to thank you for looking after him. For being his friend."

"You're welcome. Although I have to admit the 'looking after' has been mutual." Especially when it came to morning coffee. A thought hit her. "You two aren't one of those married couples who only have married friends, are you? This isn't, 'Thanks for playing but we need four for bridge'?"

"No, we're not like that. Eamon and I are the old married couple who detests hanging around old married couples." Orla vanished then rematerialized on the couch. "Something else bothers you."

Gethsemane denied it.

Orla persisted. "I can tell. I see it on you. A faint shimmer, like you see on your southern highways at summer's peak."

The air quivered on hot, sticky days in the thick of Virginia summers. Humidity. Was telling her she shimmered Orla's nice way of saying she sweat? She checked an armpit.

Orla leaned closer. Faint outlines of the fire shown through her chest. "What's wrong?"

"Will you and Eamon try to stop Maja?"

Puzzlement distorted Orla's regular features. "Why wouldn't we?"

"Competing priorities. You just reunited with your husband after a quarter-century forced separation. No one could blame you if you left us mortals to fend for ourselves."

"I came back to help my husband defend people he cares about in the village we both love and call home against an invading force. We won't let Dunmullach down." Her aura morphed to a joyful red. "Besides, we'll have eternity to reacquaint ourselves after we send Maja packing back to hell."

At the theater, Maja raged.

Energy had gone from the atmosphere, sucked out like a yolk from a blown egg. A large dose of her strength went with it. A powerful force had entered the equation, one she'd have to deal with. They would try to stop her. They always tried to stop her. But she always won. She only had to bide her time until the dying started. Which one of their sons would succumb first? The one with the hat? The bearded redhead? Better for her if one of the young boys went. The young ones always worked best. Their deaths caused the most grief. The grief on which she fed. The grief that matched her own at being walled up in a desolate tower and left to starve. Her corpse denied a decent burial, left to rot. But she'd taught them a lesson, hadn't she? She revenged herself on the family who betrayed her. She'd continue to revenge herself upon generation after generation. She would rise from the ashes of despair and make them all rue her murder. She'd wait. Six hundred years taught her patience. A firstborn would die soon enough...

In the meantime, she needed sustenance. A boost to replace what was taken from her. Luckily, that loud woman with the ridiculous hair left several of her silly gadgets scattered about.

An EMF pod lit up. It shone as bright as daylight for a few moments then dimmed as Maja fed. She flicked a blue orb at the spent pod. It burst to pieces.

Gethsemane passed a terrible night. Nightmare followed nightmare. Murderous ghosts chased students through carnival fun house theaters while she played the piano until her fingers bled trying to find the sympathetic vibration to banish the ghost. Music critics bearing plates of rancid truffles lurched about with construction tools protruding from their foreheads.

She gave up on sleep and made her own coffee downstairs. An eerie stillness toyed with the base of her neck. No sign of Eamon and Orla, and it was none of her business where they were. Too many questions might lead to the TMI zone. Venus hadn't come home but texted to say she remained among the living.

A shower restored some sense of being human. She went to the hospital to check on Niall, but the cadre of gardaí clustered around his door convinced her to settle for a nurse's assurances that the inspector "hung in there." She hoped for better luck seeing Frankie in the infirmary.

Nineteen

Gethsemane turned on the road to St. Brennan's. Sylvie stepped out of a shop several yards ahead.

"Sylvie! Mademoiselle Babin!" Gethsemane shouted to get the other woman to stop.

"I ain't got nothing to say to y'all," the diva drawled. French toast had given way to Georgia peach.

"You spoke to Venus?"

"That writer with the too-bright lipstick and those ridiculous heels? No, and I'm not speaking to you, either." Sylvie resumed walking.

Gethsemane followed. "Please, mademoiselle."

"You know my name's Sadie. Did y'all think y'all could dig up my past without me finding out whose hands held the shovel? In a town the size of Attapulgus? I have friends, too."

"Sadie, please. A moment of your time. Tell me again how you met Bernard."

"I don't want to talk about that toad." She turned to walk back to the shop.

"Not the details. Just about the restaurant you said he reviewed. Josephine's, wasn't it?"

"Why do you care about a French restaurant that closed two weeks after it opened?"

"Closed. After Bernard's bad review?"

"Yes, and some others." Sylvie/Sadie stepped closer to

Gethsemane and scrutinized her with one eye closed, the way Gethsemane's grandma used to do when she suspected she or her siblings had been in her pantry. "What's this about? Not food."

Gethsemane persisted. "Did Bernard say why he wanted to get out of the restaurant review business and switch to music reviewing?"

"Not in detail, no. I assumed it was because my friend edited a music magazine. If my friend had edited an auto mechanics rag, Bernard would have gone after a job as an automotive reviewer."

"He didn't mention anything, gave no specific reason, why he didn't want to write about food anymore? You were in Paris, the food capital of the world. No shortage of review opportunities."

"One time he babbled about the food industry being fickle, people turning on you, that kind of thing. We were at my apartment getting drunk after a performance of 'Tosca.' Drunk on brandy I paid for." Sylvie tapped her chest with her thumb. "I recall him mentioning something about people blaming you for things that weren't your fault. Same things we all say when the world ceases to operate the way we want it to. I guessed he'd been fired and thought he didn't deserve to be."

"Did he say why he was fired?"

"No, or if he did, I was too drunk to pay attention. Did there have to be a reason? Publishing's as fickle as music."

"Did he tell you he used to write under the byline Ben Schlossberg?"

That stunned her. Sylvie gawped. "Ben Schlossberg? No, he certainly never told me he wrote as Ben Schlossberg."

"He wrote most of his food reviews under that name."

"Y'all don't say? Seems I'm not the only one around here with a secret past."

Far from it. "Think. Try to remember. Did Bernard say anything at all that might give a hint why he changed his name as well as his career?"

"I've no clue," Sylvie said. "I could hazard a guess sprung from the well of personal experience. Maybe he was hiding from an enraged ex-lover. As one of the enraged, I'd have gone after him if I thought I could've gotten away with it. Or maybe an ex-lover's cuckolded ex-husband wanted his head on a platter."

"He really left a wake of destruction, didn't he?"

"Like a nuclear missile."

Gethsemane climbed back on her bike. "Thank you for your time. I won't hold you up any longer. I've got to get to the infirmary to check on my friend and my students."

"That weird sickness from the theater? I'm sorry about all that. Such young boys affected. How are they doing?"

"Holding their own, from what I've heard. I haven't seen them for myself yet."

She'd only pedaled a few feet when a voice called her back. "Hey."

Sylvie jogged up to her. "I just thought of something. Maybe Ben Schlossberg became Bernard Stoltz because Ben couldn't get another job. Maybe he'd been blacklisted, stricken from the rolls of reliable food reviewers."

"Why would he be blacklisted?"

"I dunno. Maybe one of the restaurants he reviewed gave someone ptomaine poisoning."

St. Brennan's had last filled its twelve-bed infirmary in 1918 when the great influenza pandemic struck. Since that time, all its beds, save one or two used for the occasional boy with gastroenteritis or chicken pox, lay empty. Until now. Boys of all ages, all firstborn sons, all suffering from unexplained wasting—failure to thrive in her mother's medical books—occupied eleven beds and two cots brought in to accommodate the overflow. Frankie occupied the twelfth. His red hair seemed brighter against his pallor, and his normally bright green eyes appeared dull and bloodshot.

Gethsemane pulled up a chair next to his bed. "How do you feel?"

"Worse than I look. How do I look?"

"Um, well..."

"That bad."

"Has the doctor been around? What did she say?"

"She uses lots of fancy doctor terms that all mean she's got no idea what's got hold of us."

No surprise. The typical med school curriculum didn't cover spirit possession.

"She's talking about calling in consultants from WHO and the American CDC."

And they'll come, ask questions, order tests, then go home without finding a solution. But they'll get a nice case report write-up. She fished in her bag. "I brought you this."

"My MP3 player." Frankie took the device. "Thank you."

"And these." She handed him a set of earbuds. "Don't want to get in trouble with the nurse for disturbing the peace with loud music."

Frankie smiled.

"I loaded it up with Miles Davis."

"You're starting to scare me."

"You would have preferred Coltrane?"

He barked a weak laugh. "You're being nice. Say something snarky or I'll think I'm dying."

"Fresh out of snark today. I'll hit you up with a double dose when you get out of here." When. Not if. Eamon and Orla had to beat Maja. The alternative...

"Jaysus, Mary, and Joseph, are those tears? I really am dyin'."

She punched his leg through the thin hospital-style blanket. "Don't flatter yourself, Grennan. You wish I'd cry for you."

"That's the mean Sissy I know and love."

She glanced around to make sure the nurse wasn't watching then pinched him. Hard.

"Ouch." He laughed as he jerked his arm away. "Now I feel better. You'd never attack a dying man."

"Dr. Brown."

Gethsemane recognized Ruairi's voice. She turned to see him

seated at the far end of the ward between two beds. Colm lay in one and Feargus the second. Aengus sat on Feargus's other side.

"Hey, guys." She excused herself to Frankie and went over to the boys. Colm and Feargus shared the math teacher's pallor. Blond-haired Colm seemed to disappear against the white bedsheets. Aengus's brawn contrasted so much with his brother's wasting, if Gethsemane hadn't known they were twins she wouldn't have guessed they were related. Thin, wiry Ruairi seemed the picture of health. She dug her nails into her palm to keep the tears at bay. Jokes weren't enough. "I'm sorry you're not feeling well. I miss you in class."

Ruairi tapped Colm's shoulder. "Tell her."

"Tell me what, Colm?"

"I tried to call our parents, but I couldn't reach them and the nurse won't let me call again. Not unless I tell her why I want to speak to them."

Gethsemane leaned close to the boy. "But you're going to tell me why you want to speak to them, aren't you?" She suspected it wasn't to ask them to bring him a teddy bear.

"About Saoirse. She came to see me."

"When did she come by?"

"A little while ago. She had one of Father Tim's weird books. She said she was going to do something to get rid of this sickness."

"Do what?" She didn't need to do anything. Eamon and Orla could handle it. "Where's Saoirse now?"

"We don't know," Aengus said. "Ruairi and I looked all over for her, but she's nowhere."

"The devil couldn't find her if she didn't want to be found," Colm said.

"I peeked at her book," Feargus whispered. "I learned enough at my Latin lessons to see it had something to do with magic."

"Which is why I can't tell the nurse to let me use the phone. She'll think I'm a header." Colm squeezed Gethsemane's hand. "Will you look for Saoirse? Please?"

"I don't have to look for her, Colm. I'm pretty sure I know

where she is."

"Damn it." Gethsemane recognized the SUV parked on a side street opposite the Athaneum. Kent said he'd finished with Dunmullach. What changed his mind?

She expected to find the entire *Ghost Hunting Adventures* entourage when she entered the auditorium but saw only Ciara and Poe. They snapped pictures of empty corners, pausing every now and then to change cameras.

"What are you two doing here?" Gethsemane asked. "Kent said you were leaving."

"Kent said." Poe aimed an old-fashioned flash camera at Gethsemane and depressed the shutter button. Gethsemane flinched as the bright pop of the flash temporarily blinded her. The click-whir of the shutter sounded loud in the otherwise silent auditorium. Poe advanced the film and loaded another flash bulb.

Ciara pushed Poe's camera down. "We are leaving. Kent and Hardy and the others are packing now. But Poe and I just had to have one more go at Maja Zoltán or whatever this is."

"You know it's Maja," Poe said.

"I know it's making children sick, and I'm not okay with that," Ciara said. "Isn't there something Poe and I can do to help you stop it?"

"Speak for yourself." Poe moved off to take more pictures.

"You started the party without me." Venus stepped out of the shadows of the wings onto the stage. "Or am I unforgivably late?" She stopped halfway to center stage and retraced her steps. She reached behind the curtain. "You, too, party girl." She pulled Saoirse onto the stage and put her arm around the girl.

Gethsemane climbed onto the stage and grabbed the girl by the shoulders. "Saoirse, go home. Now. I know all about your spell book. Colm, Ruairi, and the twins told me what you were up to. Not happening."

"You don't understand—" Saoirse began.

"I understand this is no place for you. I don't care how brilliant you are or how prescient you are or how old you think you are, you're twelve and this is dangerous."

"Dangerous for Mr. and Mrs. McCarthy."

For Eamon and Orla? "Dangerous for them how?"

Saoirse pulled a leather-bound book, smaller than the one she'd brought to the cottage, from her pocket. Latin letters in faded gilt marched along its spine. "Book Two. It contains the second part of that spell, the part that explains the consequences. If the McCarthys unite to create enough energy to overload Maja and blast her into the netherworld—"

"Maybe we should discuss this somewhere—" Venus began.

Too late. "That's a cheap shot, brat." Poe cursed and scowled down at Saoirse. "Maja can't help what she is."

"Back off, Poe," Venus said. "You want to get in someone's face, pick a face that belongs to someone your own size."

"You?" Poe snorted and craned her neck. "You're nobody's size."

"You little—"

Gethsemane pushed between the statuesque author and blue-haired photographer. "Stop it, both of you. A fist fight won't help."

Venus stepped back. "But it'd make me feel better."

Ciara, hands on her hips, cocked her head at her colleague. "Poe! Maja's infected half this village with her poison or anger or whatever. Children, Poe. She's sickened children. Someone needs to stop her. Someone needs to fight for the children."

"Not me." Poe fiddled with a camera lens. "I don't even like kids."

Gethsemane looked back and forth between Saoirse and the ghost hunters. What the hell? They'd see proof of Eamon and Orla's existence soon enough. "Don't mind Poe. Finish what you were telling us, Saoirse. What do you mean the spell has a second part?"

"It was split between two books. Like in that movie about the magician where the warning about the spell was on the page after the spell so the magician recites it without knowing—"

"The short version, kid," Venus said. "We're trying to avoid Dunmullach's own Armageddon. We're on a tight timeline."

The girl opened the book and displayed a page full of Latin lettering and cryptic symbols. "If Mr. and Mrs. McCarthy short-circuit Maja, they'll burn themselves out."

"Burn out, like," Venus searched for a word, "burn out?"

"They'll use up all of their energy. There won't be any left for them to use. They'll stop existing."

"Are you sure, Saoirse?"

"Pretty sure. The book's handwritten, so some of the words are hard to make out. But I'm pretty sure. Like ninety percent."

"What do we do?" Venus asked.

"You do exactly as you planned," Ciara said. "I'm sorry if these ghosts are—friends—of yours, but children's lives are at stake. Living children. Nothing's more important."

"It's not up to you, Ms. Save the Children." Poe laughed. "The ghosts get to decide for themselves. Maybe they're not as selfless as you are."

Ciara knelt in front of Saoirse and held her by the arms. "Sweetheart, isn't there something in your little book to force the ghosts to go through with it?" Her grip tightened. "Some spell that puts them in your power, so you can make them do what you say?"

"No, ma'am." Saoirse yanked her arms free and backed away from her.

"Finally, something you can't be the boss of, Ciara," Poe said.

Saoirse mumbled, "There might be a loophole." No one paid attention to her.

Poe jammed a hand into a cargo pants pocket and pulled out a phone. A phone Gethsemane hadn't seen her with before. A phone that looked a bit like Hardy's special one. Poe swept it across the scene, capturing a panorama.

"You're recording this?" Venus asked.

"Nothing will show up," Gethsemane said. "It never does."

Pure malice lit up Poe's smile. "You think Hardy's the only one who gets special cameras?"

Gethsemane lunged at Poe. She grasped air as Poe dodged.

Poe sneered. "Nice try, school teacher. But I didn't bring Maja back to have nothing to show for it. Bet I get a million hits after I upload this."

"You brought her back?" Ciara flew at her. She missed and crashed into a chair. "How? Why?"

"Why?" Gethsemane said. "Because she's bat shit crazy. How?" She stepped toward Poe. "With the grimoire you stole from Father Tim." No point in telling her about the overture and the aria and sympathetic resonance. God only knew who she'd call up if she had all the ingredients for ghost conjuring.

"I borrowed the book. I gave it back."

"He took it back. But not before you had time to do a little speed reading. Or did you take a photograph?"

"Whatev—"

A noise from Ciara cut Poe off. She rushed the younger photographer again. Poe bobbed out of reach just before Ciara's fingers closed around a handful of blue hair.

"Easy," Poe said.

"Poe, I swear—"

"Shh." Gethsemane held up a hand. "This conversation is about to become academic." She pointed at the blue haze that formed in a rear corner of the stage.

"What are you pointing at?" Ciara asked. "I don't see anything."

"Me neither," Poe muttered. She moved toward the stage and shouted. "Maja Zoltán, show yourself to me! I'm on your side. You wouldn't be here without me."

"Some claim to fame," Venus said.

Poe swore and glared at Gethsemane. "Why do you get to see her and I don't?"

"Clean living."

Gethsemane and Venus watched as the haze grew dense and morphed, first into an outline, then a transparent shade, then the solid form of an enraged Maja. Her eyes blazed red and her hair flew around her in a whirlwind fury. A blue aura enrobed her. Sparks popped and sizzled, and orbs twice as powerful—and deadly—as any Eamon ever launched hovered at her fingertips.

"Game on," Venus said.

"Where're your goody-goody ghosts?" Poe called from the rear of the auditorium where she'd taken refuge from Ciara. She continued filming with her phone's camera. "Did they decide they preferred to exist after all?"

A blast of leather and soap comingled with white roses and vetiver filled the theater. Gethsemane collapsed against a wall with relief. "You came."

"We're here, darlin'," Eamon's voice boomed through the auditorium. He materialized center stage. "You knew we wouldn't let you down."

Orla materialized next to her husband. "Go back to hell, Maja. You can't claim our fellas."

"What's happening?" Ciara asked. She stared where Gethsemane and Venus stared. "What's happening?" She turned to Saoirse. "Sweetheart, can't you do something to let me see what's going on?"

Saoirse shook her head. "I can't see them, either."

"Orla McCarthy told the bitch to eff off," Venus said. She glanced at Saoirse and apologized. "I mean, Mrs. McCarthy asked Maja to go away." She turned to Gethsemane. "Can't we help? We must be able to do something."

Maja spoke words neither of them understood.

"Does anyone know what that means in English?" Venus asked.

"Duck," Orla said.

A blue orb grazed Venus's head and exploded against the floor. The force of the blast knocked Venus flat. Ciara screamed.

"I saw that! I saw that!" Poe shouted from her vantage away from the line of fire. "That's so cool. So effin' cool. I totally got that on camera." Another orb landed on a chair a foot from the blue-haired photographer. Wisps of smoke rose from the singe mark on the velvet. "Hey," Poe said. "Watch it. I voted for you."

Gethsemane helped Venus stand. "Get Saoirse out of here," she said to Ciara.

"Why don't they do something?" Tears ran down Ciara's cheeks. "Why don't they stop her?" She pulled Saoirse to her and held her close.

Orla extended a hand to Eamon.

"Don't they deserve to hear the truth before they destroy themselves?" Poe shouted.

Ciara screamed at her. "Shut up! Shut up! Shut up!" She pushed Saoirse away and leapt from the stage. Poe dropped her phone and ran for the balcony, Ciara close behind her. Venus and Gethsemane dodged orbs which exploded around them in protest at missing their targets. Saoirse crept from the stage and retrieved Poe's phone.

"What's she on about?" Eamon gestured at Poe. "What truth?"

They had a right to know. "Saoirse's fairly certain—almost positive—that if you and Orla take out Maja, you also take yourselves out. Permanently."

"And if we don't..." Eamon said.

Then Niall, Frankie, Colm, Feargus, all the others...Gethsemane ducked behind a curtain as another orb went off nearby.

"Don't is irrelevant, my love," Orla said. "Because we will. How could I spend the rest of eternity knowing I let that creature destroy this village? That wouldn't be any kind of existence at all." She held her arms out to Eamon.

Eamon's dimples worked overtime as his aura radiated an ecstatic crimson. He spoke to Gethsemane but had eyes only for his wife. "Take care of yourself, darlin'. The cottage, too. Meeting you's been the second-best thing that's ever happened to me." He walked to Orla, his feet moving through the floor like a samurai sword through silk tissue. Her hands, arms, and body melded into his as he embraced her. He bent his head to kiss her, and the two became one.

Light exploded like a thousand of Poe's flashbulbs going off at once. Circuits in the theater sizzled, then the lights went out. A shockwave began as a faint tremble, then broadened and expanded and rolled out over the stage, flattening Venus and Gethsemane in the wings and Saoirse in the orchestra section's front row.

Ciara and Poe both swore. Gethsemane heard their footsteps thundering as they ran down from the balcony. The theater lights snapped on. She raised her head and looked around. Center stage stood empty. No Eamon, no Orla, no Maja. Venus stirred near the curtains opposite. Where was—"Saoirse?" Gethsemane called out. She rolled to the edge of the stage.

The girl lay face down near the orchestra pit.

Gethsemane dragged herself up and half-crawled down the stairs to where Saoirse lay. Venus followed. Ciara and Poe joined them.

"Is she...?" Poe let the question trail off.

Gethsemane laid a hand on Saoirse's back. She felt her torso rise and fall. Still breathing. She whispered her name. "Saoirse?"

She couldn't decipher the muffled reply.

Louder. "Saoirse?"

"I'm okay," the girl said, without raising her head. She worked her arm out from underneath her, slowly, something grasped tight in her fingers.

Poe noticed it first. "That's mine." She grabbed at Saoirse. Ciara grabbed Poe.

Saoirse held her arm aloft, Poe's phone in hand, like a runner holding the Olympic torch on its last lap before lighting the cauldron. "I got them," she said. "I got them."

Twenty

"What do you mean, 'you got them'?" Gethsemane asked.

Saoirse sat huddled in an orchestra seat. She clutched Poe's phone to her chest and kept a wary eye on the phone's owner. Venus ran interference between the two, bobbing and weaving to block Poe's attempts to retrieve her device.

"Mr. and Mrs. McCarthy are in here." Saoirse tapped a finger on the phone's edge. "On the SD card."

"Is the kid saying she's got ghosts in the machine?" Venus feigned right. Poe smashed into her.

"What are you saying, Saoirse?" Gethsemane asked. "That you recorded Eamon and Orla destroying Maja or that you've literally got Eamon and Orla McCarthy trapped inside a smartphone?"

"The second part. They're on the SD card."

Gethsemane held up two fingers. "Look at me, Saoirse. How many fingers—"

Venus halted her dance with Poe long enough to stare at Gethsemane. "We've seen a woman who's been dead for six hundred years visit a plague on the firstborns of the village, dodged orbs like dinosaurs in a meteor shower, and watched two ghosts use the nuclear option, and you're having trouble believing the genius?"

Good point. "Can you explain what you did in simple terms that a merely not-too-dumb person like me can understand?"

"I deciphered another spell in that." She pointed at the leather tome, forgotten in the excitement, lying open and face down against the orchestra pit rail. Ciara picked it up. "Once, alchemists used to trap ghosts in devices they made out of copper, quartz, and silica."

The clock-like device Father Tim told her about. The horologist's spirit catcher. What did he say? Something about trouble getting the spirits out of the device once you'd gotten them in. Why hadn't she paid more attention?

"I tried making one of the devices, but I ran out of time. Then I realized that the stuff they used was the same kind of stuff used in an SD card. When Miss Poe dropped her phone, I grabbed it and recited the spell over it. I would have used yours, Dr. Brown, but it's got crap memory. I didn't know how many bytes ghosts would need. Poe has a terabyte."

Plus a little something extra by way of MIT. Maybe Hardy's spirit was looking out for them. Gethsemane said a silent thank you.

Poe lunged at Saoirse. Venus stuck out a foot and tripped her.

Poe protested. "It's my phone."

"Say that one more time and I'll feed it to you," Venus promised.

"We don't need the whole phone," Gethsemane said. "Do we?" she asked Saoirse.

Saoirse shook her head. "Just the card."

Gethsemane opened the phone and pulled out the card.

"That's my evidence," Poe snatched at the card.

Gethsemane stiff armed her. "These are my friends."

Venus snorted. "Don't think Poe's familiar with the concept."

"Give me my phone," Poe demanded.

Gethsemane let it fall to the ground. Poe tried to scoop it up, but Gethsemane's heel found it first. She ground it to pieces. "Oops."

Poe cried out and scrambled to collect the remnants. Tears moistened her lashes as she gently placed shattered bits into various pockets in her cargo pants.

Gethsemane handed Saoirse the card. "Do you know how to recover the McCarthys?"

"Not yet. Once I figured out the alchemical formulas for the trap, the binding spell was easy but the release spell, well, some of the formulas don't make sense. I think an equation is missing. The one to reverse the silica bond." Saoirse slipped the tiny memory storage device in her pocket. "But I can figure it out. At least, I'm pretty sure I can figure it out." She lowered her gaze and her voice. "I hope I can figure it out."

"I've got faith in you, kid." Venus patted her on the back. "You're who I want to be when I grow up."

"Then let's get out of here," Gethsemane said. "I want to get Saoirse home, then get over to the infirmary and hospital to see how everyone's doing." Everyone had to be better. If Eamon and Orla had sacrificed themselves for nothing...

"I need my book." Saoirse slipped out of the seat and over to the railing to pick up the spell book.

Ciara shouted. "Look out!"

Gethsemane, Venus, Poe, and Saoirse froze. Ciara flung herself at Saoirse and pushed her out of the way seconds before a large piece of plywood, damaged by one of Maja's orbs, tumbled from the prop castle. It speared the place where Saoirse crouched just before Ciara pushed her out of the way.

Ciara's momentum carried her forward. She banged her head on the pit rail and fell back, stunned. A trickle of blood stained her silver hair pink. The other women rushed to her.

"Jesus, Ci, are you okay?" Poe asked, animosity set aside.

"I'll call an ambulance," Gethsemane said.

"No, no, please don't do that." Ciara shrugged off Venus's attempt to keep her seated and stood up. "I'm not seriously hurt. If I go to the hospital they might want to keep me. I don't want to spend the night there."

Gethsemane understood the feeling.

"I just want to go back to my room and lie down." Ciara accepted the rag Poe produced from her gear bag and pressed it against her forehead. "We leave tomorrow. No offense, Dr. Brown, but I've had enough of your charming village. I'm ready to get on with my life. Poe, will you drive me back to Sweeney's?"

"I'm going to the pub. I'm going to get mind-bogglingly drunk. How do you say that in Irish?"

"Stocious. Ossified. Plastered. Fluthered. Langered," Gethsemane said. "You have options."

"I want all those." She turned to Ciara. "You can take the SUV." She held her hand out to Saoirse. "I want my card back."

"You can't have it," Gethsemane said.

Poe responded with words a twelve-year-old shouldn't hear, collected her cameras, and stormed from the auditorium.

"I'm not up to driving," Ciara said.

Gethsemane offered to drive. "We'll walk back to the cottage. Or call a cab," she added before Venus could protest.

Ciara leaned hard on Gethsemane's arm as Gethsemane and Venus escorted her to her room. Her head had stopped bleeding. A reddish-brown crust spread along her hairline and flaked off in her hair.

"I must look a right mess," she said.

"You look like a woman who just saved a child from death by impalement." Venus used Ciara's key to let them into the room, then volunteered to go for ice.

Gethsemane pushed aside a half-packed suitcase and lowered Ciara onto the edge of the bed. "Do you want me to call Kent?"

"No, don't. He and some of the others went to return rental vehicles. We only need the SUV and a sedan to get everyone to the airport. He'll be worried enough when he gets back and sees me. No point scaring him with a phone call."

"Where are you going? To the States? On another ghost hunt?"

"I'm done with ghosts for a while. Kent's going back home to New York. I'm headed to New Zealand. I need to get away, to rest, and New Zealand's on my bucket list."

"You and Kent aren't—"

Ciara shrugged. "It was fun while it lasted. But, between us women, Kent's getting too old for me." She laughed, then winced. "My head."

"Have you got any aspirin or ibuprofen? If not, I can run and see if the front desk has some."

"Paracetamol's in my dopp kit by the bathroom sink." She stood.

Gethsemane waved her back to her seat. In the dim light with blood-stained hair, Ciara seemed to have aged twenty years since Gethsemane saw her that first day with her hand on Kent's arm. Her eyes appeared sunken, skin hung loose under her chin. Deep sulci in her shoulders highlighted her collar bones. She looked as if she'd lost weight. "I'll get it," Gethsemane said.

She rummaged through the kit for the paracetamol—acetaminophen in the US. She set several other pill bottles aside. Prednisone, ferrous sulfate, ondansetron. She found the over-the-counter pain killer in the bottom of the bag, next to something else. A bottle of sufentanil, a powerful sublingual prescription pain medication. A narcotic. Why would Ciara have such strong meds? She seemed to be one of the heartiest members of the crew. Gethsemane studied the labels. The name of the person they were prescribed for had been blacked out with a marker. Were they Ciara's prescriptions? Or had she obtained them illegally? Gethsemane read the drug names again. Sufentanil certainly had street value. Maybe prednisone did—the milligrams on the label indicated a high dose. But ondansetron? Her sister had taken the medicine for severe vomiting with her pregnancy. Was it something addicts used to fight withdrawal symptoms? And ferrous sulfate, a fancy name for iron tablets. What possible abuse potential could iron tablets have?

Ciara called from the other room. "Are you all right in there? Did you find it?"

Gethsemane stuffed the other bottles back in the bag. "Right here." She handed Ciara the paracetamol and a glass of water.

"Thank you." Ciara downed the pills in a single gulp. "I'll feel better with that and a nap."

Venus returned with a bucket of ice and some towels. "Snagged 'em off the maid's cart."

Gethsemane wrapped some ice in a towel and she and Venus left Ciara lying down with an ice pack on her head.

"What's wrong?" Venus asked as they headed down the hall. "You've got that 'something's bothering me but I can't think what' look."

"Ciara's got more going on than a headache." She described the meds she'd found.

"Sufentanil. Wow. I remember a story I did on prescription narcotic diversion. Stuff's no joke. It's stronger than fentanyl. It's used for people who are dying. What's she using it for?"

"She asked for paracetamol."

"Maybe it's not hers. Maybe it's boy toy's. If she hooks him up, maybe that's the attraction."

"You think Bernard found out she's dealing? Maybe he was blackmailing her. Or Kent. Having the news break that your girlfriend and photographer sells drugs or that you use them couldn't be good for ratings."

"Drug exposés are off Bernard's usual beat," Venus said. "But I wouldn't put anything past that snake."

"One problem. Well, two. Ciara doesn't have enough of a supply to be a serious dealer, and Kent doesn't behave like an opiate addict. He's never late to work, nor absent. He's never strung out. And he's intense, not mellow or euphoric like you'd expect someone high on opiates to be. Intense like a cocaine user, maybe, but not opiates." Gethsemane pulled out her phone.

"Who are you calling?"

"I'm texting my mother. She's a physician. Maybe she can tell me what that combination of meds might be used for. In the meantime, between murderous ghosts and murdered journalists—"

"If you can call Bernard a journalist."

"—I've got enough to deal with. I still haven't found anything that points away from Aed as the killer."

"You've found plenty to point to everybody else as equally

suspicious. Including me."

"The gardaí won't want to hear, 'I found a dozen other birds in the bush so let the one in hand go.' They'll want to hear, 'The man you've got couldn't possibly have done it because this other fella's guilty.' Maybe 'want' isn't the right word, but you get my meaning."

"You've done the best you could."

"I promised Hardy I'd do better. Speaking of whom, we should check on him while we're here," Gethsemane said. "He looked rough last time I saw him. In all honesty, I worried he wouldn't make it."

They approached the front desk. Gethsemane recognized the clerk as the one who'd given her Kent's—Konrad's—room number. The haunted house fan. "Good to see you again."

"Hello, Miss. If you're looking for Mr. Wayne—"

"Actually, this time I'm looking for Hardy Lewis, one of Mr. Wayne's colleagues. He's been ill. We want to check on him, see how he's doing."

"You mean the fella who looks like walking death? He should be in hospital."

"You know how stubborn men can be," Venus said.

The clerk giggled. "Don't I just? You could cut my husband's arm off and he'd tell you he'd be fine with paracetamol and plasters. My brothers are just as bad."

Gethsemane leaned closer to the desk. "I know you're not supposed to give out room numbers but..."

"But, seeing as how it's you and seeing as how sick Mr. Lewis is..." The clerk checked her computer monitor. "Room seventeen. Maybe you can convince him to go to A and E. He'd get head of line privileges, as bad as he looks." She lowered her voice. "Don't want guests dying in the rooms. Bad publicity."

Gethsemane and Venus thanked the clerk and started down the hall.

The clerk called after them. "Oh, Ms. James, an envelope came for you." She reached under the counter and pulled out a large, thick manila envelope. "We hoped you'd return to stay with us so we held it for you instead of sending it on."

"Thank you," Venus said and tucked the package under her arm.

Gethsemane led the way to room seventeen. She knocked. "Hardy? Are you there? It's Gethsemane and Venus. We wanted to check on you, see if you felt better. Hardy?" She knocked again. "Hardy?"

"He could have gone out."

"As sick as he was, I'm amazed he could stand up, never mind go anywhere." She repeated the knocking. A guest next door stuck his head into the hall. "You didn't notice if the guy in this room went out, by any chance?" she asked him.

The man shrugged. "If he's in there, he's been quiet. Haven't heard any noise other than your pounding." He pulled his head back in.

"Let's get the manager," Gethsemane said.

"And if he's taking a nap, we'll look stupid for bothering him."

"And if he's lying unconscious with a fever of a hundred and four, we'll look stupid for not bothering him."

They retreated to the front desk and returned with a manager and a key. "Should I dial 999?" the manager asked as she slipped the card in and out of the electronic reader.

"Let's see how he is first. He may not need an ambulance."

The manager opened the door.

Hardy Lewis did not need an ambulance. Hardy Lewis was plainly dead. He lay in the middle of the floor with a knife protruding out of his chest. His phone—the remains of his phone—lay smashed and scattered beside him.

Twenty-One

The next few hours blurred in the now-familiar ritual of going to the garda station to give a statement about a recently discovered dead body. Several of the guards greeted Gethsemane by name as she passed by them on her way to the interview room. She took it as a sign of her rising status that she only waited twenty-five minutes for someone to remember her instead of the usual ninety. She recognized the officer from the Athaneum the day she—Eamon—found Bernard's body.

"Inspector Bill Something, isn't it?" She shook his hand. "We've met."

"Sutton." He pulled out a chair and sat opposite. "You know how this works, so the floor is yours."

Gethsemane described finding Hardy. "He'd been so sick. I half expected to find him laid out from his illness, but stabbed? No, to save you from asking, I have no idea who'd want to stab him. He was a decent guy. Always willing to lend a hand, do the jobs no one else wanted. Poe, I can imagine someone stabbing. The line forms on the right. Kent, maybe. But not Hardy."

"Poe?"

"Blue hair, cargo pants, camera, bad attitude."

"Have you seen Poe tonight?"

"She's at the Rabbit learning new slang words for drunk."

"You were at the pub this evening?" He flipped through his notes.

"Sorry, no. I'm tired and upset, and I apologize for being flip. I saw Poe some hours ago. She said she planned to go to the pub. I assumed she followed through on her plan."

"Where did you actually lay eyes on her last?"

"At the Athaneum." Where her otherworldly friends had destroyed themselves to save guys like Hardy.

"We had some calls about strange noises at the Athaneum earlier this evening." He flipped more pages. "What do you know about that?"

"We—myself, Venus, Ciara, and Poe—were there. Ciara and Poe were trying to capture paranormal evidence on film. We, uh, tried to help them out by making noises to trigger a spectral manifestation. No luck though." No reason to mention Saoirse's presence.

"What time did you get there?"

"Early-ish. Around five."

"And you and the other three women all remained at the Athaneum for how long?"

An eternity. "A couple of hours." She anticipated his next question. "No, none of us left. The four of us were together until Poe headed for the pub and Venus and I drove Ciara back to the inn."

"None of the male investigators were present?"

"No. Ciara said they were packing. The crew is planning to leave tomorrow."

"That remains to be seen. You and Ms. James went to the inn to check on Hardy—"

Gethsemane corrected him. "No, we went to Sweeney's to drop Ciara Tierney off. She bumped her head and wasn't feeling well and wanted to lie down. Since we were there, I decided to check on Hardy."

"And you saw no one near his room?"

"Just the guy next door who complained I knocked too loudly."

"And you saw nothing in his room—"

"Except him lying on the floor with a smashed phone and a

knife in his chest."

"Did you touch anything in the room?"

"Venus checked his pulse. I called you guys."

"A number you've memorized by now." Sutton closed his notebook. "Any idea how to get in touch with Mr. Lewis's family?"

"I know how to contact his father. Go downstairs to your holding cells and speak to Aed Devlin. He's Hardy's dad."

Inspector Sutton narrowed his eyes. "Are you coddin' me?"

"Aed didn't know. I mean, he knew he had a son. But he didn't know it was Hardy. He and Hardy's mother never married, and Aed left when Hardy was less than six months old."

"Devlin's the one man who couldn't have killed Hardy. Being locked up downstairs gives him a solid alibi." He drummed his fingers on the table. "Niall said you had a habit of doing this."

"Doing what?"

"Monkeying about in people's investigations, bollixing them up."

"Bollix how?" For once, she'd stayed away from the gardaí. With her only police ally in the hospital, keeping her snooping on the down-low seemed wise.

"You've taken my nice, tidy, already arrested the prime suspect case and turned it into a double homicide by person or persons unknown."

"You're suggesting the two murders are connected."

"Not suggesting, stating. You think we've got two people running around the village stabbing fellas? You're sure you don't have any idea who might've stabbed them?"

"None. And I don't know of any connection between Hardy and Bernard."

"He didn't write any nasty articles about anybody? Hardy, I mean."

"I don't think he wrote. Tech was his thing. Lighting, sound, cameras."

"Maybe he took some dirty pictures of someone." Sutton stood. "That's all for now. You'll make yourself available if we need anything else." A statement. Not a question.

"Before you go, have you heard how Niall's doing?"

"I have. Spoke to him about an hour ago. He's coming 'round. Seems this dose he got's going away as sudden as it came on."

Relief hit Gethsemane like a gut punch. She gasped.

"Are you all right?" Sutton asked.

"I'm fine. I just, I'm fine." She couldn't force the grin from her face. She was about to ask if Niall was allowed to have non-garda visitors when the new message alert sounded on her phone.

"I'll let you get that." Sutton excused himself.

She looked at the message ID. A Virginia number. Her mother. She tapped the envelope icon. Her mother, always economical in her speech, had texted a single word in response to Gethsemane's inquiry about Ciara's meds: *cancer.*

Dawn broke as the uniformed garda dropped Gethsemane and Venus at Carraigfaire. Venus offered to make coffee.

"Poor Hardy." Gethsemane collapsed into a kitchen chair. "Wonder if he lived long enough to realize the curse was broken?" Had he felt better before being stabbed or had he died miserable?

Venus sat across from her. "Did the cops give you any idea of when he was murdered?"

"No. Did they say anything to you?"

Venus shook her head. "I did trick a good-looking sergeant into telling me the knife came from the inn's kitchen. So Aed is the only one in the clear. Anyone could have gone to the inn and stabbed Hardy, including you and me."

"Not me. Why would I kill Hardy?"

"Why would anyone? He didn't philander, steal, blackmail, bully. He didn't keep secrets."

"Except the huge one about his paternity." Gethsemane went to the study and retrieved Hardy's envelope from the desk. She handed it to Venus.

Venus opened the envelope and held up a photo. "Is this...?"

She handed it to Gethsemane.

Gethsemane studied the photo. A young man, barely out of his teens, sat on a bench in front of a grand piano on stage in an empty auditorium. A poster in the background announced Aed Devlin in recital. An infant slept cradled in the man's arms. A woman whose dark hair and facial features mimicked Hardy's stood next to them. "Aed, when he was younger than Hardy. Hardy can't have been more than a few days old when this was taken."

"Poor Aed." Venus took the photo back. "I'll take this when I visit him at the station. What a crap way to reunite with the son you haven't seen since before he could walk. On a metal table in a morgue." Venus waved the photo. "But no one had motive to kill Hardy to keep this particular secret, not even Aed, who couldn't have done it, anyway. No inheritance is at stake. And having a child out of wedlock is hardly scandalous these days." She slipped the photo back into the envelope, then noticed something caught in one of the envelope's seams. "What's this?" She shook a small black chip onto the tabletop.

"The microSD card from Hardy's phone. It had some pictures on it he thought I might like to have." She flipped the data card back and forth in her hand. "Why smash his phone?"

"What are you talking about?" Venus asked.

"Hardy's phone. Pieces of it lay scattered around him. Why was it smashed?"

"Maybe he tried to call for help and the killer grabbed it."

"Or maybe there was something on it the killer didn't want anyone to see. A callback number or a photo or—" Her eyes widened as light dawned. "Duh." She smacked her forehead. "Our killer wanted this—" She held the phone's SD card between finger and thumb. "They had no way of knowing Hardy had already given it to me."

"That still doesn't explain why the phone was smashed. You can take the card out without destroying the phone."

"Not if you're in a hurry. Not if you care less about seeing what's on the card than you do about keeping anyone else from seeing it."

"What's on it? What pictures did Hardy think you'd want?"

She hesitated. True, Venus could see Eamon. Also true, Eamon was gone, maybe forever if Saoirse couldn't pull him off the card she took from Poe. Don't think about that now. She still didn't want anyone to know, especially anyone who might appreciate the commercial value of the evidence, that she possessed proof that ghosts existed. Venus waited for her answer. She stared at the card, then back at Venus. Why did Venus want to know? Was she afraid the pictures were of her? Was she afraid Hardy captured her shoving a trowel into Bernard's back? Would she have had time to kill Hardy before meeting the others at the theater?

"I didn't kill Hardy," Venus said. "Or Bernard."

"I didn't say you did."

"But you thought it. Or you should have thought it. Almost anyone who was at the theater on Monday could have stabbed Bernard, and almost anyone who was in the village yesterday could have stabbed Hardy. And I certainly had reason to want Bernard dead. And if your theory is right about what's on that thing," Venus pointed at the SD card, "Hardy was collateral damage. I've been writing true crime for a while now. I know who makes a good suspect and who doesn't."

With Eamon gone and Niall and Frankie out of commission...hell, she had to trust somebody. She laid the card on the table between her and Venus. "Footage of Eamon. Hardy captured high-def footage of Eamon by the orchestra pit when I—he—found Bernard's body."

"Hardy wasn't murdered for that," Venus said. "Not even the most rabid paranormal investigator would kill a fellow believer to steal his proof. Not even Poe would do that. There's a strange bond between these people."

"Speaking of Poe..." Gethsemane took a closer look at the label on the card. "This is like hers. It holds a terabyte of information. Eamon's segment lasts a few seconds, ten at most. That leaves a lot of space to record something worth killing for."

"Then we should see what's on it. And don't look at me like that. If I was the killer, wouldn't I have hit you in the head with the coffeepot and run off with the evidence by now?"

"Probably." Gethsemane pulled her phone from her bag. "Damn."

"What?"

"Saoirse's right. Mine's crap. It won't accept a data card this size."

"Use mine." Venus pulled out her phone. A sheaf of papers fell to the floor.

Gethsemane bent to pick them up. "What's this?"

"The contents of the envelope the desk clerk gave me. I stuffed them in my bag to keep the cops from asking about them, and by asking, I mean confiscating." She unfolded the papers and slid them toward Gethsemane.

"What's in them?" She fiddled with the phone's media player app.

Venus pulled the papers back. "Didn't get a chance to look at them. Here's a magazine article by Bernard, written when he was still Ben Schlossberg. An interview with the CEO of a frozen food importer. Reads more like a love letter. Wonder how much the guy paid." She set the article aside and picked up another paper. "This is—" She sat up straight. "This is interesting. Take a look."

Gethsemane swapped the phone for the photocopy Venus handed her. "A newspaper article about a salmonella outbreak." Salmonella, another one of those germs that, like e. coli, spread fast and furious and often killed the weak, the old, and the young. She skimmed it. "Contaminated chicken fingers. Almost a hundred children got sick. A dozen died."

"Check the name of the company who imported the chicken."

"The company owned by the guy Bernard interviewed. Let me see that article." She ran a finger along the pages as she scanned them. There, near the bottom of page three. "Bernard went out of his way to say the company's food was safe. Swore he ate it. Even included a couple of recipes."

"Now look at this." The final piece of paper in the stack.

"It looks like some sort of inspection report."

"From the food safety inspector. I ran across a few of these back in the day when I worked for the station. The inspector cited the company for numerous safety issues, including improper food storage temperature."

"Which would turn chicken fingers into petri dishes." She compared the inspector's report to the magazine article. "Look at the dates."

Venus looked. "The article was written three months after the inspection."

"And was published one month before the outbreak."

"If I trusted someone who vouched for a company's product—"

"And that product killed my kid—"

"I'd want to sue the company—"

"But kill the person I'd trusted." Gethsemane grabbed the newspaper article. "Are any of the children or parents named?"

Venus read over her shoulder. "A few. None I recognize."

Gethsemane gasped.

"What? You recognize someone?"

"This quote, from the mother of one of the kids who died. 'Children's lives are at stake. We need to put these monsters away to save other children. Nothing's more important. I'll never rest until the children are safe. Those monsters will pay.'"

"Where have I heard such overwhelming concern about saving children?"

"Last night, at the Athaneum. Ciara."

Venus sat back in her chair. "Neither you nor I have kids, yet neither of us would want to see one hurt. Even Poe probably would pull one out of the path of a speeding train if it came down to it."

"But Ciara seemed particularly passionate about protecting Saoirse. More passionate than you'd expect someone without kids to behave."

"But not more passionate than a mother who lost a child. Lost a child to a preventable cause."

Gethsemane scanned the article again. "Is there a picture of the woman?"

Venus pointed. "Grainy. Not close up. Can't make out much detail. She seems to have dark hair. Says her name is Karen Rourke."

"This was twenty years ago. Ben changed his name to Bernard. Why couldn't Karen Rourke change hers? What color was Ciara's hair before it turned white?"

"The outbreak happened in New Jersey. Ciara's Irish."

"Irish people sometimes move to Jersey." Gethsemane recalled her inability to place Ciara's accent. "And maybe she's not really Irish. Sylvie faked a French accent."

"Badly. But I see what you're getting at." Venus picked up her phone. "What do you think's on this?"

Gethsemane launched the media player. "Let's find out."

The screen went black for a few seconds, then a video started. Images formed. The scene was filmed from a high vantage point. Gethsemane saw herself leaning over the orchestra pit rail. Next to her a faint, but unmistakable, semi-transparent Eamon McCarthy balanced on the rail. His feet disappeared into the brass. Down in the pit, legs protruded from under the Steinway.

"Damn," Venus said. "Hardy gave this to you? There's mensch, then there's sap."

She watched her friend-who-she-might-never-see-again and forced back tears. "Hardy offered me the card in exchange for exonerating Aed. Then he gave me the card anyway because he is—was—a mensch."

"Wait, what's that?" Venus tapped the phone's screen to pause the image. "There, almost off camera."

Gethsemane swiped to enlarge the image. She hit rewind and played it again. No mistake. At the edge of the image a woman with silver-white hair ducked behind the piano and out of the pit.

"Ciara," Venus said.

"And no sign of Aed—Wait. Yes, there is. Over by the stage. You can just see him."

"Ciara's near the body and Aed's not. How did Hardy not notice this?"

"Maybe he was so hung up on capturing a ghost on video he didn't register two humans on the periphery. Honestly," Gethsemane handed Venus the phone, "if you'd filmed this, which would you have paid most attention to?"

"The ghost. But I might have realized later, while I was lying around sick and wondering if I was dying, what else I'd recorded."

"And asked the person in the video what they were doing in the vicinity of a murdered man. Especially if that person was about to flee to New Zealand."

"Prompting the person to stab me in the heart and try to find the evidence."

Both women rose and said, in unison, "Back to the hotel."

Twenty-Two

Gethsemane and Venus burst into the lobby of Sweeney's Inn. Gethsemane grabbed Poe coming down the stairs.

"Where's Ciara? Have you seen her?"

Poe shook her head and brushed off Gethsemane's hand. "No. Why would I have? She's not my mother. I didn't check in with her when I got back from the pub."

"I saw her," Kent said. "Last night. She told me about the theater. Thank you for helping her."

Thanks for helping a murderer. Had anyone told them about Hardy? "I'm sorry about, you know."

"Yeah," Kent said. "Me, too. Hardy and I didn't always see eye-to-eye, but I liked him. He deserved better than what he got."

"We all did." Poe hefted her bag onto her shoulder.

Kent turned on her. "Shut up, Poe. For eff's sake. Nothing's about you. Nobody's wronged you. You didn't get sick, you didn't get murdered."

"I didn't get my evidence. And Maja got shafted."

Kent leaned close to Poe. His breath made her blue bangs flicker. "Do me a favor. Change your flight. I don't want to be trapped in a metal tube thirty thousand feet in the air with a sociopathic, what's the word?"

"Gobshite," Gethsemane offered.

"Gobshite, who cares more about a toxic ghost who damned near wiped out half a village than she does about a decent human she worked with for two years. So please do me, and the flight crew who will have to keep me from choking you, a favor and book a different flight. And you're fired, in case you hadn't figured that out."

"You can't fire me. I'm your partner. I own part of your production company."

"I can fire, and am firing, you from my television crew. Check the contract, I have that right. And while you're at it, read the terms for buying me out of the production side of the house. Or let me buy you out. Doesn't matter."

Poe gawped then started to speak. She looked at Kent, and instead, wiped a sniffle on her sleeve and stomped out of the hotel.

"I'm glad I got a chance to say goodbye to you," Kent said. "I know you'll be glad to see the back of me. You'll also be happy to know this episode will probably never air. Out of respect for Hardy and because the cops confiscated most of our footage."

"The gardaí are letting you go?" Gethsemane asked.

"Some of us, the ones whose alibis they verified."

"Ciara, did they give her permission to leave?"

Kent shrugged. "They must have. She cleared out early." He teared up. "She left without saying goodbye."

Venus glanced at her watch. "Should we try the airport?"

"Do you think she could have made it to Cork already?" Gethsemane asked. She turned to Kent. "The SUV? Is it still here?"

"Yeah, the car, too. We'll return them to the rental place at the airport. Why?"

"Ciara couldn't have gone to the airport yet," Gethsemane said. "The train doesn't leave until this afternoon and she wouldn't have gone on foot."

"Cab?" Venus suggested.

Gethsemane hooked her fingers in her hair and pressed her palms against her temples. What to do? These days, the airline wasn't likely to give out information about a passenger over the phone. Nor the cab company. How much time would they waste if they went to the airport and Ciara wasn't there? If they guessed wrong, she'd have time to go to ground. She could be halfway to New Zealand, or wherever she was really going, before anyone noticed. They could go to the gardaí, show the video to Sutton—but he'd see Eamon. Probably. Maybe. Could someone unable to see ghosts in person see them on camera? Isn't that why the *Ghost Hunting Adventures* boys did what they did? No time to find out for certain. She grabbed Venus's phone.

"Hey, I'm making a call."

"You can have it back." She opened the media player and advanced to the portion of the recording that featured Eamon.

Kent peered over her shoulder. "Hey, is that—"

"Nope." Gethsemane used the editing functions to crop and delete frames so only images of Ciara and Aed remained. "Not anymore, it's not."

She removed the SD card and took it to the desk clerk. "Miss, call the guards. Tell them Gethsemane Brown—trust me, they'll know the name—has proof Ciara Tierney murdered Bernard Stoltz. Tell them I don't know where Ciara is, but I'm trying to find her. Ask for Inspector Bill Sutton." She pressed the card into the clerk's hand. "Give that to Inspector Sutton. No one else. Hand it to him personally, understand?"

The clerk nodded.

Kent had followed her to the desk. "What are you talking about? What do you mean, Ciara killed Bernard? Are you nuts?"

"I'm serious," Gethsemane said. "She probably killed Hardy, too. I'm sorry. I wish I had time to explain."

"You're wrong. Ciara loves life. She'd never take one."

"I don't have time to convince you—"

"Ciara went through some health challenges recently, but she'd turned a corner. She made plans, decided to start checking items off her bucket list. She actually wrote it out, showed it to me. Murder wasn't on it."

Was revenge? Did anyone start working their way through their bucket list unless they thought they were..."Did Ciara take any meds, Kent?"

"A few."

"A powerful narcotic pain medication? Sufentanil?"

"I don't know. I never saw them. She kept them in her bag."

"You never peeked?"

"I trusted Ciara."

"I'm sorry. Do you know what was wrong with her?"

"Something to do with her bones."

"Like bone cancer?"

"No. Not cancer. She would have told me." He hesitated. "At least, I'm pretty sure she would have told me." His shoulders slumped. "I would have hoped she would have told me. Trusted me. Maybe I didn't know her as well as I thought."

Venus tapped Gethsemane on the shoulder. "I know where Ciara is. At least I've narrowed it down to two places. She's either at the school's boathouse or the abandoned asylum."

"You know this how?" Gethsemane asked.

"I just hung up with my Dublin informant. One of his, er, associates, a guy who specializes in customized travel and identity documents—"

"You mean a forger."

"A service provider. Anyway, this guy's meeting a client here in Dunmullach. A client who wants to buy a new identity. The meeting's either at the asylum or the boathouse. My informant didn't know which. Seems his associate likes to surround himself with a bit of mystery. He had to promise him three referrals for future business and a bottle of Barry Crockett to get as much out of him as he did."

"Ciara's the Dunmullach client. She has to be. How many people can there be in this village who need to become someone else?"

"What about Sylvie?" Kent asked. "Or Sadie, or whatever her name is? Maybe she's the one you're after. I'm telling you, there's no way Cee would—"

Gethsemane interrupted. "I'm sorry, Kent, but Ciara's the one Hardy's camera caught near Bernard's body." She turned to Venus.

"Didn't your informant give you a description of the buyer or any other details? No names?"

Venus shrugged. "He's an informant, not WikiLeaks."

"It's Ciara," Gethsemane said. "We both know it's Ciara."

Kent scuffed his shoe at the floor and swiped at his eye with the back of his hand. A damp trail glistened on his cheek.

"We all know it's Ciara," Gethsemane whispered.

"One way to find out for sure," Venus said. "School or asylum? Home team gets first choice."

St. Dymphna's. Gethsemane's head throbbed just thinking of the place. She touched the small scar above her eyebrow. Not even Hank Wayne's entire fortune could get her to go there again. "I'll take the boathouse." She grabbed Kent's arm. "Don't leave. Wait here. When the police arrive, tell them what you just heard."

She didn't want to place odds on whose rescue the guards would rush to.

Gethsemane pressed herself against the wall of the boathouse. She peered around the corner at the empty dock. Normally full of students and faculty celebrating the arrival of spring, the entire lake area had been put off-limits during the quarantine. The only noise came from metal cleats banging against empty flag poles in a sudden chill wind. She shuddered. "Eerie" would have been an atmospheric improvement.

She pulled her jacket tighter and inched toward the boathouse door. She peered into a window but saw only nondescript shapes hulking in the darkness. Ciara must not be here. Wouldn't you need to turn on a light to buy a new passport?

Gethsemane tried the door. Unlocked. She slipped her arm inside and found a light switch. The bright overheads revealed the shapes to be racing sculls, suspended on racks, and sailboats. Water lapped on the sides of the sailboats open to the lake. No sign of anyone. She crept in, pausing to grab an oar from a rack near the door.

Should she call Venus? Warn her that Ciara was most likely there? What if Venus was hiding, waiting for Ciara to show? A ringing phone would give her away. What if Ciara was coming to the boathouse but Gethsemane had gotten there first? Where was Tchaikovsky to warn her when she really needed him? She'd wait until the police showed. Oh, please let Kent be trusted to tell the guards where she and Venus had gone.

A noise made her catch her breath. It came from the rear of the boathouse, behind the sailboats that had been pulled out of the water. She gripped the oar tight like a bat. Her usual trick of reciting Negro League baseball stats failed to slow her heart rate or quiet her nerves. With the oar held high and her back to the boats, she crept toward the noise.

She heard it again, louder this time. A moan. She stooped and saw a pair of legs splayed on the ground. A boat obscured the legs' owner. She crept closer. A man lay crumpled in a corner. His head lolled and blood trickled from his mouth. A fishing spear extended from his chest. She guessed Ciara had come and gone.

"Don't move, sir. I'm calling for an ambulance now." She set the oar down and pulled out her phone. It might be crap in terms of memory card capacity, but it worked well enough to call 999.

The man moaned again. His eyes darted to something behind her.

She turned and saw Ciara bringing an oar down on her head. She managed to move enough to keep the bludgeon from cracking her skull. It landed on her arm and sent her phone skittering under a boat. Pain shot up to her shoulder. She tried to grab her oar with her uninjured arm, but Ciara kicked it out of the way as she swung again. Gethsemane rolled and the oar glanced off her ankle. She waited until the stars faded and warded off tunnel vision while she wriggled far enough beneath sailboats to be out of target range. She saw her phone. Ciara saw it, too, and kicked it hard enough to send it splashing into the water.

Ciara ran. Gethsemane heard her shoes against the tile floor moving away from her toward the door. Then the lights went out.

She saw a slice of natural light for a few seconds as the door opened. She heard a motor start, then the door slammed, leaving her and the injured man in darkness.

It took her a minute to sort it out. Ciara had left them in the boathouse with a running motor to suffocate. Gethsemane rolled until she could hold her head over the water. The boathouse wasn't completely closed off—Ciara hadn't had time to think her plan through—but who knew if the ratio of fresh air to carbon monoxide was enough to prevent her demise? She didn't intend to wait to find out. She cursed Ciara for knocking her phone in the water and half dragged herself, half limped to the crumpled man.

Not that he'd last until an ambulance came. Probably wouldn't last until she dialed the emergency number's second nine. Ciara had claimed her third victim; damned if she'd be the fourth. She tried to stand up, but the man grabbed her wrist with the last of his strength. He made a faint gesture toward his breast pocket. Gethsemane reached around the spear. She felt small plastic cards and what must have been a passport. Ciara hadn't had time to collect her spoils. Gethsemane pulled the documents from the man's pocket. He had passed the point of noticing. She rummaged and found his phone in a pants pocket. For all the good it did. Password protected and no emergency call option. Because why would a forger want to call the cops or let anyone use his phone? She tossed it aside and groped her way to the door. The pain in her arm and ankle had subsided to a dull throb. She could still use them, so no broken bones. She'd have some godawful bruises though. She tried the door. Jammed. The window framed the tip of the oar Ciara had wedged through the door handle. She followed the chug, chug, chug to find the motor in a corner and shut it off, then found a light switch. She guessed Ciara hadn't gone far; she still needed the identity documents now in Gethsemane's pocket. If she stayed put, would Ciara come back, hoping she was dead, or near enough, to claim the keys to her new life? Gethsemane grabbed an oar and hid behind the door.

Minutes passed like eons. Something scraped and slid across

the wooden deck outside the boathouse. The door inched open.

Gethsemane sprang, back in action to her softball days. This former star pitcher had been none too shabby at bat. She went for the home run and swung the oar as hard as she could.

The door created an awkward angle, and the brunt of the blow landed on the door jamb. Ciara jumped backward. As she fell, she grabbed the oar she'd used to block the door and thrust it into the boathouse. Gethsemane deflected it with her own oar. She kicked Ciara in the shin which knocked Ciara away from the door but set her ankle throbbing again. She struggled to put weight on it as Ciara geared up for another oar strike.

Gethsemane braced herself—

No blow. Ciara made a muffled noise and fell sideways. Gethsemane waited. Seconds passed with only incoherent sounds coming from the other side of the door. She poked her head outside. Venus stood over Ciara's moaning, fetal-positioned form, shaking her hand in the air and massaging her knuckles. Blood streamed from Ciara's nose.

"I'll pretend I didn't see that." Inspector Sutton stepped into view.

"Defense of a life, Inspector," Venus said. "It's allowed."

The inspector grinned and knelt by Ciara. He advised her of her rights.

Cuffed and on her feet, Ciara asked Gethsemane, "Why couldn't you just let me go? Ben Schlossberg deserved to die. He killed my daughter." Efforts to press her nose to her shoulder failed to stop the crimson liquid dripping onto her lip. Sutton fished in his pocket, then pressed a handkerchief against her face.

"Did Aed deserve to take the blame for it?" Venus asked

Ciara tilted her head back to speak under Sutton's hand. "Aed abandoned his son."

"Who you killed," Gethsemane said.

Ciara hung her head. A uniformed garda led her away.

"There's another body inside," Gethsemane said to the Inspector.

"Three's about your average, isn't it?" He squeezed past her and disappeared into the depths of the boathouse.

"It's not like I do this on purpose," Gethsemane called after him. "It's your informant's associate," she said to Venus. She pulled Ciara's identity documents from her pocket.

"Passport, New Zealand driver's license, credit cards, social," Venus called out as Gethsemane went through them. "Guess Ciara was serious about the Kiwi thing."

"Look at the name she was going to travel under." Gethsemane held up the passport. "Karen Rourke."

"Why'd she do it?" Venus asked. "I mean why now? After all these years?"

"You said it. Sufentanil's prescribed to people who are dying. The text I sent Mother about those meds in Ciara's dopp kit? She answered. Mother's bridge partner is an oncologist. They share some patients; Mother treats their depression and anxiety so she has to keep up with the oncology meds. Prednisone, ondansetron, iron supplements, and powerful narcotics? They're used for cancer, for palliative care. Ciara's dying. Guess murder was on the version of her bucket list she didn't show Kent."

Twenty-Three

"Are you sure you're up to this, Frankie?" Gethsemane held the hospital door as he navigated an over-sized floral-balloon display through and into the lobby.

"Don't."

"Don't what?" She retrieved an errant balloon.

"Don't fuss. I'm fine, completely recovered." He smothered a yawn against his shoulder. "Almost completely."

His color and irascible nature had returned to normal since his release from the infirmary two days prior. "You're recovered enough to be a grump. And I'm not fussing. I'm expressing concern for your well-being. You and Niall are the ones who fuss whenever I plan to do something unladylike." She pushed the elevator "up" button.

"Get out of here with that. Neither the inspector nor I have ever suggested you limit your pursuits to those suited for the fairer sex. Niall may have recommended you avoid situations liable to get you killed or arrested. I, on the other hand, have allowed you to goad me into joining you in your not-strictly-legal endeavors."

Gethsemane stepped into the just-arrived elevator car. "You're giving almost as good as you get. Now I believe you're recovered."

"You carry this." Frankie handed her the flowers and balloons.

"It's from both of us."

"Which is why you can hand it to Niall as well as I can. Guy thing." He batted a bright yellow balloon. "Bet he'd rather have a pint, anyway."

"You can't bring a pint into a hospital."

Frankie tugged at the over-sized blazer he'd resumed wearing with wrinkled khakis, Venus's style influence apparently having worn off with the sickness. He grinned. "You'd be surprised what you can hide in here."

The elevator door opened to reveal a nurses' station—and a robust Niall leaning against the countertop, chatting up the nurses. He wore street clothes, and a duffel bag lay at his feet. His dimpled smile spread to his eyes when he saw Gethsemane and Frankie. "'S that for me?" He nodded at the flowers.

"No," Frankie said. "It's for the nurses who had to put up with you."

"Of course, it's for you, Niall." Gethsemane handed him the arrangement and pulled a greeting card from her purse. "But you don't look like you need any get well wishes."

"Well enough to convince my sister to go back home to her husband. The doctor examined her while she was here, by the way. The baby's fine. No signs of whatever it is that I had. They discharged me an hour ago. Taxi's on the way."

"Cancel the taxi," Frankie said. "I drove."

Niall eyed the other man up and down. "You're looking fit."

"Slammed death's door and locked it."

One of the nurse's chimed in. "The doctor will call you, Niall, once the final test results come in. I hope they provide some clue as to what felled you."

Heads turned as Gethsemane made a noise. All the blood tests in the world wouldn't explain Maja-sickness. "Sorry, something in my throat. Um, you know they can't always identify the exact cause of an illness. They even invented a term for it, Medically Unexplained Physical Symptoms."

"MUPS? What kind of a name is MUPS?" Frankie asked. "Coined by an American, no doubt."

"You've a medical background?" a nurse asked Gethsemane.

"Her ma's a doctor," Niall said. "And I don't really care exactly what caused the dose, as long as it's gone. Time to get back to my normal life."

"Cold cases, weekly poker games, and warning me to keep my nose out of dangerous situations?" Gethsemane asked.

"You forgot craic at the pub and shoe shopping." The inspector winked.

"The nurses really do deserve those flowers more than you."

"No argument from me." He presented the arrangement to the nurse who'd told him about the lab results. "For you ladies with apologies for any aggravation caused."

Blushes and giggles spread through the nurses' station. "You were never any trouble, Niall."

"As for you two," he said to Gethsemane and Frankie, "pints on me. Let's head to the Rabbit."

A few days after celebrating Niall's and Frankie's return to health, Gethsemane gathered with Saoirse, Father Tim, and Venus around a table in the parish house. Venus's phone lay mid-table, a grimoire next to it.

"Eamon and Orla are in there?" Gethsemane ran a finger along the edge of the phone.

"On the SD card," Saoirse corrected. "But we can use the phone to communicate with them."

"Like the compass needle on the alchemist's device," Tim said.

"Better than that, Father," Saoirse said. "We can see them on the screen. Not very clearly, but clearly enough to tell it's them. They can also use the energy from the phone's battery to send text messages."

"Like one of those pods the paranormal investigators used." Gethsemane snapped her fingers as she tried to recall the name. "You know, the whoosis whatchamacallit. The thing with the database programmed in so ghosts can choose words to display on its screen."

"Why don't we use one of those instead of my phone?" Venus

asked.

The other three stared.

"The phone's not paid off yet."

"Kent's crew took all of their equipment with them," Gethsemane said. "I insisted on it."

"You have a phone, why not use it?"

"Because your phone's better, Ms. James," Saoirse said.

Gethsemane bristled. "Why is everyone so down on my phone? It does what it's supposed to do: sends and receives calls and texts, takes photos, and provides me with apps for when I'm in need of a timesuck."

Saoirse wrinkled her nose and stage-whispered. "It's still not a very good phone."

Tim patted Venus's hand. "I'm sure Ms. James doesn't begrudge the use of her technology if it helps us communicate with the McCarthys."

Venus looked away from her phone but said nothing.

"Proceed, Saoirse," Tim said.

She opened the grimoire to a page covered in the strange formulas Gethsemane had seen earlier at the theater. Some additional formulas, in a girlish handwriting, had been penciled in the margins. "I translated the alchemical formulas into mathematical equations, then solved them." She tapped the phone's screen awake then tapped numbers on its on-screen keyboard.

They waited. Three seconds, five seconds, ten. Tim said a prayer.

A soft, green glow emanated from the phone, followed by a faint image onscreen.

"Eamon!" Gethsemane exclaimed. "Saoirse, you're a genius."

"I know," the girl said in a matter-of-fact tone.

A text box popped up and words appeared: *Hey darlin'. U miss me?*

"Can he hear me?" Gethsemane asked Saoirse.

"Through the microphone."

She spoke to Eamon. "You've no idea, Irish. I thought I'd never see you again."

A text: *Can't see U*

Gethsemane turned to Saoirse.

"The screen only displays images. It doesn't receive them."

"What about the phone's camera?" Venus asked. "Can't we use it so McCarthy can see us?"

"No, the camera won't broadcast images into the phone. And photos and videos will take up storage space on the SD card."

The screen flickered and Orla's image materialized next to her husband's. Both images' intensity diminished.

"What happened?" Venus asked.

Saoirse explained. "Two ghosts use more of the phone battery's energy. So the images aren't as sharp. And the texts won't be as long."

"How do we get them out of the phone?" Venus asked.

The others stared at her.

"I didn't mean it like that," she said.

"Technically, they're on the card and not in the phone. If you remove the card from the phone," Saoirse said, "you remove the ghosts, too. But they won't be able to communicate. They need the energy from the phone's battery and the phone's screen and keyboard for that. The card just stores them."

"Can you get them out, out? Out of the card, back floating around in the atmosphere or wherever?"

The phone vibrated. A text: *Ghosts don't float*

"Sorry," Venus said. "I'm still not well-versed in spectral terminology."

"Saoirse," Tim said. "Can you release the McCarthys from the card?"

The girl dropped her gaze.

"Saoirse," Tim said again.

"It's the silica bonds. I can manage the copper and quartz. But the spell binds the ghosts' essence to the silica so tightly you couldn't slip an atom between them. That's the secret of getting the ghosts into the device. The silica bonds seem to be irreversible.

None of the writings I deciphered reported any success in breaking the bonds and releasing the ghosts from the device."

"You mean they're trapped," Gethsemane said.

"That's why the spell's called 'An Incantation, with Formulas, to Trap Ghosts.'"

A text appeared: *Shite*

Another followed: *Language, dearest*

"There's nothing you can do?" Tim asked Saoirse.

"I'm not sure you want to hear the answer."

Another text: *Say it*

Saoirse pulled a book from her pocket, a slim, red volume the size of an index card. "I found this." She laid it on the table.

Tim opened it. "German."

"A German monk wrote it. It's mostly recipes for beer and bread and rules for living in the monastery, a few complaints about the other monks, lots of prayers but, also, a couple of spells."

"What kind of spells?"

"For protection, for good beer—"

Venus laughed. "Herr Monk knew what mattered."

Saoirse continued. "And one spell—Ein Zauber, der ein großes Opfer braucht—that might do it. Maybe. Possibly. Sort of—"

"All right, Saoirse." Tim held up a hand. "We understand there are no guarantees. Tell us about the spell."

"What does Ein Zauber whatever mean?" Venus asked.

Gethsemane knew some German. "'A spell requiring great sacrifice' is how the title translates. What kind of sacrifice? From who?"

"One person can pass their energy to another person to save the other."

"Save the other from what?"

"Death."

Venus lowered her voice. "But the ghosts are already dead. Aren't they?"

"The spell was written for humans, however," Saoirse referred to the alchemical formulas, "I managed to re-calculate one of these and combine it with the sacrifice spell to make the spell work with ghosts. I hope. I haven't tried it."

"Let's assume your alterations were successful. What happens?"

"One ghost transfers all its energy to the other. That should oversaturate the silica bonds and release that ghost."

A text: *Great sacrifice?*

"The person who transfers their energy dies. The ghost who transfers their energy dissipates. Ceases to exist."

"A great sacrifice, indeed," Tim said. "Such as a parent might make to save a child or a soldier to save a comrade."

Would one spouse make it to save the other? "What's the alternative?" Gethsemane asked. "Stay trapped in the SD card? Isn't that better than non-existence? Especially since they can communicate through a phone or laptop or tablet. Anything with an SD card slot, really."

"About that," Saoirse said. "Every playback degrades their image quality. Every text does, too. I haven't calculated how long it will take but, eventually, they'll be reduced to static."

"Aren't you a bundle of good news?" Venus said.

"So," Gethsemane said, "they can remain bound to the card, potentially forever—"

"If no one deletes them."

"—but they can't communicate with each other or the world without turning themselves into static."

"Not themselves, only their images. Well, they'd also turn their texts into nonsense. But they'd remain stored on the card."

"Incommunicado. Like old files no one's able to access anymore."

"Yes."

"Or one of them could give up their existence for the other. And the one who was released from the card?"

"Would be a regular ghost again. Like Mr. McCarthy was before."

Not much of a choice. Stay trapped in a prison smaller than a thumbnail knowing that every time you reached out to contact anyone, you moved one communication closer to becoming white noise. Or, stop being, period, to give the one you love a chance at—

"The ghost who's released?" Gethsemane asked. "Can they cross over or are they stuck on this side of the veil?"

Saoirse shrugged. "Father Tim's got a lot of grimoires I haven't gone through, yet. One of them may contain a crossing over spell."

This was a choice Eamon and Orla would have to make for themselves. Gethsemane spoke to the phone. "Guys? This one's up to you."

A text: *Save Orla*

Another: *No. Not without U*

Card worse hell than limbo

Save Eamon

No. Won't let U do it

Not asking, dearest. Telling

Without U 2 long already

Not 2gether in card

But

U stay. Have friends who ♥ U

Can't bear thought

Ssh. All will be well, my ♥

Would die 4 U

I would cease 2 B 4 U. Save Eamon

"Are you sure, Mrs. McCarthy?" Saoirse asked. "If this works, I can't undo it."

"And if it doesn't work?" Tim asked.

"They might both stay trapped in the card or they might both cease to exist. I can't say for sure. Some of my equations are, um, hypothetical."

Terrific. Her friend's—she might as well admit it, her best friend—fate and the fate of the wife he loved more than life hinged on a twelve-year-old genius's ability to translate German, Latin, and alchemical formulas into mathematical equations which she hypothesized would work. But if Saoirse didn't at least try...would being trapped indefinitely and unable to communicate be worse than not existing? She remembered how ecstatic Eamon seemed when he first realized he could communicate with her after a quarter-century of isolation. She picked up the phone and spoke softly into the microphone. "Eamon, Orla, I'll support whatever choice you make."

The phone's screen went dark. Gethsemane set the phone on the table and they waited. A yellow glow surrounded the phone.

A text appeared, all caps: *SAVE EAMON*

Eamon never could win an argument with her.

A second text followed: *I'm nothing without him, anyway*

The screen went dark again.

Saoirse turned to Gethsemane. "Release Mr. McCarthy?"

Gethsemane inhaled deeply then exhaled until her lungs felt empty. She nodded.

Saoirse sat and pulled the grimoire to her. She positioned the phone mid-table while she read the notes she'd made in the book's margins. She brought the screen to life with a tap, then tapped numbers. She sat back. No one moved. Seconds passed, but nothing happened.

"What's wrong?" Venus asked. "Why isn't it working?"

Gethsemane laid a hand on Saoirse's shoulder. "Try again."

The girl tapped more numbers. Still nothing. She pressed the phone's power key and hit restart.

All four held their breaths with an audible intake of air. A minute passed. Saoirse started to cry noiselessly. Another minute passed. Five.

"It didn't work," Venus said. "Damn." She reached for the phone.

Gethsemane stopped her. "Just wait. What's ten minutes versus eternity?"

Seven minutes, eight. Just as Gethsemane began to lose faith, the phone vibrated. The acrid smell of an electrical fire filled the room. Gethsemane touched the phone.

"Ow!" She drew back her hand and sucked the tip of her forefinger. "Hot."

The phone sparked, and a puff of smoke wafted from the battery compartment.

Father Tim pulled Saoirse up from her chair and stepped back. "Perhaps we should go. I'll call the fire brigade from the church."

"No, wait." Saoirse broke free from Tim's grasp and pointed at the phone. The service provider's logo filled the screen. The sparks and smoke abated.

Nothing else happened.

"Is it over?" Venus asked. "What about the McCarthys?"

"I warned you it might not work." Saoirse sniffled.

Had they destroyed both Eamon and Orla? Had Maja claimed a pyrrhic victory? Gethsemane cursed the vengeful harridan. May she burn in—

Venus dug her nails into Gethsemane's arm. "Do you smell that?"

Gethsemane took a deep breath. Leather. Hay. And the freshness of soap.

Twenty-Four

A new bottle of Waddell and Dobb hovered in mid-air in the kitchen. The bottle tipped and filled two old-fashioned glasses with a generous pour of bourbon. One glass levitated to Gethsemane, the other to Venus.

Gethsemane raised her glass in toast. "Thank you, Irish."

Eamon materialized next to the range. "Anytime, Sissy." He pointed at the oven door and it opened a crack. "What are you making?"

Gethsemane slammed the door shut. "Chocolate chip cookies, what does it smell like?"

"No comment," Eamon said.

Venus hid her laugh behind her glass.

"I go away for a little while and you turn into a domestic goddess? What's going on with that?"

Gethsemane took off the apron she'd found in the linen closet and shoved it under the sink. "I'm just making some cookies for Niall and Frankie to celebrate their recovery. No big deal."

"I'm guessing they'd both rather have a bottle of their favorite."

She turned to Venus. "Aren't you going to help me? Female solidarity?"

"They're burning." Venus gestured at the oven.

"Shite." Gethsemane yanked open the oven and grabbed the cookie sheet. The searing pain in her fingers reminded her she needed an oven mitt. Hand appropriately garbed, she pulled out a sheet of steaming cookies with charcoal-colored edges.

"On a positive note," Eamon said, "Your brogue has improved."

She gave him a few more examples of how much her brogue had improved. She held up a cookie. "I'll stop by the off license tomorrow."

"You can ride with me," Venus said. "The cab can drop you on the way to the airport."

"Off to your next assignment?" Eamon asked.

"Nope, off to a vacation. Aed and I are on our way to Ibiza. He plans to start another opera."

"Not seriously, not after all that's happened?"

"Not seriously, actually. I mean his new opera won't be serious. It'll be an operetta. Think Gilbert and Sullivan instead of Verdi. It's a commission from a small opera company just outside Chicago. Not the Met, but a start."

"I never thought I'd say this," Gethsemane said, "but I'm sorry to see you go."

"I never thought I'd say this, but," Venus raised her glass in toast to the others, "I'm going to miss both of you. I'm not used to having friends. Real friends, instead of contacts and informants. It's kind of nice."

"When's the new edition of the book coming out?" Gethsemane asked. "I promise to read the whole thing this time."

"In a few months. The publisher's going to rush the production."

"What's after that? A book about Ciara and Bernard?"

"Yes, but not a sensational one. Legit reporting on the e. coli outbreak and how lax oversight of the safety inspectors and an industry rife with bribery led to preventable deaths. Ciara's daughter will get some justice. I just hope Ciara—Karen's alive to see it." Venus drained her glass. "Time for bed. Got an early flight."

Early? "About sharing the cab," Gethsemane said. "I'll walk to the village later or ride my bike. I plan to sleep in."

Eamon laughed himself green. "Some things stayed the same while I was away."

"Welcome home, Eamon." Venus blew him a kiss. "And goodnight." She headed upstairs.

Gethsemane toyed with one of her ruined cookies. "What she said."

"Goodnight?"

"Welcome home." Gethsemane threw a cookie at him. It passed through his chest and landed on the floor. He pointed at it and sent it floating back to the cookie sheet. "It's good to have you back. I'm sorry Orla couldn't be here, too."

His aura dimmed to a dull yellow. "I had her back for a little while. I'll miss her every day. But at least she has no more worries. I'm satisfied she's in heaven teaching the angels to mind their manners."

"And Father Tim granted you absolution, so now you can go visit her."

"Shouldn't you be off to bed? Tomorrow's a school day."

"Nope, day after tomorrow. Now that all the boys have recovered, Headmaster Riordan's scheduled a 'clean team' to go through the infirmary, the dorms, and the classrooms, and disinfect anything that can't run away fast enough."

"Are you going to tell him Father Tim would do him more good than antiseptics?"

"Nope, not saying a word."

A knock at the front door interrupted the jovial mood. Neither moved.

"Are you going to answer it?" Eamon asked.

"It's late in the day for good news, and I can't handle any more bad."

The knock repeated.

"They know you're here."

She opened the door to find Billy on the porch. "Let me guess, I've got five minutes to pack and hit the curb."

"Nope." He took off his hat. "May I come in?"

"It's your house." She ushered him inside.

"I apologize for the lateness, but I wanted to tell you before I leave town. Business trip to Germany. You may stay at Carraigfaire as long as you like."

She threw her arms around him in a bearhug. "What happened? What changed?"

"You've been getting a lot of attention, lately."

"Don't I know it?"

"It means I've been getting some attention, too. Mostly from people interested in Uncle's music. Is he back, by the way?"

"Yes. He's in the kitchen now, criticizing my cooking."

"D'you think you can convince him to start composing again?"

She raised an eyebrow.

"Some of these folks showing interest in Uncle's music are interested in licensing it for things like movies and television ads. Some are interested in buying his catalog. The bigger the catalog, the bigger the sale."

She heard swearing from the kitchen and smelled leather and soap. "I don't think he's going to go for the sale idea. The licensing..." She winked. "Leave him to me."

"I heard that," Eamon called.

"You're serious about letting me stay here?" she asked Billy. "You mean it?"

"Yeah. Truth is, I've gotten used to having you here. Can't imagine anyone else taking care of the place. You belong." He glanced at his watch. "Oops, gotta run. Catching a red eye to Berlin. Welcome home."

ⴕALEXIA GORDON

A writer since childhood, Alexia Gordon won her first writing prize in the 6th grade. She continued writing through college but put literary endeavors on hold to finish medical school and Family Medicine residency training. She established her medical career then returned to writing fiction.

Raised in the southeast, schooled in the northeast, she relocated to the west where she completed Southern Methodist University's Writer's Path program. She admits Texas brisket is as good as Carolina pulled pork. She practices medicine in North Chicago, IL. She enjoys the symphony, art collecting, embroidery, and ghost stories.

The Gethsemane Brown Mystery Series
by Alexia Gordon

MURDER IN G MAJOR (#1)
DEATH IN D MINOR (#2)
KILLING IN C SHARP (#3)

Henery Press Mystery Books

And finally, before you go...
Here are a few other mysteries
you might enjoy:

ARTIFACT

Gigi Pandian

A Jaya Jones Treasure Hunt Mystery (#1)

Historian Jaya Jones discovers the secrets of a lost Indian treasure may be hidden in a Scottish legend from the days of the British Raj. But she's not the only one on the trail...

From San Francisco to London to the Highlands of Scotland, Jaya must evade a shadowy stalker as she follows hints from the hastily scrawled note of her dead lover to a remote archaeological dig. Helping her decipher the cryptic clues are her magician best friend, a devastatingly handsome art historian with something to hide, and a charming archaeologist running for his life.

Available at booksellers nationwide and online

Visit www.henerypress.com for details

MACDEATH

Cindy Brown

An Ivy Meadows Mystery (#1)

Like every actor, Ivy Meadows knows that *Macbeth* is cursed. But she's finally scored her big break, cast as an acrobatic witch in a circus-themed production of *Macbeth* in Phoenix, Arizona. And though it may not be Broadway, nothing can dampen her enthusiasm—not her flying cauldron, too-tight leotard, or carrot-wielding dictator of a director.

But when one of the cast dies on opening night, Ivy is sure the seeming accident is "murder most foul" and that she's the perfect person to solve the crime (after all, she does work part-time in her uncle's detective agency). Undeterred by a poisoned Big Gulp, the threat of being blackballed, and the suddenly too-real curse, Ivy pursues the truth at the risk of her hard-won career—and her life.

Available at booksellers nationwide and online

Visit www.henerypress.com for details

THE SEMESTER OF OUR DISCONTENT

Cynthia Kuhn

A Lila Maclean Academic Mystery (#1)

English professor Lila Maclean is thrilled about her new job at prestigious Stonedale University, until she finds one of her colleagues dead. She soon learns that everyone, from the chancellor to the detective working the case, believes Lila—or someone she is protecting—may be responsible for the horrific event, so she assigns herself the task of identifying the killer.

Putting her scholarly skills to the test, Lila gathers evidence, but her search is complicated by an unexpected nemesis, a suspicious investigator, and an ominous secret society. Rather than earning an "A" for effort, she receives a threat featuring the mysterious emblem and must act quickly to avoid failing her assignment...and becoming the next victim.

Available at booksellers nationwide and online

Visit www.henerypress.com for details

COUNTERFEIT CONSPIRACIES

Ritter Ames

A Bodies of Art Mystery (#1)

Laurel Beacham may have been born with a silver spoon in her mouth, but she has long since lost it digging herself out of trouble. Her father gambled and womanized his way through the family fortune before skiing off an Alp, leaving her with more tarnish than trust fund. Quick wits and connections have gained her a reputation as one of the world's premier art recovery experts. The police may catch the thief, but she reclaims the missing masterpieces.

The latest assignment, however, may be her undoing. Using every ounce of luck and larceny she possesses, Laurel must locate a priceless art icon and rescue a co-worker (and ex-lover) from a master criminal, all the while matching wits with a charming new nemesis. Unfortunately, he seems to know where the bodies are buried—and she prefers hers isn't next.

Available at booksellers nationwide and online

Visit www.henerypress.com for details

OCT 2 2018

CPSIA information can be obtained
at www.ICGtesting.com
Printed in the USA
LVHW08s0055080918
589551LV00008B/81/P